"So, tell me, how did you end up in Dunmow, as guest of my friend Lord Adrien?"

Rowena remained  his guest, milord."

Then, from within the Lifting the damp he past him, and Stephe door for her.

She flinched at his raised arm. Rowena was scared. Hurt, also, but mostly frightened. Stephen stepped aside as she ducked into the hut.

Wandering from the door, Stephen looked again at the vandal's work. The cur had crushed an egg, had laid waste to late season herbs and had trampled the roots under his boots. *Saxon* boots. The simple style was unmistakable.

Why would a Saxon destroy this young woman's food stocks? Because she was rumored to have allied herself with the Normans? It had been two years since William's victory at Hastings. This Rowena would have been barely into womanhood back then.

The door behind him opened again. Stephen turned to watch Rowena step outside with a babe in her arms.

The babe had dark hair and olive skin—the father could not possibly be Saxon.

His heart sank. So that was how she was aligned with the Normans.

Barbara Phinney was born in England and raised in Canada. After she retired from the Canadian Armed Forces, Barbara turned her hand to romance writing. The thrill of adventure and the love of happy endings, coupled with a too-active imagination, have merged to help her create this and other wonderful stories. Barbara spends her days writing, building her dream home with her husband and enjoying their fast-growing children.

Books by Barbara Phinney

Love Inspired Historical

Bound to the Warrior
Protected by the Warrior
Sheltered by the Warrior

Love Inspired Suspense

Desperate Rescue
Keeping Her Safe
Deadly Homecoming
Fatal Secrets
Silent Protector

Visit the Author Profile page at Harlequin.com for more titles

Sheltered by the Warrior

BARBARA PHINNEY

♦ **HARLEQUIN**® LOVE INSPIRED® HISTORICAL

Recycling programs
for this product may
not exist in your area.

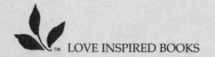 LOVE INSPIRED BOOKS

ISBN-13: 978-0-373-28300-2

Sheltered by the Warrior

Copyright © 2015 by Barbara Phinney

This edition published by arrangement with Love Inspired Books.

® and TM are trademarks of Love Inspired Books, used under license.
Trademarks indicated with ® are registered in the United States Patent
and Trademark Office, the Canadian Intellectual Property Office and in
other countries.

www.Harlequin.com

Printed in U.S.A.

And straightway the father of the child cried out,
and said with tears, Lord, I believe;
help thou mine unbelief.
—*Mark* 9:24

Chapter One

Kingstown, Cambridgeshire, England
Autumn, 1068 AD

She will surely starve this winter.

The mists of the early morning lingered as Rowena stepped from her hut and found herself staring at the plunder around her. Little Andrew hadn't yet awakened, so she'd taken this time to pray, as her friend, Clara, had once suggested.

Her shaking hand found the door and she shut it quietly. Her other hand grasped the cut ends of the thin thatch that reached from the roof peak almost to the ground. In this village, 'twas cheaper to grow thatch for roofs than to make daub for walls, so the hut's walls were short, barely coming to her shoulders. Only those in the manor house were rich enough to have fine, straight walls that reached two stories up to the thick, warm thatch above.

Stepping forward, Rowena gaped at the devastation around her. How could someone have ruined her harvest? And in the middle of the night? Aye, the villagers gave her the cold shoulder, but to move to such destruction? Why?

Gasping, she tossed off the hood of her cloak and forced the crisp air into her lungs to conquer the wash of panic. Last night, when she'd locked up for the evening, she'd wondered if there would be a killing frost, but had remembered with gratitude that she had a good amount of roots dug and neatly stored under mounds of straw, and enough herbs drying to make strong pottages. With the pair of rabbits and the hen Lady Ediva had given her, she'd truly believed that she and her babe would not just survive the winter, but mayhap even flourish.

Nay, this cannot be happening!

Rowena bit back tears as she stepped toward what was left of her garden. The heavy dew soaked through her thin shoes, and her heart hung like the wet hem of her cyrtel and cloak. All her hard work of collecting herbs and gathering straw and burying roots in frost-proof mounds was for naught.

As she looked to her right, wisps of her pale hair danced across her cheek. Both the rabbit hutch and henhouse had been torn apart, the animals long gone. Someone had wrenched off the doors and crushed the early morning's egg beneath the hard heel of a heavy boot. Chicken feathers flipped in the misty breeze.

She hadn't heard a thing, but since her babe had begun to sleep through the night and her days were long, she was oft so exhausted that sleep held her till morn. Hastily, she scanned her garden, her eyes watchful for movement, her ears pinned to hear any soft clucking of a distressed hen. Nothing, not a breath of life amid the shredded vegetation.

"Nay," she whispered in the cold air, "come back, little hen. You're safe now."

No answer. Just a ruined cage. But that was fixable, at least. Clara, who'd left yesterday to return to her own home, had shown her how to weave various plant stalks into strong netting. Being a fisherman's daughter, Clara knew these things.

Rowena already knew how to soak and shred the leftover stalks until the soft fibers could be spun into threads. She'd seen her older sister weave cloth that way and looked forward to making baby clothes this winter, for Andrew was growing fast and she had no one to offer her their children's castoffs.

At the thought of her family, a knot of bitterness choked her. Rowena tried to swallow it, for Clara had warned that bitterness caused all measure of illness. But 'twas hard to forget the fact that she had no kin willing to help her. 'Twas hard to forget that her parents had sold her as a slave to a Norman baron, ridiculously boasting that her pale hair and eyes were a promise of many strong sons within her.

Nay, she thought with watering eyes, 'twas hard to forget that the baron had then tried to murder her and steal the son she'd birthed, as part of a plot so villainous it still terrified her.

And the men in Colchester, the town to which she'd fled, had no wish to defend her. They'd wanted her along with Clara to leave and take their troubles with them. So she'd left. Now here in Kingstown, she knew that heartache and pain had followed her.

Rowena looked toward the sun that strained to pierce the rising mists. *Lord God, Clara says You're up there. Why are You doing this to me? Are You making me suffer for not knowing You all these years? I know You now.*

When she received no answer, Rowena set her shoulders and pursed her lips. She'd resettled in this village, been given her freedom and a hut that had with it a decent, albeit overgrown, garden. Clara had brought with her some provisions from Dunmow and had offered Rowena a final prayer to start her new life. 'Twould be difficult for her as a woman without a husband, and a babe too small to help, but Rowena had been determined to succeed.

She'd thought she would do well.

But now? She peered again at the ruined henhouse. Each day she'd found that one egg brought joy, and she'd offered thanks to God for it. A hope of a new life.

Not so anymore. The fair-headed Saxon villagers here had taken one look at Andrew and his mixed heritage and prejudged her. She'd heard the whispered words: "Traitor." "Spy." "Prostitute." They didn't even care to ask for the truth.

Rowena stifled a cry as she turned her gaze back to her garden. All the roots she'd stored in a straw-covered mound were scattered, snapped or crushed to a useless pulp by heavy boots. Nay, only one certainty settled over the awful, angry scene.

Someone wanted her to starve this winter.

Stephen de Bretonne accepted the reins of his courser and swung his leg up and over the saddle to mount the large chestnut beast. The mail of his hauberk chinked as he settled down. The horse stirred, expecting battle, or at least a good run, but Stephen kept the reins tight as he turned around to survey his village. Kingstown looked peaceful, very different from the politically charged dangers that flowed through the court in London.

Ha! Despite the gentle morning here at his holding, Stephen knew the lifting mist and soft dew masked the day's intrigue. These villagers could rival even the suspicious courtiers in Lon—

"Milord?"

Stephen snapped his attention to his young squire, a boy named Gaetan. The boy offered up a dagger. Reluctantly, he took the extra weapon. Wasn't it bad enough that he needed to carry his long sword each day? And now a dagger for extra measure? Beside him, atop another stallion, one of his own guards also accepted a dagger from a second young squire. With a scowl, Stephen led his mount from the stables. Along with other villages, this estate had been his reward for his bravery at Hastings, two years before.

Ha! What was bravery on the field at Hastings, when a man could not even save his own brother? Corvin had fought alongside him there, but one moment of distraction on Stephen's part and suddenly Corvin was dead.

And shortly after, King William had bestowed on Stephen many estates. Corvin should have been the one to receive them. He'd fought boldly until the end.

Now Stephen had more than enough land. With a tight jaw, he shoved the remorse back where it could not sting him, for the work ahead required his full attention.

He kept the seat of his holdings here in Kingstown, for none of the others had a manor house. Now he put his home behind him as he trotted along the road leading through the village, his sword scraping his saddle on one side, his dagger snug on the other. His chain mail sat heavy on his shoulders, as if expecting a battle instead of the quiet mists of morning.

Stephen was not afraid of fighting, for such was a part of his soldiering life. But he was not here for battle. His was a shrewder reason—to seek out those local agitators who would defy the king.

When William had ordered the task, Stephen had accepted it with a flick of his hand, but he'd soon learned 'twould not be easy. At court, he'd enjoyed the sly machinations of those who would try to outmaneuver King William, but here, the Saxons were craftier, feigning ignorance and hiding the troublemakers who oft taxed his soldiers to exhaustion. He was sick of Saxons, each pale face hiding secrets. For all he knew, one of these men had been the one to deal Corvin his fatal blow. Aye, the chances were slim, but they still remained.

Stephen felt the expected wash of terrible memory. 'Twas as if the moment Corvin died had been winked out, replaced by a blur and then a stretch of time where all Stephen saw was Corvin on the ground.

And in the weeks and months after, word reached him of their mother's reaction. Her accusing words to him still tore his heart. He'd lost both his brother and his mother that day at Senlac.

Nay, enough! There were chores to do.

And checking the defenses each morning he was here in Kingstown had become a distasteful chore. But King William was due to visit before winter, and Stephen knew his liege would order an embankment and palisade be cut through the forest to the north. 'Twould not be a popular command, and Stephen would not impose the task on the villagers yet, for they needed to finish storing their provisions for winter. But 'twould have to be started soon.

"Which way, milord?" the guard asked, pulling his horse up beside Stephen.

"'Tis my first day back and I must inspect it all." Stephen had been in London all summer, leaving this estate in his sister's capable hands. "It makes no difference. To the north, I suppose." Always the most unpleasant task first. There, the village wrestled constantly with the encroaching forest. Beyond it, the land dipped into the marshes and fens that reached all the way to Ely. Another backwater full of dissidents.

As he and his guard walked the horses, the mists rose to block the sun, and the day grew duller. Disgusted, Stephen spurred his horse to a trot through the thinnest portion of Kingstown. Ahead stood the village fence, the dilapidated weave of wattle designed to hold back marauders from the north. It sagged, rotting where it flopped into low spots. William would take one look at it and demand it be replaced immediately. Mayhap the trees cut to create a palisade could be used to—

Movement beyond the fence caught Stephen's eye, and he reined his horse back to a walk. Wisps of silver-blond hair danced in the light breeze as a woman stooped to lift something from her garden. With an almost forlorn air, her small hut stood behind her. The woman dipped again and her pale hair flipped like a feather in a breeze.

'Twas too early for anyone to be roused. Stephen had already noted that these Saxons preferred to sleep in on the misty days that hinted of winter. So what was the woman doing at this hour?

He halted his horse at the gate as the guard leaned forward in his own saddle to flip open the latch. All the while, Stephen remained stock-still, entranced by the woman's hair. 'Twas so unique a color, he would not have believed it existed if he'd only been told of it. But she was quite real, standing bareheaded in her garden, her whole demeanor one of sadness, like one of those minstrel girls who visited the king's court to entertain with songs of lost love.

"Milord?" his guard prompted him quietly.

Something squeezed Stephen's heart, but he ignored

the odd sensation. He hadn't been given Kingstown and its manor because he was an emotional clod. This village lay directly in the path between London and the rebellious north. A calculating tactician was needed here to draw out instigators who would bring down more from Ely. Extra troops would help, aye, but such had been discussed already in London, to no avail. They were still needed elsewhere.

Nay, until Stephen had eliminated all malcontents who would threaten the king's sovereignty, any softness of heart could get him murdered, and 'twas best ignored.

Still curious, though, he swung off his horse and walked through the gate toward the woman. Ah, this must be Rowena, the woman who'd taken this hut. His friend Lord Adrien had sent him a missive asking if he could find a home for her here. Only the hut beyond the fence had been vacant. Its proximity to the forest made it undesirable, for everyone knew the woods harbored thieves and criminals, worse than those who lived in the village.

Having been in London when Adrien's request arrived, Stephen had dispatched his brother-in-law, Gilles, to handle the issue of land and hut, and to set out the terms of tenancy. All he'd heard of this Rowena was that she'd been a slave, made free by order of the king himself, and that her rent for the next year had been paid in full by Adrien.

As Stephen passed his guard, the man dismounted, also. "'Tis the woman Rowena, milord."

"I know of her. I should like to meet her."

"She is of ill repute, sir," the guard warned.

Stopping, Stephen shot the man a surprised look. "Why?"

"The villagers say she's allied herself with us Normans. Did not Lord Adrien pay for her to be here?"

With a brief laugh, Stephen rolled his eyes, remembering one short conversation he'd had with his friend this past summer. "That means nothing. Lord Adrien is generous to all Saxons because he's besotted with his Saxon wife." Stephen shook his head, then peered again at the woman. "What is she doing?"

The guard stepped forward. "I will find out, milord."

Hand raised, Stephen stopped him. "Nay. I will. 'Tis time to introduce myself."

"Milord, she's Saxon and not to be trusted. For all we know, she'll sink a dagger into your heart the moment you speak to her."

Chuckling, Stephen touched his chain mail. "Yet she allied herself with us? You make no sense, soldier. Besides, the woman is barely out of girlhood and she's far too skinny to have enough strength to pierce my mail. Ha, if I were fearful of every Saxon, I would not leave my bedchamber. The king gave me this holding to—" He stopped. 'Twould not do well to say the king's reasons for bringing him here. He continued, "I should at least meet all of this village's inhabitants."

Without waiting for an answer, Stephen strode up the lane toward her. The guard led the horses, but Stephen also heard the slow scrape of steel leaving a scabbard. The man had freed his sword.

Stephen's courser whinnied loudly at the sound so akin to war. And at both harsh noises, the woman ahead spun. Again, Stephen was struck by her hair as it flowed with her movement. Aye, Saxons were towheaded, thanks to their northern ancestry, but never had he seen hair so free and so pale. This Rowena hadn't even braided it yet, something that would have appalled his mother.

She looked up at him and he found her eyes were almost too light to look upon. A blue as delicate as in the stained-glass window in his home church in Normandy. Stephen watched her body tense. She twisted the broken root she held into a deadly grip one might reserve for a dagger.

"Planning to bury that parsnip in my chest?" asked Stephen as he opened the short gate of the hut's small fence. Then he halted, shocked at the disarray. The pen at the far end had been tossed on its side, its door hanging by one hinge. Roots and vegetables were strewn about, some crushed as if a furious giant of lore had turned his wrath upon this garden.

Rowena said nothing, only keeping her grip on the parsnip tight as she backed away. Immediately, Stephen regretted his sharp tongue. He had no desire to frighten her.

Still in English, he tried a lighter tone. "'Tis not the best way to preserve your crops for winter, or to keep your fowl from escaping."

She tossed the root onto the ground. "You think I do not know this?"

"An animal in the night?"

"Ha! Only one who wears boots," she snapped. She quickly brushed the back of her hand across her glistening cheek, leaving a smudge of tear-dampened dirt in its wake.

"Who did this? Did you see them?" Stephen asked.

"Nay. I heard nothing, so they must have done this late into the night. Cowards!"

Stephen stepped gingerly around the garden, close

to the door of her hut, to survey the mess. "Why would anyone do such a thing?"

Rowena said nothing. Stephen watched her. Though silent, she carried a wealth of information in the way she stood. She knew the reason for this vandalizing, he was sure. "Have you any enemies?" he asked.

She stiffened. "I should not have any! I have been here a month at best, and tried to speak with the other women, only to be treated like an outcast. That I can deal with, but this? I shall surely starve this winter because of their evil!" Her voice hitched slightly.

"I'll see to it that doesn't happen."

"Who are you that—" Her gaze flew up and then narrowed. "You're Baron Stephen." Rowena's cold whisper scratched like brambles, leaving it to feel more of an accusation than a statement.

"Aye. And you are Rowena, late of Dunmow."

"I did not live in Dunmow. I came from a farm in the west, near Cambridge."

Relatively close. Stephen pursed his lips. Most of this county had suffered greatly under William's scorched-earth policies when he'd marched north to fight after taking London. But Cambridge had fared moderately better, for 'twas nothing but a backwater village as rude as any wild moor that lay to the south. Though the manor houses in the king's path had been razed and the holdings would suffer much for years to come, the most isolated farmers, those with little contact with civilization, had escaped total destruction. Had she come from one of them?

Rowena threw her arms out to the mess around them. "We Saxons live hand to mouth here, barely affording a grain of barley. You offer food where you should be finding who did this!"

Aye, 'twas exactly his reason for being here. "'Twill be easy enough to discover. My experience in London has taught me several techniques of extracting the truth."

She gasped. His calm answer was guileless, although he was not one to employ brutal punishment to acquire information. 'Twas better to keep one's eyes and ears open and, for the most part, one's mouth shut. A calm manner was more apt to lure out subterfuge than a harsh beating.

"So, tell me, how did you end up in Dunmow, as guest of my friend Lord Adrien?"

Rowena remained stiff. The breeze dropped and her hair fell, a single flaxen curtain of sword-straight locks. She went still, and if 'tweren't for the light breath that streamed from her lips, he'd have thought she'd turned to stone. Finally, she said, "I was not his guest, milord."

Stephen didn't want to know what she wasn't. Odd that she wouldn't answer his question directly. Was there a hidden reason, or was he seeing intrigue where only shadows of Saxon distrust lay?

Then, from within the hut, a babe cried loudly. Lifting the damp hem of her cyrtel, Rowena swung past him, her chin tipped up and her mouth tight. Her eyes, too wide set and too large for her face, turned icy blue, adding to the chill of the morning. Yet, by their sheer size alone, they offered only innocence.

Stephen reached forward to open the door for her. 'Twas not required, but his mother's training had been drilled into him long before his promotion to baron.

She flinched at his raised arm. 'Twas merely a blink and a slight jerk back, and so swift he would have missed it had his gaze not been sealed to her face.

Then 'twas gone, replaced by wariness. But he knew what he saw, and though not uncommon in a land where women had few rights, he disliked seeing fear in any woman's eyes.

Aye, Rowena was scared. Hurt, also, but mostly frightened. Stephen stepped aside as she ducked into the hut, her cloak wafting out as she passed. The youthful screams within were soon replaced by soothing murmurs.

Wandering from the door, Stephen looked again at the vandal's work. He bent several times to study and measure the boot prints he spied, while noticing their tread. The clear imprints of heavy boots all the same size told him that only one man had done this. The cur had crushed an egg, had laid waste to late-season herbs and had trampled the roots until they were completely inedible. Not just any man's boots, Stephen noted as he straightened again. A *Saxon* man's boots. The simple style was unmistakable.

Why would a Saxon destroy this young woman's food stocks? Because she was rumored to have allied herself with the Normans? She was far too young for such subterfuge. It had been two years since William's victory at Hastings. This Rowena would have been barely into womanhood back then. But still, a Saxon? One from the village, too, for the boot prints retreated toward the huts rather than disappearing into the forest to the north. This attack made no sense.

The door behind him opened again. Stephen turned to watch Rowena step outside with a babe in her arms.

The babe had dark hair and olive skin, and only one lineage with men of that complexion was in England right now. For some reason, his heart sank.

So that was how she was aligned with the Normans.

Chapter Two

Though not ashamed of her babe, for he brought such great joy to her, Rowena knew that his dark hair, bred into him from his father, gave away a parentage she'd have preferred to hide.

She sagged. She'd seen Lord Stephen's surprise. Soon, suspicion would follow and then, distaste evident, he would walk away, putting the woman with no husband behind him. She'd seen it often enough in this village.

"Aye," she muttered, tugging Andrew's cap back on after he'd reached up to yank it off. With the other hand, he caught her rough wool cloak. "He's my son." She held back the urge to explain. Nay, 'twas no one's business. She'd already learned that few people would believe her, anyway. To those scoffers, she was a simple farm girl with a wild tale of slavery and scheming, something unbelievable from a creature looking for sympathy because she'd found herself pregnant after a shameful tryst. She leveled her stare at him. "Aye, his father is Norman."

Rowena looked away, not wanting to see the shadow of turning in his expression. This tall, strong man was just another Norman—untrustworthy. Lord Stephen may not be Taurin, who had been exiled to Normandy for his treacherous plan to use her babe to usurp the king, and, aye, that same king had agreed to her move here, but she would not trust this man one jot. Only Lord Adrien had shown her any kindness. He was the exception, having a Saxon wife of great influence, whom he loved very much.

Her friend, Clara, though, had taught her to hold her head up high. 'Twas not her fault she'd been an unwilling partner in the creation of her beautiful babe. With that reminder, Rowena straightened and lifted her chin.

The look of surprise on Stephen's face dissolved like mist under a hot sun. "The boy's paternity is of no concern to me."

No concern? She wet her lips, suddenly perplexed by his calm reaction. Did it really not interest him? Or did he hide it well? She wasn't sure.

He cleared his throat. "As you know, I am Baron Stephen de Bretonne. This village is my responsibility."

"Then you are failing, sir," Rowena replied softly, with a furtive glance to her ruined garden and with a measure of relief that he didn't turn away in disgust.

"Apparently so," he answered. "But in my defense, I have been in London for the summer and just arrived home last night."

Rowena could hear only the slightest French accent in his English words. He was surprisingly fluent in her mother tongue. "And what exactly is your responsibility now that you're here?" Despite her bold words, Rowena battled the sting of fearful tears. She walked to the garden, hoping in her survey of the damage that she might find some salvageable food, for surely this man would do little to help her, despite his promise. Setting Andrew on the ground, and making sure there was nothing around him he could choke on, for he was apt to put everything into his mouth, Rowena began the grim task of sorting through the disarray. She set aside the few roots that remained mostly whole, whilst those mashed would either nourish the soil or be rinsed in the river before being boiled into a pottage. She refused to waste anything. Everything here had been a gift to start her new life, and she would not treat poorly a single portion of it.

Behind her, deprived of her attention, Andrew squawked. Then squawked again. With a sigh, she turned in time to see Baron Stephen scoop the babe into his arms.

With a gasp, she leaped to her feet and snatched Andrew from the tall Norman's grip. "Nay! He's mine!" Then, with one free hand, she shoved him back with all her might. The hauberk's chain mail bit into her palm.

Immediately, the guard burst forward to shield his lord. He pressed the point of a long Norman blade against her throat. She cried out, clutching her babe close as she stared at what could be the instrument of her death.

Stephen reacted swiftly, grabbing the blade and pulling it away from Rowena's neck. In the same fluid movement, he drove the weapon into the soft, damp earth. "Stand down, soldier!" he ordered, planting himself between the guard and Rowena. He then turned to her.

Her arms protecting her child, Rowena flinched again. Terror flooded her expression. Stephen tightened his jaw. In the past, any fear he'd caused, especially due to his height, had pleased him. He'd even cultivated it occasionally, for intimidation alone often kept his king safe. As captain of the King's Guard, Stephen had made William's safety paramount. 'Twas the only reason the Good Lord had given him life.

But today, seeing Rowena's fear, he found his belly

souring. 'Twas obvious, based on the way she shied from him, that the man who'd fathered this child had done so using that same fear and intimidation Stephen employed in court. His belly churned further. She was hardly aligned with *any* Norman. 'Twas only a filthy rumor against her.

He glanced swiftly around him at the shambles. So someone in this village felt that she needed to be taught a lesson? Immediately, an idea blossomed. Tightening his jaw, Stephen turned to his guard. "Return to the horses."

As the man reluctantly retreated, Stephen focused his attention on Rowena again. With no blade at her throat anymore, she should have been relieved, but fear still lit her eyes despite her uptilted chin and the squareness in her shoulders.

Father in heaven, take away her fear.

"'Tis all right, Rowena," he stated calmly. "My guard thought I was threatened."

Her eyes flared. "You were! By me! You grabbed my babe!"

Stephen shrugged mildly. "He was fussing."

"I wasn't paying attention to him, that's all. He'd have stopped in a moment. 'Tis often so with babes. Sometimes, they want their mother and nothing else will do."

She spoke with an accent Stephen didn't recognize. But he'd learned that here in England, each tiny village had its own unique way of speaking. "I don't remember fussing when my mother turned her back."

Rowena flushed and shifted the boy in her arms. Away from Stephen. Again, she fixed the babe's wayward cap.

"Please don't mock me, my lord. You would not remember fussing." Then, with a glance behind him, she added, "And please, if I have satisfied your curiosity, will you depart? Your presence here is rousing the interest of my neighbors, and I don't wish to be seen in any Norman's company."

Stephen spun. The family living in the hut closest to the village fence was now standing by the gate, each person peering with unabashed interest. The father, a belligerent Saxon Stephen had met several times, scowled the worst. If there was ever a troublemaker, this man was it. But Stephen had no proof yet. However, with William's new edict, Stephen didn't need much evidence to arrest anyone. 'Twas only his personal integrity that he have adequate reason.

Like this attack on Rowena's harvest? Stephen glanced back at her. He mentally counted the distance. Her home was closest to the forest, outside the wattle fencing and at least twenty long strides from her nearest neighbor. Hers was a hut set apart long ago for some unknown reason. And judging from the foul expressions on her neighbors' faces, not far enough.

Noticing his return glare, the Saxons retreated from the fence. Stephen faced Rowena again. "Do you think those people vandalized your garden?"

She shook her head. "I cannot say. I heard no one last night." She cleared her throat as she avoided his eyes. "My lord, I must return to my task and salvage what food is left. If you have no more questions, please excuse me."

Her fearful expression shot up to him again, one that set his teeth on edge. Knowing he could do nothing about her reaction in the next few moments, Stephen nodded and strode back to the fence, sending the neighbors scurrying into their hut. As he mounted his courser, he noted several other Saxons, having been roused from their pallets, poking out heads and peering at the odd scene he'd created.

Deliberately swinging his horse and his harsh glare around that end of the village and being successful in forcing the curious back into their homes, Stephen returned his attention to Rowena. She, too, had retreated into her hut.

He sighed, the air leaking from his lungs like a pierced skin of cider. 'Twas for the best that everyone here remain intimidated and therefore subdued, but to have Rowena fall into that category left bitterness on his tongue, a taste he knew would linger until he broke his fast. And that would not happen until after he'd inspected the forest's edge and made note of where to start the work on the embankment that would keep this village safe should those rebels at Ely attack.

At the gate, Stephen hauled in the reins of his courser and noticed that Rowena had once again slipped outside. Her soft, pale hair danced in the morning breeze as she stooped to return to her task.

She'll find little food in that mess, and the two cages she'd owned are destroyed. She would have had a hen, but what else? Rabbits, maybe? 'Twas rare for a Saxon to own rabbits. Mayhap jealousy spurred the attack?

Stephen's jaw clenched as he watched Rowena search around the pens for her livestock, all the while furtively sweeping tears off her cheeks. Once she dropped onto her knees and covered her face. He jerked forward, his fingers tightening on the wooden pommel of his saddle. The only reason he did not leap from his mount was because he knew she'd only ask him to leave again. Out of the corner of his eye, he spied his guard watching him closely, his eyes dark under the rim of his steel helmet.

Stephen turned his courser and the animal snorted and stamped its feet impatiently. He knew he could do nothing more until he completed a new task. 'Twould be one that, if employed properly, could serve both *his* needs and Rowena's.

Aye. Then those Saxons who would make trouble for the king would think twice about supporting those fools at Ely in their losing cause.

Startling even his guard, Stephen galloped his horse back to his home to carry out his plan.

Slack-jawed, Rowena stared at the sight of the wrapped stalks of grain and the gunnysack of root vegetables. She blinked when the young woman in front of her set half a cheese round atop the load. Someone had wrapped the expensive treat in leaves and tied it snugly with thin vines. Everything was secured by a fraying rope that had been tied at many points.

Her visitor smiled expectantly at Rowena, but she couldn't return it. She had seen this girl near the manor house, but had not approached her. Why should she? The rest of the village had scorned her and her babe. Why go looking for more of the same? Finally, words formed and Rowena muttered, "What is all this?"

"'Tis a gift from Lord Stephen," the woman answered in English with an accent that told Rowena she was a local. "He said you have need of it." Her smile increased.

Automatically, Rowena glanced to her right where she'd spent the better part of the day. So far, she'd recovered only a meager portion of her harvest. Her attempt to rinse the crushed roots had met with little success, for grit and dirt were imbedded deep in the mash of vegetables, and often the current in the nearby stream broke apart the delicate pieces. Tears choked her again but she fought them back.

The woman followed her gaze, and her hopeful expression fell into dismay. "What happened?"

"'Twould seem that I am not welcomed here."

As if to remind her why, Andrew cried out from where he was seated nearby. The woman's attention snapped to him and in that instant, her expression turned to joy. "Oh, such a beautiful child! Look at that lovely thick hair!"

About to answer that his hair came from his father, Rowena stopped her words. She'd be stating the obvious and adding the suggestion that she'd willingly partaken in Andrew's creation. Was that not what the people here thought?

She smiled stiffly instead. "He's a good boy, but hates it when I don't heed him."

The young woman abandoned the food to scoop up the boy. She fingered the curls that peeked out from the edges of his cap. "Aye, 'tis like all men." She bounced him a bit. For her effort, she received a squeal and a giggle. Her smile broadened so much, Rowena was sure 'twould split her face in two.

"The villagers see this babe as the result of you conspiring with the Normans." The girl's expression turned compassionate as she glanced back at Rowena. "They are hated here. I know. I work at the manor and was also born in this village. Those who destroyed your winter provisions are probably my relatives, I'm ashamed to say. Sometimes, they even scorn me for working as a simple housemaid for Lord Stephen. They oppose everyone living at the manor. But we need the work and they forget the sacrifice that saved them from King William."

Rowena shook her head. Who had saved them? What sacrifice? This woman's? Or Lord Stephen's? Immediately, she crushed her curiosity, for she would not get cozy with anyone here. This woman might be offering genuine friendship, or she might be a spy sent to see if more damage could be inflicted.

Still, the maid seemed kind and there was never any reason to be rude. Rowena walked over to the young servant and took Andrew from her. "What's your name?"

"I'm Ellie. It's short for Eleanor, but that was my grandmother's name and I think it sounds old," she answered cheerfully. "Your name is so pretty. But it doesn't match your hair, I don't think. To me, it sounds like a red-haired woman. You know, like the color of rowan berries."

Rowena grimaced, and not because her name meant "white one." Nay, 'twas because her hair had attracted Taurin, whose own wife was also fair-haired. Even Master Gilles, who'd set forth the terms of Rowena's tenancy, had light hair, but 'twas uncommon among the Normans she'd seen. Most had medium to dark hair, and none as light as Saxons'.

Her hair was so fine, she could barely keep it braided, and she hated the way it would fly around at the slightest breeze. She may as well have duck down on her head. 'Twould be warmer at least. 'Twas why she hadn't bothered to do anything with it this morning.

Forget the hair. She turned to the food that sat in a cart Ellie had towed here. From the corner of her eye, she noticed some villagers had gathered. *Again.* All stared her way. *Oh, dear.* 'Twas a repeat of earlier today, when Baron Stephen visited. And 'twould be easy enough for even a child to guess where this bounty came from.

Thankfully, no one appeared ready to reprimand Ellie for being there. Mayhap because she was on her master's business. All well and good now, but what would happen tonight? Would those men return to destroy these gifts?

They, too, were gifts from a Norman, like what she'd

brought with her from Dunmow, where Lord Adrien held his seat. He and Lady Ediva had given her livestock and the vegetables she'd stored in those destroyed mounds. Though she had convinced herself that 'twas Saxon wealth donated to her, Rowena couldn't deny it was also in part Norman.

But today's offerings were all Norman. They'd have to be taken into her hut for safekeeping. What would her attacker do then? Burst in? Rowena squared her shoulders. "Take them back, Ellie. I don't want them."

Ellie's jaw fell. "Back? I can't do that, Rowena! Lord Stephen himself ordered me here. He listed all the provisions I was to collect. 'Tis his gift to you!"

"I have had quite enough 'gifts' from Normans. I was bought by a Norman once, and I won't be bought again."

Confused, Ellie protested, "You're not being bought!"

"But I am! First 'twas with coinage. Now 'tis with food. I won't accept this." To prove her point, she grabbed the sling Clara had fashioned for her and hoisted Andrew into it. Brushing past a dumbfounded Ellie, she wheeled the old, wobbly cart across the yard and through the village gate. Locals stepped out of her way as she bumped the cart over the dirt path that led to the manor house. It loomed tall, from its stone foundation to its thickly thatched roof. The entrance jutted from the end, with carved stone columns that forced her gaze up to the strong, straight chimneys high above the fine thatch. The front bore grand windows with panes of skin vellum thin enough to allow in much sunlight.

Forcing away hesitation at such grandeur, Rowena called out over her shoulder to Ellie, "Is Lord Stephen at home?"

Hiking up her cyrtel, the shocked maid hurried up beside her. "Aye. Rowena, you must reconsider! You'll starve this winter without food!" As they approached the manor, Ellie glanced around and lowered her voice. "And you know my menfolk won't help you."

Babe bouncing in the sling, Rowena kept trudging, refusing to acknowledge the doubt pricking her decision. 'Twas a dangerous and bold move, one born of an impulse, but nay, she would not be owing to another Norman!

The guard lounging by the front door of the manor house straightened when she approached, but not for her. The solid arched front doors opened suddenly and out walked Stephen.

Before her courage drained away, Rowena rotated the cart toward him and handed him the well-worn handle. "I thank you for this gift, milord, but I cannot accept it."

Stephen looked down at her. He'd exchanged the chain mail he'd worn earlier for a tunic of fine linen, dyed a rich blue. Dark leggings were secured with new leather thongs, revealing his powerful legs. The cloak he'd tossed over his shoulders was also made from a material finer even than what she'd seen in Colchester, which boasted good weavers. Its embroidered hem lifted a bit in the increasing breeze. He was an imposing figure, and Rowena battled the foolishness now creeping in. She stepped away from the temptation of relenting. "I will not take your gift, milord."

"Why not?" he asked calmly.

"'Tis wrong for me to accept food from your house and your family."

He lifted his brows. "My family won't starve this winter."

Rowena could see the brawny upper-arm muscles pressing against his sleeves. And the wind brought from him the scents of mint and meadowsweet, a mix that encouraged her to inhale deeply. She refused.

"I have already accepted a hut from you, and the gift of rent money from another Norman." She clutched Andrew closer, smoothing his cap as if 'twould strengthen her. "Not to mention what the first Norman I met gave me. I'm seen as siding with your people, and I want the village here to know that I am not."

"How will you do that? By starving to death?"

"You know nothing of me. I have always survived and I will do so this winter."

Stephen appeared unimpressed by her boast. Galled, she wondered if he had any reactions at all within him. "How?" he asked finally.

Rowena shut her mouth, refusing to enlighten him. When she was younger, she'd been sent to the barn at mealtimes, to wait for crumbs and leftovers, whatever the dog rejected, because she wasn't worth the food. She was too small, too weak, a runt best left to fend for itself. Eventually, she was told to sleep there, as well.

She shuddered. Nay, she would not linger on what her family had done to her simply because she'd had the misfortune to be born last and a female. And she would not allow that bitter memory to weaken her stance now.

With determination she answered, "There is still time to gather food. I know how. I am farm stock. We Saxons have weathered droughts and storms that destroyed our provisions, not to mention a Norman invasion. I *will* survive!"

Chapter Three

Stephen could hardly believe his ears. This arrow-thin girl was refusing his offer of food? And with a babe in her arms? If someone had told him yesterday this would happen, he'd have burst out laughing.

Then he saw one of the reasons for her addled answer. The villagers, whose names were harsh Saxon words nearly unpronounceable, had stopped their work to watch the conversation with more frost in their glares than a cold winter's day.

One of them had vandalized Rowena's home. For a heartbeat, vengeance scorched him, but Stephen was not given to acting on impulse, for in London, as well as in King William's home in Normandy, doing so could lead to enemies. And when one had enemies, one tended to die mysteriously in the night.

"I can force you to take this food," he countered coolly, his words providing the buffer of time needed to consider his options.

Her shoulders stiff, Rowena answered in the same cool tone, "Nay, you cannot, nor will you waste your provisions by leaving them out for wild animals to scavenge." She gazed over at the villagers. "Or worse. Who-ever saw fit to ruin mine may finish off yours."

True, he thought. He would not waste food when win-ter was coming and mayhap also his king, with extra men for him. Dropping provisions into her lap may have been a misstep on his part, he added to himself.

Mayhap not. The idea that had budded in his mind earlier now returned ready to bloom. William couldn't afford to put soldiers in every corner of this land, but he could put people like Stephen at strategic points to root out those who would want to stir up trouble for the new sovereign.

Arresting those persons would go far to subdue these Saxons. They'd soon learn to behave after seeing their loved ones who still defied the king thrown in jail, flogged or worse.

Stephen studied Rowena. She was hardly a traitor to her people, but her stubbornness refused to allow her to admit her true story to anyone. Aye, he told himself. She could be useful here. Using her to lure out the per-son who attacked her would be the same as luring out those who would defy the king. 'Twould be best for all here if he found that person, for the alternative was to raze this village, something no one wanted.

Stephen paused in his planning. The people knew their lands had not been razed because of the dowager baroness, whose family had had influence with King Ed-ward. She'd requested an audience with William when he'd marched through. Stephen had watched the events unfold with interest, for her son had fought against Wil-liam at Hastings. But the dowager had been charming and genteel, perhaps reminding William of his own mother, and she'd convinced the king to spare her vil-lage in return for her prayers and role here as anchoress.

Though not privy to the conversation, Stephen had later suggested Udella remain within the manor proper. She may prove helpful in finding the local trouble-makers. Of course, the wily old vixen would not will-ingly reveal them, despite her pious promise to the king to work for peace here, but Stephen was confident he could coax the names from her.

Aye, 'twas a good plan forming. With Rowena as bait and Udella wanting peace and knowing that it may have to come at the sacrifice of the agitators, Stephen now re-alized that giving this woman food would certainly rile up the locals enough to cause them to reveal themselves. But first, he had to get her to accept his offer.

"What, then, are your plans," he asked, "since you don't want this food? Have you considered the dead of winter? The snow can be quite harsh, and that babe will want solid food by then."

If Rowena wouldn't take the food, he knew he may have to force her. 'Twould do her good, for she would surely starve otherwise. 'Twas not a thought he liked, for some reason. And it certainly would not be good for his plans.

As Stephen watched her, Rowena wet her lips and swallowed. With that sword-straight spine of hers, he thought, she obviously had not considered winter at all.

Someone behind him broke into a heavy coughing fit, something caused by a mild fever that had started through the village. Stephen had to do something fast, for more villagers had begun to congregate. He caught a glimpse behind Rowena of Ellie, the essence of remorse for being unsuccessful in her task. "Take half the grain and roots to the larder," he told his young maid. "Leave the cheese."

Then, to the guard, he barked, "Since these villagers aren't interested in doing their own work, they can work for the crown. Assemble them in the north forest. Have them begin cutting the trees. The palisade must be started before your king arrives. Oh," he added, "save the saplings for the fence. It needs to be repaired."

Stephen waited patiently until the guard and the villagers moved out of earshot, his gaze sealed on Rowena the whole time. She stood stock-still, with only her short breathing lightly rocking the drowsy child she carried. Her gaze stayed on his chest, not at his feet, where the servants kept theirs, nor in his eyes as a person of equal rank may look. Nay, she wanted to defy him, yet didn't dare do so.

He unfolded his arms. "What is the real reason for this refusal, Rowena? You *need* food. We both know that."

She blinked and sniffed. Still, she shook her head. "Nay, I refuse to accept any more charity from you Normans. I have taken quite enough, thank you."

"And if I were Saxon?"

She didn't answer, though a gentle shiver rippled her light frame as she glanced away. Would she not accept aid from her own people, either?

"'Tis just as well," he finally said. "For I expect that he who vandalized your home last night would lay siege to it again should it be filled with provisions." 'Twas exactly what he wanted, but he would not tell her that.

Rowena reacted with a wrinkled chin and tightened lips and yet added steel in her spine. "Aye, 'twould do nothing but ruin good food."

"We wouldn't want that," he murmured.

But he would like to find who had done so last night. Stephen had discovered enemies of the king before, traitors who would sooner slit your throat than smile at you.

Though William ruled with an iron fist, the king had to put his trust in someone. Sometimes that was Eudo, his steward, or that monk William de St. Calais, but for the most part, protection came from Stephen and his watchful eye and subtle machinations, guiding the people around him to work for, not against, the king. He may be captain of the King's Guard, but he was also William's best spymaster. 'Twould be more than easy to root out troublemakers here by using a simple maid.

Stephen extended his hand toward the front door. "Mayhap we can discuss this over some strong broth and a portion of good cheese?"

"Nay, there is nothing to discuss," Rowena answered with a stubborn lip. "I won't take your charity, my lord. And do not be concerned for me."

"And when you get vandalized again?"

Finally, with brows lifted, her eyes met his. That remarkable pale color clouded with apprehension. "I will not, for there is nothing left to vandalize."

Stephen paused. *True.*

Oddly, the thought of Rowena starving turned his stomach, a compassionate feeling so alien to him, it took him a moment to recognize it. He wasn't used to reacting with emotion. His portion in life was to think with his head, not his heart.

But if he could get Rowena to take even some of the food, 'twould satisfy both his plan to stir the pot of dissention *and* his compassion.

However, he'd discovered two years ago that Saxons were not a logical people. They fought with their hearts, not their heads. Rowena was acting on her foolish pride in refusing this food.

Did you not already react with emotion to the thought of her being hurt? Or hungry? Or with another man?

Stephen stiffened. Nay, he was acting on his king's orders, plain and simple.

"One small request, then?" he countered, thankful that only the two of them lingered at the door. "A bit of food, sold to you?"

"I have no money, milord."

"Few have until the bills are collected at Michaelmas."

"When the taxes take all?"

"Your taxes and rent have already been paid for this year. I have often sold food and wood, and not taken the payment until collection time." He frowned, realizing that she probably had nothing to trade for coinage. "Is it not the way at your farm, where goods and livestock were bought and sold?"

At the mention of her home, her gaze hardened. He noticed it immediately. "I had nothing to do with such dealings," she snapped. "I was to care for the livestock and weed the gardens. Because of that, I know I can forage for enough food to last all winter."

He shouldn't have, but still, Stephen laughed. "'Tis easy to say you won't accept food when your belly isn't crying out for it in the cold of winter." He dropped his smile and softened, doing his best to make his tone mild. "Did you have a good evening meal last night? Was it so filling that you aren't hungry even now?"

Rowena's throat constricted and she glanced once more at the corner of the manor, around which half the provisions had been carted. Her delicate eyes glistened. Stephen hated to reprimand her pride, however gently, but 'twas more necessary than simply working through his latest plan. This was her life and the life of her child at risk.

She glanced up at him. *Don't let your pride over-*

rule your good sense, he pleaded silently. "You have no money now, but do you have a skill with which can earn you some?"

She paused. "Aye, milord. I can make rope. Good rope, strong enough for the North Sea."

"The North Sea? I have not seen it, but I hear 'tis violent."

"I was taught rope making by the daughter of a man who fished it."

Stephen watched Rowena's eyes stray to the food on the flagstones. Ellie had secured the bundle to the cart with a worn, knotted rope. Good rope went to the various training pulleys his soldiers used to keep their muscles toned. Aye, this manor could use all the new rope it could get.

But the issue wasn't about rope. "'Tis good to break one's fast in the morning with a thick slice of hard cheese and a cup of hot broth," he coaxed companionably. "Such food lasts a body all day."

Again, Rowena glanced at the cheese resting between them. Her babe squealed. Finally, she offered, "Very well. I will take a small portion of food from you, but I will repay you in rope *and* netting."

Stephen nodded blandly. "Every estate needs them. Can you make enough?"

"Aye, if I begin today. I have not taken charity from the Normans, and I won't start now."

His brows shot up. Proud, indeed, but didn't she just tell him she'd taken enough charity from the Normans? "What about Lord Adrien?"

"Nay, that charity came from Dunmow Keep. 'Twas Saxon wealth."

Stephen smiled. Let her think that way if it justifies her decision. But his smile dropped as quickly as it came. Why would someone want to hurt her, when it could be argued that she had not aligned herself with the Normans?

Rowena fought back tears as she lay on her pallet in her dark hut that night. Her babe had finally drifted off to sleep, and she'd tucked away all the food she'd bought from Stephen. Tucked it from her sight and hopefully her thoughts in the coming days, for surely she would gobble it all down otherwise, she was that hungry.

Instead, after collecting the weed stalks she needed for her rope making, she'd stirred to a slurry the pottage made from the salvaged roots in her garden. She'd hoped she'd rinsed away all the grit left behind by the boot prints, but on the first, crunchy bite, she knew 'twas not so. The meal had to do, however. She wouldn't dip into those winter provisions. She would do that in the dark cold of a winter's eve when once more, hunger won over her shame and trusting another Norman didn't sour her empty belly.

Lord God, strengthen me to survive the winter, to be able to make enough rope and nets to sell.

Not for the first time since Rowena returned to her hut, Lord Stephen's big frame and cool, impenetrable gaze visited her thoughts. He was too hard to read. She'd learned to decipher her father's thoughts early on, his calculating dealings with other farmers or the way his mouth would tighten before he backhanded her for not moving quickly enough. She'd also learned Taurin's subtle hints that his mood had shifted and her evening would become a frightening ordeal.

Yet Lord Stephen's face remained a mystery. Those dark eyes, smooth lips and broad shoulders revealed nothing. All she'd seen was the merest hint of compassion when she'd said there was nothing left to vandalize. But the softness was brief and darting, like a nighthawk at dusk.

Kindness scared her as much as seeing her father's lip curl or Taurin's lustful squint before he took what he wanted. Nay, she didn't dare even think on Lord Stephen's generosity, for surely it came with a hefty price.

In the dark of her hut, shameful tears pricked her eyes. She'd given in to her hunger, taken the food and had done exactly as Lord Stephen wished, despite her promise to refuse the gift.

Lord, why am I so weak?

She'd done much the same with Lord Taurin, when he'd held back food to ensure compliance. Only when he'd realized she was pregnant did he take better care of her, but 'twas just for his evil plan.

Livestock, that was what she'd been to him. But what was she to Lord Stephen?

Nay! Lord God, not the same thing!

But nothing about him suggested he was like Lord Taurin. 'Twas not slyness or lust in his eyes. He gave her his full attention, and the way he moved his body did not alert her of evil to come.

Still, he was a Norman. And a man.

Ensuring her babe was warm and tucked into his sling close to her chest, Rowena curled around him on her pallet. She pulled the wool blanket and her cloak around them to stop up any drafts. Mayhap someday, she would put all the horrors of the past year and the shame of today behind her.

But now, within the dark hut, she lay awake, eyes shut to tempt the elusive sleep, all the while refusing to move for fear of awakening Andrew.

She'd let her small fire die, knowing that in her spark

box was an ember that would glow all night, and with it she could rekindle her fire in the morning. 'Twas wise to conserve fuel before winter.

Had the fire died? Rowena sniffed the cool air. Was that smoke she smelled? She opened her eyes and turned her head.

A glow lit up the thatch above the door just as acrid smoke stung her eyes.

Then, on the section above the door near where the spark box sat, a tendril of glowing smoke kindled and a flame burst upward.

She gasped in horror.

Chapter Four

Rowena wrapped one hand around her babe and bolted upright. Her house was on fire!

Despite the damp days, the old thatch burned readily. For one horrifying moment, she stared hypnotically at it, at how easily the fire consumed her roof while dancing provocatively in front of her.

Then, as if shoved hard, Rowena reacted. She had but a moment to escape. Throwing open the door, she plowed head down under the flames and into the dark of the evening. With a series of stumbling steps, she ran beyond her garden before a spasm of pain tore through her ankle.

She cried out as she sank onto all fours. Andrew, tucked safely in his sling, protested the sudden jerking. As she rose, a new spike of pain wrenched her ankle, but she ignored it enough to scream, "Fire!"

'Twas a farmer's worst nightmare. Years ago, fire had destroyed her family's barn, killing livestock and burning feed and foodstuffs. 'Twas Rowena who'd awakened and escaped the burning barn to rouse her family. Their home would have been consumed as well and all would have died otherwise.

Several hut doors flew open, with one man calling out to another as they surged into action. Men poured through the village gate. A woman pulled Rowena out of the way. Within a short time, people were everywhere, soldiers, Saxons, even Lord Stephen himself passing forward buckets of water to toss on the small house.

Someone raked the roof, pulling down the thatch for others to stamp out the fire that hit the dirt. Rowena could barely see them through her stinging tears. A woman beside her gripped her tightly, and at one point, when the fire flared into the night sky and the noise of men was the loudest, Rowena turned to see her companion's face.

'Twas Ellie, the young maid who'd delivered food to her. She was blinking back tears herself, her arms tight around Rowena. Crushed between them, Andrew cried, and Rowena stepped back to bob him up and down.

Finally, the glow of fire died. The last of the burning thatch was pulled away from the hut and extinguished, and a collective sigh raced through the villagers.

"Are you all right? What happened?"

Swiping her face, Rowena blinked. Lord Stephen stood in front of her. Someone nearby lifted a lantern to cast a light now that the wild flames were gone.

Dressed only in light braes and a pale shirt, he was as soaked and muddied as the rest. His height and strength showed as fierce as in any Norman she'd met. Rowena stepped back, her arms tightening around Andrew. What did he ask her?

Stephen caught her arm. "Rowena?" His voice softened. "Are you all right?"

Mutely, she nodded, glancing around him. Aye, she was fine. But her home…gone?

His tone still quiet, he asked, "Can you tell us what happened?"

With a shake of her head to dispel the fog of shock, she tried her voice. "I—I don't know. I was down for the night when I smelled smoke. I turned and saw the thatch above the door glowing." Her voice caught a short hiccup. "Then it just burst into flames!"

"Above the door? What is there to start a fire?"

She shook her head. "The spark box. But I hadn't done anything to it, except to ensure the piece of bone was still aglow."

Another male voice cut in, saying, "She must not have closed the lid properly, Stephen. A piece of dust probably dropped into it and caught fire."

Rowena squinted into the dark, smoky night. Who was this man, just beyond the circle of light, that he would call Lord Stephen by his Christian name? She could see only the outline of a fair-headed man. Master Gilles? For a moment, he looked like one of the villagers, his clothes soaked and muddied.

"Mayhap," Stephen answered him. "'Tis fortunate that we saved all but the front part of the roof. The thatch can be replaced. Less so the beams and braces." He turned to one of his soldiers and ordered a fire picket for the remainder of the night.

Then he turned again to Rowena. Even in the dim light of the lamp's low flame, his dark eyes drilled into her, sending a shiver through her as cool as the night.

What did he want?

Oh, Lord God, please let it not be—

"Come," he said, breaking apart her thoughts. "You can finish this night with Ellie and the other maids. There is nothing more we can do until morn."

At the manor house? Rowena turned. A sharp pain stabbed at her ankle. "Oh!"

Stephen grabbed her as she drooped. Ellie took the babe as Rowena grimaced down at her foot. "My ankle. I must have turned it running outside." She cried again as she tried to put weight on it, and she gripped Stephen more tightly.

Immediately she was lifted up. She started, catching the damp linen of Stephen's simple shirt. She was in his arms! Hastily, with the other hand, she pushed her undertunic down to cover her legs.

"Go ahead," he ordered Ellie in French. "Prepare your pallet for Rowena."

"Nay, I can't take her pallet," Rowena answered in the same language.

Stephen stopped and looked down at her. "*Tu parle Français?* You speak French?"

Rowena clung to him, realizing how much she disliked being so high and putting her safety in this man's arms. *"Oui,"* she whispered, peering over her shoulder at the ground that seemed too far away.

"I thought you were a farm girl. Where does a farm girl learn French?"

Heat flooded her face. Could she tell Stephen she'd learned French out of necessity? To answer him truthfully would be admitting too much. Would it give this Norman the same idea that Taurin once had?

If only Lord Stephen could read her thoughts and save her the humility of an explanation. For as he stood there his frown deepened, his handsome face cut with moving shadows as the lantern that someone had raised swung about.

She couldn't speak the full truth. "You Normans invaded our land, remember?" she finally whispered. "'Tis how I learned. From a Norman."

Stephen tightened his mouth. Aye, he and his fellow Normans had come to this land, but 'twas his king's right to rule England. The crown had been promised to William. And in the two years since, had they not brought order to these unruly villages?

But just because the Normans were scattered about did not mean that all Saxons had learned French, especially not a simple farm girl. Why her?

The babe in Ellie's arms fussed and then he remembered. Rowena had given birth to a Norman child. She must have learned the language during the course of her pregnancy. Or mayhap before. But one thing he was certain of, if given the choice, Rowena would not have learned a single word of French. And seeing the dark pleading in her eyes, Stephen would stake his life that Rowena's heart did not belong to the child's father.

Still, 'twas an uncharacteristic emotion that ripped through him when he should be feeling nothing. He picked up his pace. Best not to think with his heart, he reminded himself. Without exception, it gave bad advice. He'd seen many fooled by it.

"My lord," Rowena whispered, her face so close to his that he could have stolen a kiss should he'd so desired. "Please put me down. You're hurting me!"

Stephen stopped. A guard approached and lifted a lantern again. Horror bled into him as he saw her pained expression.

She blinked. "Your grip is too tight, my lord!"

He relaxed. "My apologies. I…I didn't want you to slip."

"I have my own good grip, milord." She shook her

head. "Please, let me try walking. We're at the manor house now, anyway."

Stephen looked up, surprised to find he'd reached the grand entrance to his home. Inhaling, he set her down just as a woman opened the large oak door. It was his sister, Josane, who was also his chatelaine. Staring openly at the pair, she held the door back for him. "Ellie has just come in with a child, Stephen!" she exclaimed in French. "Have we lost a family? Was there a fire? I can smell the smoke—"

"*Oui*, Josane, 'twas a fire, but no one was hurt. The child belongs to this woman, Rowena."

Josane peered at Rowena, her expression concerned but cool. "*Oui*, Gilles told me he'd given her a hut, as you'd requested." She looked over Rowena's shoulder at the villagers slowly filtering away. Then, lifting the skirt of her fine linen cyrtel, she swung out her arm impatiently. "Come in. Come in. 'Tis cold and damp out."

Stephen stepped forward to scoop up Rowena again, but she lifted her hand. "Nay, I'll walk."

She tried one hobbling step, only to reach for the door. Impatient like his sister, Stephen lifted her again and carried her over the threshold into his manor house. "We'll take you to the maids' chamber. 'Tis small, but your son will be there with Ellie."

Josane hurried ahead of them, through the narrow corridor to where it opened into the great hall. Stephen listened to the sound of her shoes crunching the rushes strewn about. Josane's cyrtel swayed back and forth in rhythm with her steps. She preferred a practical, shorter hem than what other ladies of the manor might wear. As chatelaine here, she was always busy, and the longer hems of ladies of leisure often snagged the rushes.

Torches soaked in tallow lit the way down the far

corridor, infusing the air not with the oily scent of animal fat, but with sweet herbs and dried flowers. Josane hated the smell of burning tallow and had concocted an infusion to mask the odor. Now it swept along with them as he carried Rowena the length of his home, deep into the servants' end.

Ahead, Josane opened a small door. Stephen ducked as he took Rowena inside the tiny room. Its floor was filled with pallets, except where a table, a chair and an old chest stood. Ellie had already moved a crude chair beside a pallet that held little Andrew. Stephen set Rowena down on it.

For one brief moment she clung to him, her arms still locked about his neck. Whether 'twas because she could not feel the chair beneath her or because she wanted to remain in his arms, he didn't know. But in the instant, he stilled.

Two lamps lit the room, making it easy for him to see the apprehension swimming in her pale blue eyes. She wet her lower lip, then held it tight between her teeth.

Sympathy—something he did not want to own— washed through him as he held her close. Immediately, the sermon from the previous Sabbath echoed within him. *Be ye kind, one to another, tenderhearted.* He felt his jaw tighten.

Why this sudden piety? Stephen had never felt conflicted with his faith before, even when trapping plotters against the crown. His God-given duty allowed him to punish evildoers without so much as a blink of the eye. Was it because he'd erred here? He hadn't expected that the malcontent bent on hurting Rowena would return so quickly.

Stephen found himself saying "'Tis all right, Rowena.

You're safe here." His whisper was for her ears only, and in response, she nodded briefly and released him.

"Thank you. And may God bless you, milord." Her voice was as soft as her eyes as she spoke to him.

Stephen straightened, regretting his warm, quiet words. They made him sound as if he cared. He didn't. He wanted only for his newly formed plan to work. He needed those troublemakers to show themselves, because next time he would be ready.

He cleared his throat. "Ellie will see to your care. I must ensure the fire is completely out." With that cool statement, he left the chamber.

In the corridor, Josane caught his arm. Speaking in French, she hissed, "You should not have brought that woman here. We know nothing about her." Her expression bored into him, the torchlight reflecting in her dark eyes. "She could be a thief. And look at her babe. 'Tis obvious already she is a prostitute."

Stephen yanked back his arm. "She was a slave, given her freedom by the king himself."

"That's ridiculous! King William banned the sale of Christian slaves three years ago. See? You know little of her! I've heard the rumors about her aligning herself with Normans. See what it got her? A life of shame. Stephen, she will bring us nothing but trouble!"

Stephen said nothing in answer to her warning. They stared at each other, and after a long minute, Josane shook her head in disbelief. "Nay, Stephen," she breathed out.

He looked away. "'Tis necessary. The king has already ordered it." Only Josane and Gilles knew of the king's order to root out rebels and quell any unrest that could threaten the crown.

King William, on his trek north shortly after Hastings, had found this village filled with sly Saxons. Although they had done nothing to warrant razing their land, they had pricked William's suspicions enough for him to assign Stephen to the task of finding agitators. Such were in every village, and William was canny enough to know they abounded here. 'Twas the only way to control this village when most of William's soldiers were fighting the Welsh.

These villagers are just waiting for us to turn our backs, the king had told Stephen after he'd agreed to spare this village. *I made a promise that I would not raze this land, but I will destroy any Saxon who defies my law. Arrest anyone suspicious. I will have no one rebel against me.*

Josane sliced into his memory. "All the more reason to foster Rowena somewhere else. You of all people know what Saxons can do. Did they not take our brother's life at Hastings?"

He inwardly recoiled. Their younger brother, Corvin, had been a fine, dedicated soldier. He'd fought hard during that battle, but his life had ended when a Saxon blade pierced his heart moments before King Harold's own death. 'Twas mayhap the reason William had bestowed so much honor on Stephen. He'd inherited his brother's share, as well.

Such a hefty price. Immediately, he tried to harden himself against the inner pain. He would die to bring his younger brother back.

Josane folded her arms. "For all we know, these Saxons set that fire themselves in order to create dissent here. And with that girl already aligned with Normans, they would gladly rid the village of her."

"'Twas an unfastened spark box that caused the fire," he responded.

His sister shook her head in disgust as she continued in French, "You may be able to handle the intricacies of court in London, Stephen, but this village is totally different. Do not allow your heart to lead you because one maid looks at you with eyes like a fawn. I fear you're getting soft away from the king."

He darkened. "My heart does not rule me, woman!"

"The villagers—"

"Will obey me," he snapped back in his mother tongue. "And you will obey, also! This is my estate, Josane, and you work as chatelaine for me. Remember that!" He tossed a look over his sister's shoulder. The maids' chamber door remained ajar, and he caught a glimpse of Rowena peering wide-eyed at him across the small room. Aye, with those great fawn eyes Josane had been kind enough to mention. He drove his attention back to his sister. "I may not be the best person to trust, especially after Hastings. But *you* will obey me!"

Josane went dead silent. He could feel her stare. "I will, but you've brought home a Saxon like 'twas a lost puppy. And I know you. You plan to—"

He pierced her with a harsh glare. "Be quiet! And be advised, Josane—Rowena speaks French."

His sister suddenly recoiled. "So the Saxons *do* have good reason to suspect her. And you dragged her here. So typical of a man to see only to his wants." With that, she stormed off.

Stewing at his sister's accusation, Stephen turned his back on her, only to have his gaze meet Rowena's again. Though her eyes were as round as bowls, they gave away nothing but innocent concern.

Was there such a thing in a Saxon dealing with a Norman? Doubting that, he was about to turn away when her voice reached him.

"Milord?"

Chapter Five

Lord Stephen turned, stretched out his arm to push the door open farther. At his sheer size, Rowena drew a long breath. Aye, this chamber's door was smaller than the others she'd passed in the manor, and he had to duck just to enter, but to have him straighten up once again in the middle of this tiny room completely overwhelmed her.

"What is wrong?" he asked tightly.

Looking up at him, Rowena swallowed her sudden apprehension. "I—I couldn't help but overhear, milord," she began in English. "I did not start that fire, not even by accident. The spark-box lid was closed, I know it! The fire was started from outside and burned its way through the thatch. I could see it." She paused. "Your sister is older than you. She expects you to respect her beliefs, but she's wrong about me."

"How do you know we are siblings?"

"She said 'our brother' when she mentioned Hastings. Milord, she doesn't want to be here, and—"

"How do you know that?"

"I can tell. She's not happy here. And angry at you. Not because of your brother, though his death haunts you." She stopped and shrugged. How did she surmise all of this? 'Twas just by looking at Lady Josane that she knew. For years she'd been able to guess people's motives. And she'd learned Taurin's emotions easily. She did not catch all of the conversation between the siblings, but she knew something serious was stirring. "'Tis of no import right now. My home is. I did not leave the spark box open!"

Lord Stephen folded his arms. When he did not answer, she tried again. "You have to believe me! Why would I put my child at risk? Why would I set fire to the roof directly above the door, my only escape? If I didn't care about my child's life, would I have shoved you back when you reached for him yesterday morning? Would I have risked punishment?"

Rowena had no idea whether her earnest words convinced him. He did nothing but stand in the middle of the room, and the only sounds were of Ellie shifting as she stood over the pallet that held Andrew. The baby had dropped off to sleep, oblivious to the events around him. Rowena thought out a fast prayer. *Lord God, help Lord Stephen to understand me. Help me to convince him.*

Finally Stephen spoke. "What do you want me to do?"

Rowena hesitated. What *did* she want him to do? She didn't want to stay in her hut, but she didn't want to stay here, either. And she certainly did not want to be bound, albeit through gratitude only, to another Norman.

When Taurin had purchased her, 'twas as if she'd gone from the fry pan into the fire. Now it seemed as though she had been tossed back into the fry pan again.

Nay. She was a free woman, and in the time she'd spent with Clara, both in hiding from Taurin this summer past and here as the midwife had helped her settle into her new home, she had learned how to stand up for herself. Clara was a good teacher. 'Twas time to put the lessons to use and make her mentor proud.

Rowena straightened her shoulders. "I have been vandalized, milord, and my life put in jeopardy. Is there anyone here who can find out who is to blame? Your brother-in-law, mayhap? He assigned me my hut. He seems to run this village. Can he not help me?"

At the mention of his brother-in-law, Stephen's mouth tightened. "Gilles is my bailiff, but he hears only civil cases. It is a bit complicated what is civil or criminal. But the major criminal cases are decided in London. We can convene a manorial court, which is a civil court, but the case must be compiled first and the culprit found. Gilles cannot investigate if he is to be the judge."

Rowena sagged. "So, I have no one to help me?"

Stephen pulled up a chair and sank heavily into it. It creaked under his weight. The two small lamps flickered warm light onto his tired features, cutting sharp angles along his jaw and cheeks. It had been a long night, and Rowena wondered if they shouldn't leave this until the morning.

But she couldn't. Any desire to delay was caused by naught but fear and shame for asking. She leaned forward again. "Who could possibly help me? I have no relatives here."

Stephen shook his head. "You are a *villein* here. Do you know what that means?"

"Aye. Master Gilles told me how I cannot leave without your permission and of my obligation to work your lands, milord, three days each week. I have started to do so! He also spelled out my right to protection. But if he cannot help me, who can?"

Stephen leaned back. After a moment when nothing

was heard but the soft breaths of expectation, he said, "I will help you."

Hearing Ellie's short intake of breath, Rowena gaped at Stephen. "You will?"

"You say that you're being persecuted but don't know by whom. I will find out who it is and why."

Hope surged in her, but there was something about his words that didn't feel as open as they should. Or was it the look around his eyes?

Still, Rowena said, "Thank you." For a brief moment, he'd shut his eyes, and when he opened them again, their gazes met. Even in the dimly lit chamber, for one lamp had just winked out, Rowena could see his eyes. The remaining lamp's flame flickered in the dark brown circles, and when he parted his lips as if to speak, she found herself drawn toward him like a thirsty animal toward water. Her heart thundered in her chest and she quickly prayed that he would not renege on his offer.

"Bienvenue," he finally murmured in French. "But 'tis not as simple as it sounds. You must trust me completely in this."

Rowena stiffened. "What do you mean?"

"You will stay here out of harm's way while I investigate these attacks."

"But—"

"No buts. You will say and do nothing." Those dark eyes hardened. "You must put all your faith in my ability to handle this situation. Do you understand?"

Indignation flared within her. Was she a dolt who needed everything spelled out? Did he expect her to trust blindly? Was he addled?

Still, Lord Stephen had promised to help her when no one else would. "I understand," she murmured. "But I can—"

"Nay. I expect your complete obedience."

Like the bone in her spark box receiving fresh air, she felt heat flare inside her. "Obedience? Am I a slave again, or mayhap a prisoner here? I know I am a *villein* and bound to the land, but why should I be punished for the suffering I've endured? I should be helping!"

Stephen stood. He towered over her like the keep at Dunmow when she'd finally met her sponsor, Lord Adrien. "You cannot! Nor are you being punished. I know exactly how to deal with this situation and these people. Nay, you are not a slave. But you will do as I say."

Rowena folded her arms. "I will not live here owing you."

He blew out an exasperated sigh. "Fine. You can be in my employ."

"Doing what?"

He rolled his eyes. Then he paused, and Rowena could see his gaze turn calculating. Her heart chilled.

"Mayhap since you are so good at identifying people's feelings, I can use you to read those who come to this manor looking for an end to their disputes." He held up his finger. "Perhaps you can tell me when people are lying."

Rowena shook her head. "Use me to read people? Am I a tool, like a pitchfork?" She stiffened. "Nay, milord. I have had my fill of intrigue. I will not be forced into the middle of it again."

"Your fill of intrigue? How so?" His brows shot up in question, but she refused to enlighten him.

Instead she dropped her gaze, wondering if she had pushed her demand to earn her stay here too much. Would he turn her out to fend for herself?

Nay. There was a goodness in him, she was sure of it. *Lord, guide me.*

"We had agreed that I could make rope in exchange for food. Mayhap I could make more to pay for my stay here?"

She craned her neck to see his face. Would he accept that instead? He met her searching gaze, but she couldn't read it. He'd been in London, he'd said before, and from what she'd learned from Taurin, London was filled with conspiracy and danger. Stephen must have learned to hide his feelings there.

Finally he nodded, stirring up all scenarios. What *were* his plans for an investigation? Why was he willing to help locate her persecutor? No man had ever just volunteered anything. Would his plans involve punishing everyone here in order to extract a confession? How could that possibly help? She asked, "What will you do to find my attacker?"

"Did I not just demand faith in my abilities?" Lord Stephen snapped. Then, with a long sigh, he rubbed his forehead. "'Tis the middle of the night, Rowena, and we are both tired. I will speak to you on the morrow."

He turned to Ellie, and her heart sinking, Rowena knew he was right. They were exhausted. "See to Rowena's needs. Her ankle will need attention, and clearly she needs some clothes. I believe my sister has given you maids some old cyrtels. One should be suitable."

Rowena drew the edges of her undertunic together at the neck as Ellie bobbed in obedience.

With a final glance around the tight quarters, Stephen bid her good-night and left.

Rowena slid her gaze over to Ellie. Still standing beside the pallet, the maid wrung her hands. "Rowena, you must not argue with Baron Stephen!"

"I didn't argue with him. I asked for his help."

The maid walked around the pallet to reach a crude

wooden box in the corner. There were several pallets packed into the room, but Rowena had yet to meet the other maids who used them. Mayhap they were busy in the kitchen? Ellie dragged the box into the meager circle of lamplight. "Lord Stephen's giving you his help, is he not?" she said, pulling out a dark blue cyrtel and holding it high to examine it. As if satisfied, she lowered it to peer pointedly at Rowena. "But you can't tell him *how* he must help you!"

Rowena folded her arms. Her ankle had begun to throb, and she was in no mood to explain her reasoning. "You don't know what you're asking," she responded testily. "I may be a foolish farm girl, but I have every right to ask how Lord Stephen plans to help me. What if his plans would hurt my son? Had I been asleep, Andrew would have died. I don't care about my own life, but I do care for his!"

Ellie folded the cyrtel and set it on her pallet close to Andrew's tiny feet. Clara had made him a warm bunting outfit, warning Rowena not to swaddle him too tightly for too long. By now, his feet pressed against the lower seam. Ellie tugged on it to help make more room for him, but 'twas a wasted effort. She then pulled up the chair Stephen had vacated to gently prop up Rowena's injured foot and lift the hem of her undertunic to see the ankle.

While wincing, Rowena fought the urge to press her point of not trusting any Norman until he'd proved himself. Should she really rely upon Lord Stephen? "Do you think he will do as he promised?"

"Aye." Ellie paused in her examination as she nodded to Rowena. The lamplight shone warmly on the girl's earnest expression. Her cyrtel fit snugly, as if she had blossomed into womanhood too soon. She needed those secondhand cyrtels as much as Rowena did. Mayhap Lady Josane had passed them down to her because she'd seen the girl nearly busting from her own cyrtel. "I understand what you're saying, Rowena. I, too, wonder what cost his promise will be to us Saxons."

Was Ellie suggesting that this village would suffer punishment for Rowena's misfortune? She wet her lips. Not a good start to living here when already the villagers distrusted her. "What do you mean?"

With a glance to the closed door, Ellie answered, "Lord Stephen is said to do the king's...how do I put it? Filthy work? His dirty work that no one else can do."

Rowena gasped. "Like murder?"

"Nay!" Ellie shook her head briskly. "Oh, I'm not explaining this right. How can I say it? The court in London is rife with intrigue, they claim. People switch allegiances as quickly as the weather turns. 'Tis said the king needs an ear to be where the schemes against him are plotted. He needs someone who can rid him of those against him."

Rowena swallowed. That did not sound good. "So Lord Stephen is as sly as a fox?"

"'Twould be wise not to irritate him. His allegiance is to God and the king, and only them. Some say he is more ruthless than the king himself."

"'Tis hardly Christian."

Ellie pressed her knuckles against her mouth and thought a moment. "I heard Lady Josane say once that Lord Stephen has never done anything unbefitting of his duty to King William, and that since God put the king on the throne, Lord Stephen's duty was also God-given."

"God didn't crown King William. Lord Taurin sa— The king crowned himself."

Setting the hem gently over Rowena's swollen ankle, Ellie went on, "'Tis a dangerous attitude, Rowena. Speak no more of it. Aye, milord is harsh, but he will keep this village safe for both Saxon and Norman. I have faith in him."

"How? He hasn't done a good job so far."

"Beyond the forest and fens is Ely. Many here feared the king would destroy us if he marched through to fight the rebels there. Indeed, he would've razed our land two years ago had it not been for our anchoress, Lady Udella, who pleaded for our safety, and for Lord Stephen, who offered to keep her here. We should be grateful that milord took this holding, instead of one who cares not for anything but power."

Rowena swallowed. Aye, she knew one baron who cared for nothing but power.

Ellie continued, "Some men in the village say that Baron Stephen is here to punish men who would try to be rid of a Norman king." She shivered openly. "I have heard talk in this manor house that the king is moving north to harry the rebels there. I pray he bypasses Kingstown. 'Tis not a good time to live here. Some of the villagers would swear fealty, then break their promise as soon as the opportunity arises. 'Twill not bode well for our village should even one of us turn our allegiance from the king."

With that, Ellie spun on her heel and left, adding a quick mutter that she would return with some knitbone leaves in which to wrap Rowena's ankle. Alone and unable to move in the near dark, for the second lamp threatened to die, Rowena fought back fear. She was to trust Baron Stephen, a man whom his own servants said was harsh?

Nay. She'd be a fool to put her faith in him during this dangerous time. Baron Stephen's sister, the chatelaine and obviously his equal, didn't want Rowena here. Saxons shunned her. She couldn't even go home to her parents' farm, for she would surely be turned away, what with bringing another mouth to feed. Not that she would return. Not after her father had sold her.

She had no champion, save herself.

She stopped her thoughts. Wouldn't God help her? Did she have so little faith? *Forgive me, Lord.*

Ellie returned with the leaves and a dark poultice to plaster carefully around Rowena's ankle. Rowena sucked in her breath as Ellie pressed the cool remedy against the swollen flesh. She would be laid up for days, a prisoner trapped by her injury, obliged to let Baron Stephen act as he would. The baron's priorities were not to find her attacker. They were to suppress a rebellion. He would hardly allow his promise to her to hinder that great task.

And, Rowena's heart reminded her furiously, she would never trust a Norman. Taurin had done what no man should ever do and had even planned to kill her afterward, lest she reveal the truth about the babe.

Fury rose anew and she gritted her teeth to bottle it, leaving her shaking. As Ellie finished her ministrations on her ankle, Rowena finished her thoughts.

She had no choice but to stay here. But count on Lord Stephen to see to her best interests? Nay. Only a fool would stand behind the horse after it had kicked him.

Chapter Six

His short nap done, Stephen rose. After quick ablutions, he threw on a light cloak and took his sword. He departed through the front door, a personal guard at his heels. The only other soul awake outside, for it had been such a late night for everyone, was the soldier on guard. Stephen had even allowed Gaetan, his squire, to sleep in. The duty guard snapped to attention, and after acknowledging him, Stephen strode down the lane toward Rowena's hut.

Yesterday had seen him weary of fighting and being ever watchful. But today Stephen felt invigorated. Now he had a plan to root out the rebels he knew lived here. They hated Rowena, and he would use the young woman to lure them out. It was the only plan that didn't include arresting every man.

But before he could use her, he had to do a quick investigation of the fire. It was probably an accident, but Stephen was not one to leave a stone unturned.

Though dawn had just begun, the day was light enough for him to start his investigation. Rowena's home looked a sodden, useless shell now, he decided as he closed in on it. Thankfully, a tributary of the Cam

River flowed east of the village, mere yards away, and the easy access to water had helped to save the building from far worse damage. Rowena's garden, where she'd attempted to salvage her food stocks, had been trodden down even further.

Ordering his guard to remain out front, Stephen walked slowly around the small home, thinking one more time of what Rowena had said. She would never be so foolish to put her son's life in danger. Hadn't she been protective of the child when he'd picked him up? She'd given Stephen a shove for all she was worth, and she'd risked punishment for it. No Saxon would dare openly attack a Norman.

Although, Stephen recalled, she was also terrified of him. In London, he could make maidens shrink back in fear with one glower and it bothered him not one jot. Rowena had flinched when he'd raised his hand to open her door.

This kitten—aye, Rowena was a kitten, fearful and yet bold at the same time—had acted in a way that had made him feel compassion, which hindered him in the way he preferred to work.

Stephen's tasks had always been to listen for dissension, coax those whose allegiances were faltering and maneuver the intrigue of court life to keep it safe for the king. He had allowed dissidents to form plans, caught them in their lies and manipulated their friends into turning them in. Stephen had drafted the Act of Surety of the King's Person to assist in arresting those who would want William dead. He was good at his job and knew without forethought he was doing his Lord's work.

So, why bother investigating a simple fire? Did Rowena need protection so much that he likened her to the king?

Nay, he needed Rowena to draw out troublemakers, and there were plenty of them around. Kingstown sat too close to Ely, which housed that unpleasant Saxon abbot who nursed an inconsequential grievance against Cambridgeshire's new Norman sheriff, all the while encouraging Hereward the Wake to come fight for England's sovereignty. 'Twould be best, Stephen thought, that he remove all rebels here. The least he could do for his brother's memory was to keep this town safe. And if it took using one Saxon woman and her babe to arouse rebels and arrest them, he would do exactly that.

An insect buzzed about Stephen's head, some late-season mosquito from the marshes around Kingstown. He swatted but missed it, and it annoyed him.

With his guard waiting patiently, Stephen finished his survey and circled back to what remained of the front of Rowena's hut. The scent of smoke lingered. The fire had been hottest here, and most of the thatch was nothing but ashes spread out on the ground. The door was charred at the top, while the wattle and daub of the short walls showed only scorching. Very little repair would be needed.

Thank You, Father, for getting her out so quickly.

The prayer came unbidden to his forethought, for he usually reserved his prayers for the king alone. With a slight frown, Stephen opened the door beneath the bared roof. Dawn was now complete and the sun high enough that he could easily see into the single-room home. Mud pooled in slurries, and as he stepped into one, something between the puddles caught the sun's first rays as they slipped through the open door.

The spark box, he noted as he picked it up. With all the water that had been tossed on the house, the box now gleamed. He weighed it in his palm. 'Twas still warm.

And fully closed. Snapped shut firmly.

Stephen's heart chilled. With a single deft movement, he flicked open the lid. 'Twas exactly as Rowena had said. A small piece of bone glowed within.

Dry bone was good in a spark box. It burned far slower than a hunk of hardwood. With the sudden breath he streamed out in a sigh, the bone flared from its slumber. Jaw tight, Stephen snapped the lid closed. He looked back toward the small front door and the shelf beside it. Only for ease of access was the spark box shelf there at all. Now, as morning lit the sky, Stephen could see how the shelf, though charred, was still intact.

Rowena had been correct when she'd said that 'twere not possible for the spark box to have caused the fire, for surely the whole shelf would have burned and the wall scorched. Stephen set the box on the mantel above the small, crude hearth. His heart hammered at the truth before him.

'Twas arson, indeed. As he'd surmised last evening, Rowena's enemy had struck two nights in a row. If he'd known that would happen, he'd have hid a guard beyond the village gate to ambush this troublemaker. But he'd thought that his presence yesterday morning would have deterred them for at least a day. His jaw tightened, his neck heated. Rowena had been vandalized and then attacked. *More than attacked.* Someone wanted her dead.

Aye, his plan to use Rowena would work well. 'Twas the only reason for his sudden interest in her, and nothing more, not a weakened heart or her fawn-like eyes, as Josane suggested. Not even that curious ability of hers to read people. 'Twas *only* how she'd fit into his plan. By openly assisting her as she convalesced, Stephen would be riling up this malcontent to attack again.

He left the hut shortly after. Movement caught his

eye, and he noticed Alfred the Barrett pushing open the village gate to approach him. The guard stopped the old cottager, but Stephen motioned the man closer. Mayhap he knew something of value to this investigation.

However, Stephen doubted it. The man lived up to his Saxon family name, which meant "quarrelsome." Stephen's servants said Alfred's father had been the same, as his grandfather before him, so the surname stuck like mud in the welt of a boot. Automatically stiffening, Stephen waited for the man to approach and speak.

"Milord," he started, "you need not be concerned with this fire. 'Twas a simple accident. We will see to it that the girl has a new roof before long, let me assure you."

Stephen felt the hairs on his neck rise but said nothing. Alfred Barrett was volunteering his village to help Rowena? Would they also give her food and lodging until she was able to manage on her own? Would they pay for a new roof, when they barely had two coins to rub together?

Stephen doubted that very much, for if such generosity existed, 'twould have been displayed last night. Aye, they saved the house, but not one villager except Ellie had even spoken to her.

"'Tis good of you to offer this. Rowena has hurt her ankle, so for the moment she will remain in my maids' quarters under my care."

The man's mouth tightened, Stephen noticed. 'Twas as brief as a blink, but perceptible. And expected.

"Would you start the work immediately?" Stephen asked, though he knew the only thatcher in the village was currently employed.

Barrett's eyes narrowed. "Mayhap with your lordship's permission, we could gather the thatch today instead of working in your gardens or building the king's palisade. We do have one thatcher in the village, but he's busy." Barrett's tone turned sly. "Rethatching one of *your* barns, milord."

Stephen nodded, pretending not to hear the change in tone. "Aye, he does excellent work."

Barrett rubbed his grimy hands together. "It costs so much to rethatch, doesn't it, milord? I don't know how this girl will pay for it."

Forming a grim smile, Stephen agreed. He'd already decided to pay for the repairs while standing in the hut, but this sly verbal dance he was doing with Barrett curbed his words.

Nay, Barrett had come here for another reason. What it was, Stephen wasn't sure, but he'd discover it soon enough. He had patience to spare, and Rowena wasn't leaving his manor anytime soon.

With deliberate heartiness, Stephen pressed his hand down on the other man's bony shoulder as he guided him out of the small parcel of land. "We are just grateful there wasn't more damage and that no one was hurt, aren't we?"

"Oh, aye, milord! But I am concerned for the work to be done, and we all know we must be about your harvest or cutting your trees." Barrett waved his hand. "But, milord, 'tis a matter for us villagers, and not your concern. We'll make the best of it. We Saxons take care of our own. In fact, I can arrange for the girl's care, if you like."

His expression calm, Stephen studied the man, wishing he had Rowena at his side to discern Barrett's motives. Stephen's first instinct was to send the man back to his home with a curt announcement that only when Rowena was well enough would she leave his manor. But he thought carefully before answering.

"'Tis a good offer, Barrett. Let us see what the day brings, as I plan to inspect the thatcher's work." With that, he strode ahead of the Saxon, hearing his guard also step past the man.

At the manor, Stephen found Rowena in the maids' chamber, mending hose with her ankle propped up. Weed stalks were drying nearby, obviously destined for rope. Her babe sat on the nearest pallet, flicking small scraps of cloth, as was a babe's custom. Stephen saw that Rowena had been given one of Josane's old cyrtels. The dark blue complemented her milky complexion and pale hair. Though Rowena didn't fill it as his sister had, the color was better on her than on his sallow-complected sibling.

At his entrance, Rowena looked up quickly, expectant yet nervous. Shifting his sword, for in his haste to come here, he had not surrendered it to his squire, Stephen sat down beside her. "Good morning."

"Good morning, milord," she whispered. "Forgive me for not rising."

He waved his hand. "No matter. How is the ankle?"

"Far more swollen than yesterday, I fear. Ellie has gone to the well for cold water." She set down her mending with a small shrug. "I had to do something while my stalks dry. Mending was the only thing I could manage, and Lady Josane was quick to take my offer. But," she hastily added, "Ellie has promised she will get everything I need to make your rope."

Stephen shrugged. "Both are always needed, I suspect. Although I have neither mended nor made rope in my life. I expect my fingers would be too clumsy."

Rowena looked down at his hands.

The urge to wiggle his fingers raced through him, just

to bring a smile to her face. But 'twas not the time for jocularity. Nor was he the type to engage in it.

"I've just returned from your hut," he said grimly.

Rowena drew in a quick breath as apprehension flashed in those pale blue eyes.

Her lips parted, then shut firmly as she looked away. In her lap, her hands shook. Would they be cool if he covered them with his own? Suddenly, the room was becoming uncomfortably warm, and Stephen was glad he'd left the door ajar.

"You found something that disturbs you," she commented.

He glanced around. Though this cramped chamber was one of many in his manor, before last night he'd not stepped foot in it, let alone sat in one of its chairs. This whole wing was new to him. 'Twas Josane's business to deal with the kitchen and maids' quarters.

He pulled in a breath and found it filled with the warm scent of sweet herbs and late-season blooms, instead of the expectant smell of smoke from the single bare lamp on the table. The hall where his soldiers slept, indeed his own room, had never smelled this pleasant.

'Twas most likely due to the many plants drying within. As Stephen stood to remove his cloak, he cleared his throat. He would not focus on such foolishness, not whilst he planned to use her as bait. "I found your spark box."

Rowena stared up with a surprised expression. "The lid was clicked shut, was it not?"

"Aye, it was shut tight." He sat down. "And the fire did start over the door. One has only to see where the center of the blaze had been to know that."

"I saw the glow over the door first! I smelled something burning and turned, and that's when it burst into flame. It had already burned through the thatch."

"The top layer of the roof would be damp with dew, so whoever set it would have had to light the cut end of the thatch, which would burn upward. That may be why it appeared to have started from the inside, but the spark-box shelf was barely scorched."

Rowena eased back in the chair. "My provisions for the winter were trampled. And my chicken let loose and the rabbit hutch ruined. But that wasn't enough for whoever did this. Someone wants me dead, at first by starvation, but when you offered me food they decided to try to kill me quickly." She dropped her head, her hands covering her face.

Stephen's fingers curled to make fists. If he'd had enough soldiers, he would have taken full, unyielding control of this village, herded all the villagers into a single group and demanded the truth from them.

But his full complement of men had not yet arrived. Stephen knew 'twould be foolish to start something he could not finish. King William had promised him a company to help build the palisade and prepare for fighting should those rebels in Ely move south. Except that the king was ready to push north to York to raze that county and prove his sovereignty there.

Stephen worked his jaw. He'd be addled to do anything drastic with only a dozen and a half soldiers at his disposal. Especially against Saxons with murder on their minds and deadly pitchforks in their hands.

"I'll continue my investigation," he said briskly, "until I discover who did this."

Rowena's eyes sparkled with unshed tears. "No one here will surrender that person, milord. They feel threatened by me, for I gave birth to a Norman child. They'll be threatened all the more by you. Who knows what will happen if they think we are working together? Even you will have to be careful."

Though she was young, Rowena seemed quite well versed in intrigue and plotting. She'd either been taught this or learned it the hard way. More likely the latter, Stephen decided as he glanced over at the babe, who'd discovered he could move to his hands and knees and rock back and forth in preparation for crawling. Why would anyone feel threatened by her? Did the answer lie with her child's sire? Did the villagers know more than he did? "Rowena, who is this child's father?"

Silence answered him first. Then finally, she spoke. "Didn't Lord Adrien tell you? I thought he would in his letter explaining me."

"Adrien and I are friends, but he is worse than I am at not volunteering information. Nay, he asked only that I find a home for you."

"Why you?"

Stephen shrugged. "Mayhap because this village is only a day's brisk walk from Dunmow Keep. Mayhap because he knows I would not say no."

Rowena's lips parted as she considered his answer. "Are you that good a friend?"

"Aye," he said with a nod. "But unless I speak directly to Adrien, 'tis hard for me to guess his reasoning. He said nothing of the child, just that you were freed from slavery by King William. This child's father is Norman, isn't he? I know of no Saxon so swarthy."

She looked down at her fingers, now meshed together in her lap. "Aye. Lord Taurin bought me from my father to be his slave. I didn't realize until later that I was to be bred because Lord Taurin's wife is barren. I remember the day my father boasted that all his other daughters had provided strong, healthy sons. I didn't understand why he was saying that to a Norman who seemed just to be passing through."

Stephen swallowed. "Did Taurin treat you poorly?"

Rowena lowered her eyes, and again her hands began to shake. "I think you know that answer, milord. At first, Lord Taurin told me I was going to have a better life, one where my father could never hurt me again. I believed him, for my father…well, he was not like other parents…"

"How so? Besides selling you?"

"Other fathers love their children." Rowena swallowed. "Even Lord Taurin had been interested in the babe within me, though only because he was a means to receive land."

She wet her lips. "My father had no interest in me. He acknowledged that I was alive, that's all. For I was a burden. I had no dowry, no prospects to bring income through marriage. I was also small and couldn't manage even the simplest farm tasks." She sniffed. "I could have if they'd fed me."

Shock rattled through him. "You mean you weren't given food?"

Rowena didn't look up, choosing only to toy with her fingers. "After the dog ate. He could herd the sheep and guard the barn. I ate what he left. The barn was a separate hut, for only the most valuable animals, breeding stock or hens that laid regularly were kept in the farmhouse." A soft sound akin to a sniffle broke up her words. She then shrugged sadly. "You don't feed the runt, for it cannot give you anything worthwhile."

"'Tis not true!"

She shot up her head and glared. "I'm not lying to

you, my lord! 'Tis a hard life with eight girls to marry off, and then get another one, a runt, no less, to care for!"

"Don't defend your father, Rowena! What he did was wrong. No Christian man would—"

"My father didn't believe in the one true God! 'Twas how Lord Taurin justified his purchase of me. King William banned the sale of *Christian* slaves. My father practiced the old pagan ways. He said that bringing Christianity to England had given Saxons bad luck. It wasn't until I met Clara that I became a Christian."

"Clara?"

"The midwife who risked her life to save me. She opened my eyes to God and how He loves me. She also petitioned Lord and Lady Dunmow to ask the king for my freedom, and then she came here with me to see me settled. Had it not been for her, I wouldn't have been freed. Taurin would have killed me for fear I would reveal his evil plan."

Stephen shut his mouth, trying to digest all she'd said. Aye, King William had banned the sale of Christian slaves, but he may not have considered that England still had her share of backward pagans in remote areas. 'Twas a cruel twist to the law. "So, you thought you'd been saved when Taurin bought you? But he was just as cruel?"

"Aye," she whispered. "Although when he realized I was carrying his child, I was given more food and a warm place to sleep. At first I thought the cruelty was over, but Lord Taurin has an evil streak."

"How did you end up at Dunmow? Did Clara help you?"

"I escaped on my own. I feared for my life, though I feared more for the life of my unborn child. So I traveled to Colchester, where I met Clara."

"Wasn't Clara in Dunmow?"

"She later moved to Dunmow to help Lady Ediva birth her son." She paused when Andrew fussed. After he settled again, she continued.

"When I realized that soon I would be too heavy with child to travel, I slipped away from Taurin's estate. He was visiting another of his holdings and there were some families passing our way to take their goods to the market in Colchester. They had spent the night in Taurin's great hall." She captured Stephen's gaze and held it. "I simply covered my head and walked out with them, right past Taurin's steward and guards."

Stephen gaped at her.

"If the gate is narrow, all the sheep jam in front of it, and if the farmer is impatient, he opens the gate wide. Then the sheep rush through and 'tis hard to count them. One man had many children, all noisy, so the guard at the village gate opened it fully and we all rushed through."

A magnificent tactic, excellent in its simplicity. He would have to instruct his own men on the dangers of impatience. "Didn't anyone notice an extra girl?"

"Nay. Besides, I watched the guards and stayed closer to the one who cared the least."

There she went again, reading people. Rowena was most likely better at it than he was, a skill forced on a victim who proved naturally talented.

"How did you get out of your chamber, anyway?"

"The servant who was to mind me forgot to lock the door. He would have returned at sunset and discovered me gone, but by then, we were far away. We were a big group and the leaders didn't want to dawdle. As for the father of all those children, he realized what had happened only after we'd reached Broad Oak."

"'Tis the king's land and well managed. The men there guard that forest well."

"All the more reason for Saxons to hurry through. But 'twasn't the only reason. Cattle plague had struck there, and the men in our group were reluctant to linger and risk the oxen that pulled their cart falling sick, as well. No one wanted to waste time dealing with me. So we hurried to Colchester. When we arrived there, the father's wife found Clara, for she had already guessed my condition by then and was anxious to be rid of me."

"Then what happened?"

"Clara protected me, even after I gave birth. 'Twas a hard summer, being hidden from Lord Taurin, who was searching for me, and knowing that Clara was also in danger just for hiding me. Only after Lord Taurin found me and tried to steal Andrew was it revealed that he planned to kill me and his wife and pass Andrew off as her child. Her family had promised to bestow large portions of land on him for giving them a son of their only child."

Ah, Stephen thought, and should this wealthy couple in Normandy lose their beloved daughter, her babe would be that much more valuable to them. He'd heard a bit of this trickery whilst at his other holding and how Taurin had been sent back to Normandy, his lands stripped from him and a heavy fine imposed, all within a few days, all at Lord Adrien's urging. Stephen hadn't seen any threat to William after the fact, for the baron was disliked all-round and was soon gone from London, so he'd not returned there. Adrien and the soldier Stephen left in charge of the King's Guard had handled the affair well.

What of the rest of Rowena's tale, though? It was astonishing, but he knew enough not to believe every story that reached his ears. 'Twas more than convenient that the Saxon father didn't want to linger at Broad Oak, with its extra Normans and cattle plague threatening the man's own oxen. But hadn't the spark box already proved Rowena was honest?

Stephen looked at her, trying to assess her sincerity, but instead saw her soft, pale hair light up in the lamp's single, unwavering flame and watched her stay as still as stone, the blue cyrtel hanging off her slight frame. She blinked and held his gaze. He watched with fascination her small, upturned nose with its dusting of fine freckles, though her complexion could surely be described as the cream that rose from fresh milk.

Milkmaids had perfect skin. 'Twas not for the milk they drank, as some might say, but 'twas the odd fact they usually caught cowpox, which sealed their skin to the perfect pale sheen he saw mere inches from him. Would it be as soft as it looked under his rough palm?

Stephen pulled away mentally. Josane had warned him not to think with his heart. Indeed, 'twas dangerous to allow his heart to think at all. Especially now that he planned to use Rowena. One didn't get attached to the bait one used for fishing.

Rowena leaned forward, her eyes still wide and her mouth still parted. "Milord, my story is true, but it changes nothing. You must be careful. Whoever wants me dead could easily kill you. How many Normans have died mysteriously since King William was crowned?"

Stephen tightened his lips. *Too many.* New rumors surfaced each week. Norman couriers, lone soldiers disappearing mysteriously. He frowned. "'Tis very generous to be concerned with my personal safety, though I question your motives. You've already demonstrated your distrust of me."

Rowena looked away. His barb had hit its target. "You say you will find my attacker, milord. If 'tis true, then I should do my best to keep you alive. But if 'tis not true, you are still Norman, correct?"

He nodded, waiting for her next words, for her thoughts were quiet, well-ordered for a simple maid.

"Then better to keep my enemy close than to face one who is unknown. Lord Taurin said, 'Know your friends well and your enemies better.'"

Stephen lifted his brows. "The mind of a warrior," he murmured, recalling an earlier thought about her, "with the face like one of those maids who sing in court."

"I've heard of minstrels traveling and singing for their suppers. Someone once said they dance high in the air and have trained animals doing all sorts of tricks, plus acts of great mystery!" She sobered. "Do they visit here? It would be wonderful to see them."

Stephen paused. An interesting thought. Although Rowena's reasons were wistful, his were far shrewder. Aye, wouldn't it irk her attacker to see her upon the baron's dais, seated in a place of honor as they watched the performers? It may stir up enough dissension to force an attack. Stephen allowed a small smile. With his men in strategic places, even hidden from view, they'd be ready to make enough arrests to quell any rebellious ideas permanently.

He nodded. "'Tis a good idea. I will consider it."

Rowena stiffened and her eyes flashed with sudden brilliance. She lowered her injured leg, then struggled up to standing, but only on one foot, for the other one, well poulticed and still swollen, hung from her bent knee. "I thank you, milord, but I can see that 'tis not for the same reason I have." She shook her head gravely. "And you want me to trust you? How can you be trusted to save my life and my babe's when you're planning something terrible?"

Chapter Seven

Rowena didn't want to hear the answer to her questions, for 'twould be as awful as any plan Taurin thought up, she was sure. Lord Stephen wanted her to trust in him, and yet that glint in his eye warned her otherwise.

Nay, don't listen! 'Twould be safer just to leave this manor house. She and the babe had survived alone so far. She would manage again.

Those years of weeding her parents' garden, scrounging for food when her empty belly ached, had taught her well. Many a day Rowena had chewed on bitter herbs to set the hunger at bay. Later Clara had taught her which greens would strengthen her through a cold, hungry winter.

'Twould be far better away from this warm manor house, all the while wondering what plan he schemed. How many lives would be lost? How would those villagers who hated her retaliate?

Stephen rose, his spine as straight as the sword dangling from his lean hips.

No answer came. Instead, Stephen pivoted on his heel and strode out, his long surcoat flaring and his sword smacking his chair so quickly it wobbled.

Rowena watched the door slam behind him and listened as his harsh footfalls died away. Shaking and no longer able to hold her weight on her good ankle, she fell back into her chair again. Beside her, Andrew cried briefly before settling down to a nap. She blew out a sigh, thankful she didn't have to deal with a fussy babe. Her hands shook so much, she'd surely drop him.

The chair that Stephen had used finally came to rest. What had just happened? He had not even answered her. Did that mean he had no wish to speak of his own cruelty? Mayhap keeping her ignorant was part of the control he'd commanded over this whole investigation. How could she just sit and wait for the terrible events to play themselves out? Did he expect her simply to look forward to a minstrel troupe like an innocent child?

Her stomach hurting, Rowena tried taking a deep breath to quell her fears.

Clara had told her God was but a prayer away. "Lord," Rowena whispered, "what am I supposed to do? What is Your will here? Should I warn someone, even one who hates me?"

The door opened again, and in breezed Ellie with a wooden bowl. Rowena jumped.

"Oh, dear, you're as white as snow! Is your ankle worse? Why isn't it propped up?" The girl dropped to her knees and looked down at Rowena's foot. "Mayhap these cold cloths will bring the swelling down."

Rowena sucked in her breath as the cold, wet strips of linen hit her hot skin. Yet they felt good. They forced her mind away from all Lord Stephen had said.

And had not said.

Should she put her faith in him regardless? Rowena choked on the whimper that rose in her throat, hating that even Stephen's silence spoke as much fear as his words demanded she trust him.

"You need to rest, with your foot up," Ellie ordered, interpreting Rowena's agony as from her injury. "See, your babe has the right idea. Look at him sleep. Let's get you down onto the pallet and I'll prop up that leg of yours. Then I'll see about a tea to ease the pain. Willow bark will help."

Ellie helped Rowena down and, after propping the leg on a stool, stood back to admire her handiwork.

Rowena swallowed another sob, hating that she wasn't sure if she should say something about Lord Stephen's silent plans. Would people like Ellie even believe her? "Ellie, you're so kind to me! Why?"

Ellie laughed, seemingly oblivious to the emotions churning within her charge. "Because you need a friend, I guess."

"'Twill be dangerous for you. Someone wants me dead. If you help me, they may want you dead, as well!"

Immediately Ellie's expression sobered and grew almost fierce. "Then you'll need a friend all the more." She dropped to her knees on the pallet and shook her head. "Why is someone trying to kill you? It makes no sense. You have nothing, and 'tis obvious that you're more in need than any in the village. With the babe, I mean." She stopped a moment, toying with the blanket that she'd tucked around both Rowena and Andrew. "They say you were a mistress to a Norman. That's not true, is it?"

"'Tis true, but not by choice." In the dim light, Rowena felt her cheeks flush.

Ellie shook her head. "I don't understand. If the villagers punish you for what happened, it would only cause them to be punished by Lord Stephen. He keeps the law here quite firmly. Besides, you wouldn't be the first

Saxon maid a Norman has—well, you know… My kin-folk must realize this. They aren't that addled."

"What if it's a Norman who wants me dead?"

Jaw dropping, Ellie sat back. "A Norman? Like Lord Stephen or Master Gilles? Why? It wouldn't gain them anything. Not even the soldiers have a reason to hurt you, and I know several of them who enjoy…um, throwing their weight around."

Rowena considered Ellie's words. What if her attacker was a soldier who was akin to Lord Taurin, or aligned with him? What if they stood to gain something from her death, like land in Normandy or money? If Andrew died, mayhap some distant relative, *who was here in Kingstown*, would inherit Taurin's property!

But didn't King William banish Lord Taurin? Hadn't he taken his land as punishment? The king had appro-priated all of her father's land shortly after the Battle of Hastings, then he'd offered her parents a chance to pur-chase a portion of it back should they have the money.

In the sudden quiet of the chamber, Rowena bit her lip. Was that why her father had sold her into slavery? To buy back his land?

Rowena longed to roll over, away from Ellie's earnest gaze. But her propped-up foot prevented any movement. Instead, she closed her eyes and tried not to think of any reason someone might want her dead.

And what Lord Stephen planned to do.

Both questions scared her deeply.

Stephen wiped his damp brow with the back of his wrist. Today had been far too difficult and the sun of this late-summer hot spell too blazing for his distracted mood.

Rowena had guessed that he planned to lure out her

attacker. She didn't guess any details, but she knew. Then she asked how he could be trusted to save her and her babe's lives while plotting something terrible.

He couldn't be, and that realization rocked him hard.

He hadn't even been able to save Corvin's life, and his brother was a seasoned soldier, good with a sword and as agile as one of those acrobats whom he planned to bring here.

Oh, Corvin, why did you die?

And the anger his death had caused. Such pain in his family still bit into him like vinegar in a wound. His mother's grieving, all the harsh words spoken, even by Josane. She missed her youngest brother, who'd been almost like a son to her. It all hurt. Was his plot to lure out Rowena's attacker driven by his own grief?

Stephen's thoughts returned to Rowena. What circumstances had taught her how to discern people's morality?

Adrien de Ries would know. Stephen pulled up on the reins of his courser as he approached the far barn. The big beast stopped, allowing him a moment to pretend to supervise the men thatching the roof. He'd already ensured that the embankment being cleared through the forest was progressing well. As soon as he returned to his manor, he'd dispatch a letter to Adrien asking for a complete explanation of Rowena's past. She had told him some, but the situation required more from another who would know the truth.

'Twas better than asking her for more, for her fawn-like eyes and innocence stirred guilt. Why did he think he could protect her?

"Milord?"

Stephen looked down at his reeve, Osgar, who'd approached when he'd ridden into view. The man reached for the horse's bridle, stilling the great beast with a calm hand. Stephen had selected Osgar last year to oversee the maintenance and repair of his buildings, including the homes of the tenants. He was a good man, but as a Saxon, he kept Stephen at a wary distance.

"There is a tenant house to rethatch," Stephen said.

Osgar nodded curtly. "I was there last night, also, hauling the water out of the stream. I have sent two men to cut more thatch."

Was there a tightness in Osgar's tone? Stephen explored the man's expression, but it revealed nothing. Was he being too suspicious? He turned his frown to the barn, where several men were climbing ladders, their backs bearing wide bundles of thatch. Two other men were pounding a long beam into place at the peak of the roof.

Stephen nodded, pleased that the man had already begun preparations to repair Rowena's roof.

Yet there was the matter of this building. "This barn is taking too long to complete."

"Aye, milord," Osgar answered, glancing over at it. "We had some trouble with one of the support beams. It had rotted and needed to be replaced, so I had ordered one be brought from storage."

Stephen grimaced. "I had hoped those new beams might be used to repair Rowena's hut, if they were needed."

"Nay, milord. The beams in storage are too fine a quality and too long for a *villein*'s hut," Osgar said bluntly. "We'll find something more suitable for that woman."

Would they? To Stephen's ear, the last comment definitely carried an edge of disgust. Hauling sideways on the reins, Stephen turned his horse. Like Barrett, Rowena's argumentative neighbor, this reeve sounded as though he wanted Stephen to allow them to take care of Rowena once and for all.

"The woman was also vandalized the night before. Do you know anything of that?"

"Why should I?" the man growled. "I work too hard all day to be out gallivanting at night. 'Tis a time to sleep."

"The woman is now under my protection. There will be no more attacks on her," Stephen goaded.

The reeve's eyes narrowed. He glanced over his shoulder to the few workers at the barn. Stephen could see the thatcher atop the peak, ordering the men. When the reeve turned back to Stephen, he grunted, "As you wish, milord."

His gut tight, Stephen ended the conversation and trotted back to the manor. Aye, he would dispatch that letter to Adrien forthwith. He'd promised Rowena he would get to the bottom of the attacks on her, and he would. Mayhap learning more about her would help his investigation. Reaching his stables, Stephen paused. Was that really the reason for dispatching a letter so quickly? Or was it because Rowena intrigued him? Sweet, yet fiery, like a kitten ready to defend itself mere days after it had opened its eyes. Nay. The wild tale she'd told him needed to be confirmed.

He'd insisted that she trust him implicitly. With the king expected to visit before winter, 'twas best that Stephen find Rowena's attacker soon. The king's life may depend on it.

Besides, no one would want King William to arrive and discover *any* dissent, even Saxon against Saxon. And should it be against a woman William had personally freed, 'twas quite possible he would lose his temper and raze the land, regardless of his promise to spare it.

The king ruled harshly, not liking his decisions mocked any more than one liked a toothache.

Inside his manor, Stephen went straight to his private office, ordering a cleaned parchment and a quill from a servant. By the light from the small window, he began his letter to Adrien on the stretched sheet of vellum. At the first word, the quill's nib broke, forcing Stephen to sit back a moment and check his impatience before taking up another prepared quill and dipping it into the gall ink.

The delicate parchment was stretched on a frame and difficult to write upon. After each missive, the skin was cleaned and restretched. Reusing these sheets thinned them more each time. He needed something more practical.

Forcing calmness into himself, Stephen penned his questions again, all the while avoiding the niceties of good letter composition. His mother would be shocked.

At the thought of his mother, Stephen stopped writing. He didn't want his hand to shake again and break another quill. Was she still angry at him for not saving her youngest son's life? He'd heard from a family friend how much she'd cursed him. Stephen was a middle child, the oldest son, and expected to do far more than had been expected from Corvin. He felt his face flush. If he could have, he'd have returned to Normandy, begged his mother's forgiveness for not doing his duty. But he'd been needed in London, and later here, where he faced similar judgment from Josane.

The vellum before him brightened when the sun broke from an errant cloud, as if reminding him why he was here. He wanted answers about Rowena immediately, and Adrien would appreciate the plainspoken words. Then, remembering Rowena's suggestion, he penned a short postscript, asking for a minstrel troupe. Stephen may not know whether she was telling the truth about her life, but he did know a good suggestion when he heard it, especially considering how well it would work into his plan.

After dispatching the courier with a guard, for Rowena's reminder about Normans disappearing mysteriously also lingered, Stephen heard a tap on his door. Young Gaetan announced that the midday meal was ready.

Indeed. The scents of roasted meat and onions, with freshly baked herb bread and soft trenchers, had wafted in around the young boy. But despite the distraction, Stephen's thoughts remained on Rowena. He doubted she'd had a decent meal in days.

And 'twould be good to put her on display in front of those who lived here at the manor. For surely they would report back to the village that Rowena was indeed in league with the Normans. Everyone knew there were few secrets in a manor house.

"Bring the woman Rowena to me," Stephen ordered his squire as he stood. "I should like to dine with her." He paused. "You may have to carry her."

Gaetan shot him a look of horror but trotted off obediently. Stephen's mouth twisted into a half smile. The boy could never handle the order, but with faith that his lord knew best, he dashed off. If only Rowena shared that kind of trust.

He should rescue him, Stephen thought. There was no reason to subject the boy to Rowena's fire. Gaetan had enough with Josane's temper, for she was quite apt to employ him for all sorts of errands.

"Lord Stephen has ordered you to dine with him, Rowena," Ellie announced hurriedly as she stood in the open doorway of the maids' chamber. Having just fed Andrew, Rowena glanced at the other maid, a young woman whose responsibilities had her up before dawn to help the cook. Her eyebrows shot up.

"In the hall?" Rowena asked, turning to Ellie.

"Where else?" Ellie answered. "Milord even sent his squire to carry you."

With a glance at the anxious young boy peering around Ellie's frame, Rowena laughed, though the sound carried a nervous ring. "Should that even be possible, I won't be carried about like some fat overlord. Nay, I'll walk." She didn't want the young boy to find himself in trouble when he could not fulfill his task.

Looking at the door, Ellie handed Rowena the crutch she'd procured, took little Andrew from her and watched Rowena stand gingerly. "Well, the compresses and poultices have worked. Mayhap you can put weight on it. Just take your time."

"And risk Lord Stephen's impatience? Not to mention the possibility of losing a hot meal." Rowena smiled. "Nay, I couldn't do that."

Ellie shook her head. "Don't make light of this. You've already risked his temper once. Plus you returned his offer of food and practically demanded he find who torched your home."

"I didn't demand anything. But Master Gilles spelled out that I am to be protected here."

After setting the babe on the pallet, Ellie took her hands and squeezed them. "Please, Rowena," she pleaded quietly with a shake of her head and another fast look toward the door. "'Tis unwise to irk Lord Stephen. For he's as cold as a winter wind and has the king's ear. We could all suffer for your insolence."

"I have done nothing wrong!" Still, Rowena paused

at the threshold, regret washing through her. True, she had annoyed Lord Stephen, and 'twould not be fair to others here if he was mad only at her. Even to the ones who wanted her dead, 'twould not be fair, as Clara had taught her to love everyone.

Andrew let out a soft whine. Behind her, the other maid wisely distracted him, allowing Rowena to limp into the corridor. Facing away from the great hall, she paused. Was it wise to accept Stephen's kindness in employing her, over and over? It certainly wouldn't be teaching Andrew how to survive on his own, for she wouldn't always be around.

Her defiance would not teach him anything, either, for Andrew could end up dead should he become belligerent. Still, Rowena looked at Gaetan. "Lead the way, and I—"

Abruptly she was scooped up, and as she had that morning outside of her burning home, she swiftly grabbed the clothing of the man carrying her. The crutch she'd taken from Ellie clattered to the floor. She gasped as she turned her head to find herself as close to Lord Stephen as before.

"I want to eat whilst my food is still warm," he announced. "So I don't want to wait for you to hobble down to the hall like an old man."

"Then you shouldn't have told your squire to carry me."

Stephen laughed, but to Rowena, it held little enjoyment. "That's why I'm here. But you didn't notice me, did you?"

"Apparently neither did Ellie."

"I indicated to her not to tell you I was here because I wanted to see how you would react. You should trust that I know what I am doing."

Rowena stilled in his arms. "I have no choice right now, do I? I have to trust you." Her stomach tightened, for as surely as she breathed, she knew Stephen wasn't talking about his promise to find her attacker.

She would never be able to eat the noonday meal now.

Stephen halted. "You must have faith that I know what I'm doing."

She looked away, for he was altogether too close to her. When she turned her head to face him again, *still too closely*, she whispered, "Then let me help you, milord, and not as bait."

He stopped, a frown deepening as he studied her. Did he guess that she suspected he had other plans? "Nay. I have the experience, not you." His lips tightened. "Say no more on that right now. I'm hungry, and I know you are, also. No one, even one as thin as you, can last for days without food, as I know you have."

Heat spread across her cheeks. Everyone ahead and behind them had stopped, obediently waiting for Stephen to resume his stride. She shut her eyes, unable to risk her gaze colliding with Stephen's.

"Rowena." His voice had dropped so low, she could barely hear it. "Open your eyes. Look at me."

Her throat hurt, her breath stalled. "Nay. Put me down. *Please.*"

"You were far more resistant when I carried you in last night," he added as quietly as his previous words. "What has happened?"

What had happened? Where was that independence she was sure she'd learned from Clara? Gone with the realization that one of her own people wanted her dead?

Mayhap she was just weak from hunger. Mayhap she should consider her babe's need for strong, healthy milk. Was she so selfish that she would starve her babe to stay proud? Oh, that should never be, but to be forced to deal with yet another Norman, another man she did not dare trust—

"Rowena!"

Her eyes flew open. "Nay, don't tell me I must trust you. I cannot bear to think on that! And put me down. Please?"

A pause stretched out before them. Then, with a heavy sigh, Stephen set her on her feet. Ellie rushed up with the crutch. Just as Rowena began to hobble down the torch-lit corridor, she glanced over her shoulder. Before she could stop her words, she added, "Do not carry me again, milord. I'm neither a babe in arms nor a crippled old woman. I'm only someone trying to start my life again."

Chapter Eight

Josane sat stiffly to the left of Stephen's grand chair, the expression she wore lethal as he followed the hobbling Rowena. Gilles arrived late, excusing his tardiness with a reason lost to everyone in his mutter. Stephen looked at his brother-in-law, noting suddenly that the man was growing his hair over his ears, mayhap to hide the way they stuck out. The inscrutable chaplain also arrived late but was far more flustered than Gilles. Stephen wasn't sure if either man even noticed Rowena.

He frowned and thought again of Rowena's ability to read people. Mayhap *she* could tell what each man was thinking, for Stephen had learned in William's court that no one save the king was above suspicion. Mayhap Stephen could sway the old priest to root out dissidents for him. Surely, he knew each man's heart?

Rowena sat quietly, her hands clasped tightly in her lap, her stare on them forceful. Stephen burned with curiosity all through grace and the serving of the meal. He practically ached to ask her more questions but wondered if the answers would be lies, and hated that he wasn't sure.

Nay, they couldn't be lies. Rowena would gain nothing from dishonesty, for she had already spurned any attempt at generosity on his part. All she wanted was to establish her life again.

Now, without her realizing it, she was the crux of his plan to fulfill the king's command to find and apprehend those who would threaten this new Norman land. What would she say if she knew?

It shouldn't make any difference. This was for her and her babe's welfare as much as 'twas for the welfare of the crown.

After glancing at Josane, a young servant set out two fine, fresh trenchers, each as thick as two fingers and still steamy from the oven. Another servant then scooped a healthy portion of meat onto each. Behind her, the cupbearer poured new cider into two goblets. Normally, he and his guest would share a goblet, good form in times when poisoning was apt to end the life of a guest or host. But not today. Had Josane ordered the separate servings without him noticing, as was her right as chatelaine? Probably. Her disgust lingered like smoke from an untrimmed wick.

Stephen glanced furtively around the room, cataloging every subtle expression that revealed how each person felt having Rowena on the dais.

The cupbearer appeared calm, but the server's hands shook. Josane stared a hole in Stephen's left temple, but he'd borne the brunt of her displeasure many times before and could allow this to slide from him.

Gilles threw a fast glance at the chaplain, who peered down the table at Rowena as if just realizing she was there.

As he gazed at her, Stephen caught Rowena staring wide-eyed at the food. She swallowed hard, then wet her lips.

Remorse soured his tongue, but Stephen successfully swallowed it away with a generous gulp of cider. Every day of his life, he'd eaten well. Good fare, rich in flavor and heavy with meat. A huge platter of fine cheeses and pastries sat in the middle of the table, artfully decorated with late-season apples and the last of this year's berries.

Rowena furtively touched her belly, pushing on it as if to quell any hunger. He should tell her she was to take all her meals with him, lest her determination to owe him nothing curb her appetite. Foolish thought. Was she not making rope and mending clothes for him? He wished he could use her skill at reading people, but apart from her being uncooperative, there was the logistics of moving her around whilst her ankle healed. Nay, she would earn her meals with rope and mending.

"Thank you for dining with me," he stated loudly as he sliced off a portion of cheese and offered it to her.

"I'm grateful, as well," she muttered back, not looking at him and still pressing her belly with her left hand as she reached for the morsel of food.

His fingers stilled over hers as she accepted it. "You're a curious mix of fear and determination. I would prefer the latter."

"And you, milord, demand that I simply put my faith in you without any proof that you can find who wants me dead."

From the corner of his eye, Stephen ensured that none of the others at the table heard his private conversation. No one appeared to be listening, though. He said, "I will do as I promised, Rowena. You are my guest."

"I've been hired to work here, milord. I'm not a guest."

She blinked. Pale blue eyes, bright with tears, and her long tresses, as white as snow, gave her a delicate air. She wore nothing on her head today, and a few fine strands had escaped her braids to halo her face.

The torches lit around the great hall warmed her skin. She was so beautiful. Had he not noticed that before? Gentle, yet determined to stand up for herself. If she'd ordered him never to speak to her again, in that single breath of time, he'd have obeyed her, for she bore such a look of purity and truth.

He mentally stopped himself. Was he addled all of a sudden?

"Rowena." Josane split open any unwanted attraction with a single chilling slice of her sharp voice. Rowena's attention flew down the length of the table.

Josane leaned forward. "Next time you are invited to this table, I will expect you to at least wear a veil. 'Tis not proper to come bareheaded into this hall."

Rowena's eyes widened and Stephen was sure she would have fled the room had her ankle allowed it. *Lord in heaven, take away her terror.* He needed her here.

"Oui, milady," Rowena whispered in French and English.

"Et tu parle Français?" Josane asked.

"Oui, madame," she whispered back.

"Est-ce Français convenable?"

"Oui, madame. Un baron et son épouse m'a enseigné."

Stephen took note. Rowena had learned her French from both a baron *and* his wife? Had that baron been Lord Taurin, the father of her child? Rowena had known his wife at the same time?

With his mouth tight, Stephen sat back with folded arms.

"Then I expect you to speak only French to the maids," Josane continued in her native tongue, her tone icy. "I may as well take advantage of your language skills while you're here. Work on their pronunciation. Their accents are terrible." With that, she resumed eating.

The chaplain frowned. Stephen knew the man spoke only English, not understanding even the simple conversation that had just transpired. But only a fool would fail to note the foul expression on his sister's face. Stephen shot her a warning look. Not even Josane, as chatelaine and his older sister, was allowed to bully his dinner guest, regardless of Rowena's status as *villein* and now servant. He would speak to her later.

The meal stretched on, with Gilles ignoring everyone except the chaplain. Josane ate efficiently and was the first to excuse herself. Rowena's hand shook as she played with her food. Finally, when Gilles and the chaplain left, Stephen turned to Rowena. "That went well."

She looked up at him as if just realizing the ordeal was finally over. "Thank you for inviting me."

"Ha! You barely ate anything."

"My friend, Clara, who is also a healer, says if you eat when you're nervous, your food will not digest." She paused. "I was nervous."

Stephen smiled. "Really? I didn't notice."

She looked skeptical. His smile widened. "Not all meals go this poorly. Josane is just protective of her position as chatelaine. She runs this manor for me. She keeps the keys and is in charge of hospitality. She's usually very gracious."

"Really? I didn't notice."

Stephen threw back his head and burst out laughing, causing several soldiers who still lingered over their noon meals to peer their way. Ah, 'twas good to see Rowena had a sense of humor, albeit a sarcastic one. As with many Saxons, her wit was as dry as the rushes on the floor. When his laugh died to a chuckle, he focused on her.

She was smiling back, a true, broad smile from unpainted lips, showing straight, white teeth. A dimple showed on each glowing, clear cheek. Her eyes sparkled.

She was truly lovely. He felt his smile die away, and he quickly cleared his throat. He could not allow any feelings for her to sway him from his king's command. The sooner he knew the truth about her life before, the easier 'twould be to deal with her. And if the truth was as bad as she'd said, he'd use that to his advantage, for surely she would agree he should root out Saxon dissidents who reminded her of the man who sold her into slavery.

But the answering letter from Adrien could be weeks away.

His hand shaking, he reached for his goblet, his other hand stopping the maid from taking away their food. "Eat your meal, Rowena. 'Tis wrong to waste it, and my sister is gone. I saw your smile, so I know you're no longer nervous."

Rowena lifted her spoon and tried the tepid stew. Most of it had long since soaked into the trencher. They both knew the food would not go to waste, for someone would gladly finish it off should she decline. Still, Stephen held his breath as she tasted her first morsel. Then she smiled and took another bite.

Again, he watched her. Around them, mounted on weighted clips on the wall, were blazing torches, for the narrow windows did not let in enough light. Grease pans below each one caught any drippings, which would be remelted for reuse. Now that the meal was over, the flames had turned long and lazy, offering a warm glow to her hair. *Amazing hair.*

"Forgive Josane," he said. "But 'twould be best if you found a veil for your hair. We are not used to bare-headed women." 'Twas a distraction for sure, and since Norman women were more inclined to hide their hair, Rowena should, also.

Mayhap a sturdy wimple, too, he thought. Anything to curb some of her beauty. The chaplain and Gilles may not have noticed, but he had. He'd also seen a few fur-tive looks cast from his soldiers.

Her head shot up as if she'd heard his thoughts. Pink flooded her face. "I had a veil in my hut. But I suspect it has been ruined. Though I hadn't worn one before I met Clara."

In his chair, Stephen leaned back. "It still surprises me to see so many Saxon women let their hair show. My mother would be horrified. She didn't even like the tips of her braids to hang below her veil."

After swallowing another spoonful of food, Rowena shook her head. "I had no need for one, though some-times I wore a cap. I had only the clothes given to me by my sisters. My oldest sister was the one who got the new clothes."

Again, compassion reared its unwanted head, but he tamped it down. "Aye, handing down clothes is a com-mon practice."

"They didn't include a veil." She bit her lip. "I will ask Ellie for one, and a wimple, as well."

She didn't protest. She was trying her best. Was he? "Don't worry," he said briskly. "She'll find something for you."

Her meal finally eaten, Rowena set down her spoon. "Thank you. 'Twas a good meal. But I should return to my mending while there is still light coming in the window. And you must have better things to do than sit here and chat."

"I don't. I spent part of the morning arranging to have your home repaired, but 'twill take some time. The crossbeam may need to be replaced and we have none prepared. The thatch has to be gathered and the thatcher must finish his current job."

She paled. "How long will all that take?"

"Longer than it takes your ankle to heal, I suspect."

Her pale brows shot up, but she was silent.

Stephen rose, thankful she said nothing, but knowing she wanted to remind him of her desire to be independent. The manor's chandler had already begun to trim the rush lights and collect the valuable tallow from the grease pans. He backed away when Stephen turned to face Rowena. "I assume you will not allow me to carry you back to the maids' chamber."

She folded her arms. "Nay, I will not."

As he suspected, he thought with sudden ill-humor. "Then I bid you a good afternoon. But I expect you to return here for the evening meal."

He strode away, irritated that he'd allowed Rowena to annoy him. Irritated by everyone, in fact.

And especially irritated by the fact that a part of him wondered if using Rowena as bait was the Christian thing to do.

Chapter Nine

Rowena needed air. She'd been indoors for more than a week and longed to get outside to breathe in the last of the autumn's warm spell. Her ankle had healed well enough; now her eyes needed a rest from mending and her raw fingers a break from twirling rope.

This air would also clear the fog that Lord Stephen's presence had left on her senses. He'd ordered her to take her meals with him, and each one had been as difficult as the first, days ago. Last night, thankfully, he did not appear. When she had entered, Master Gilles had said Lord Stephen was at the palisade being built and all were to eat without him.

Rowena was glad for it and gratefully sat with the maids far from the dais, rather than with Lady Josane and the chaplain. Though Stephen had been generous enough to foster her here and let her work for the manor while her ankle mended, he'd been as chilly as his sister at times, watching those who ate with them the way a hawk watched prey. And yet, he'd laughed heartily at her feeble attempt at sarcasm during that first meal in the hall.

He confused her. He cut a fine figure, but was he not

Norman, with his agenda to serve a king who'd caused so much grief in the short time he'd reigned over England? Nay, 'twas good to be away from so confusing a presence. Each moment with him had her mind spinning and her heart thumping.

"There's trouble in the forest," Gilles had said as he walked in and found Josane finishing her meal and Rowena trying to slip out. "Several villagers were injured while felling trees."

Gilles had turned and looked down his nose at her. "They didn't heed their orders, the fools."

Rowena had blinked at the large, stocky man. His lip had curled, and she felt foolish standing and listening. Though he was a Norman, his accent was different and his hair was much lighter.

But Lord Taurin's wife had also been fair-haired. 'Twas one of the reasons Rowena had been purchased, for her father guaranteed she would bring forth a towheaded child. Wouldn't her father be surprised if he saw Andrew, with his thick mop of dark curls?

She pulled herself up short. That meeting would never happen. Then she'd looked at Master Gilles. "I'm sure they didn't mean to hurt themselves."

Just then the chaplain had asked, "How many were injured?"

Gilles had nodded. "Two men." He'd glared at Rowena. "You Saxons are a clumsy, stubborn lot. I expect Stephen will punish them for their inattention."

With that remark, he'd stalked from the hall.

That had been last night. Now, late the next afternoon, outside, with her ankle almost completely healed and Andrew in his sling, she surveyed the manor from its backyard. 'Twas not as large as Lord Taurin's, for his was taller and had its own attached chapel. It also boasted a large solar with windows that lit the entire room. But this manor was sturdy, with two strong chimneys and thick, solid walls. Beside the maids' chamber, Rowena had been in the kitchen and the great hall only, each at opposite ends of the manor, but she much preferred the kitchen. 'Twas less formal and ruled by a stout, no-nonsense cook who clicked her tongue at Rowena's slim stature and pale complexion. The woman wasn't above telling her she needed to eat more.

In fact, today, the older woman had thrust a hard roll of sweetbread at her, telling Rowena she should eat it outside in the sunshine.

Obliging, she walked to the small stone chapel that sat across the enclosed yard from the house. 'Twas warm there and she longed to free her head of the veil, but she'd promised Stephen she'd wear it. Along the chapel's sunniest wall, late-season roses climbed, with fully opened blossoms hanging over a rough-hewed bench that faced a small cemetery.

Sitting down, she adjusted Andrew to free him from his restrictive sling. He automatically reached for one of the roses.

"Nay, young man. They have thorns." Then, with Stephen's fine form in her mind, she added, "Be careful of the things that are lovely to look at. They can be dangerous."

"So true, indeed."

Rowena jumped up and looked around. The old, weary voice spoke English, but no one was in sight. "Who's there?" she demanded, automatically shoving her son back into his sling. "Why are you hiding?"

"I'm not hiding, my dear. I live in here."

Rowena stumbled back a step. Was she dreaming? Had the wall spoken to her? She looked down at the sweet bun she'd begun to nibble. Was it poisoned, making her delirious? She tossed it away.

Looking from one end of the wall to the other, she braved another response. "You're a wall. You cannot speak!"

A throaty old chuckle answered her. "I'm not a wall. Come close, girl, to the center of the roses. See that big one that is fully opened? Move it to one side."

Rowena stepped tentatively close to the shrubbery, then stretched out her forefinger to move the largest rose. She spied an opening in the stone wall the size of a person's head. A woman's face appeared in it.

Startled, Rowena dropped the blossom.

A gnarled hand moved the branch, tucking it out of the way of the hole with surprising agility.

"There. That's better."

Rowena craned her neck to peer in. An old woman smiled toothlessly back at her. Tufts of white hair had escaped her wimple and veil and deep creases lined her face. She looked pale and thin like Rowena.

"Who are you?" she asked the stranger. "You should come out. 'Tis a fine day and you could probably use the sunshine."

"Oh, I cannot come out, my dear. I'm to spend the rest of my life here behind this wall."

Rowena gaped before taking several steps away to scan the wall, then the cemetery behind her. When she turned back to the old woman, she said, "How awful! Who did this to you? Don't worry, I'll get someone to free you!"

"Hush, girl!" The woman paused. "Lord Stephen did this."

"Nay!" Rowena rushed up to the wall, planting her hands on each side of the hole despite feeling several thorns bite into her palms. "I don't believe that! I will find him and demand you be released! I don't care what he says—"

The old woman laughed. 'Twas as if she was pleased with Rowena's outrage. "Don't do that. Sit here instead and talk to me."

"But you can't stay in there! What does he think you've done? Surely there is a door I can unlock. Lord Stephen's sister has all the keys. I will ask her. I know she doesn't like me, but if I promise to leave—"

"Nay, don't go!" A gnarled hand shot out and caught Rowena's wrist. "I'm leading you astray, my dear."

Rowena stilled. "You're not walled up?"

"I'm walled up, aye. But by choice, my dear. I was allowing you to believe that I am a prisoner."

"I don't understand. Why would anyone want to be stuck behind a wall?"

"'Tis my way to serve the Lord."

"Can't you serve Him out here?"

The old woman shifted, looking over her shoulder for a moment, before peering out again. Her words were softer. "You are new to our village, aren't you? I'm the anchoress, Udella."

Still confused, Rowena shook her head. "Why would the Lord want you in there?"

"I have my own cell here. They walled up the transept to make it."

"The transept?"

"Aye, the side part that extends outward from the rest of the chapel. See how this wall cuts in?" She pointed to Rowena's left. Indeed, the wall did cut out by two arms' span before carrying on to the front end.

Rowena swallowed. "I don't remember seeing a transept."

"Because 'tis walled up. And you didn't see me because I was ill and did not open my small door to hear the services. But I'm well now and want to talk to someone. Like you."

"Me? I'm here only while I heal."

The old woman's eyes lit up. "You must be Rowena."

"You know me?"

The anchoress, *whatever such was*, Rowena thought, looked to her right again, deep within her cell. "Come into the chapel, my dear. I want to see you properly, without bending down. It hurts my back." She pointed to the front of the small building.

Still confused, Rowena turned to her left and followed the stone wall until she reached the front door. 'Twas an old structure, its stones weathered and dark. A small, arched door stood slightly ajar, revealing the darkness inside. When she reached it, she pulled on it, and it creaked open a bit more. Its hinges needed oil. She lifted her cyrtel's hem and pressed herself through the narrow opening. Tucked in his sling, Andrew swiveled his head to peer around. Rowena knew neither of them would see anything until their eyes adjusted.

She heard a rasping sound to the right of the altar, and a small, waist-high door scraped open. Light from the hole by the roses bled into the chapel, only to be suddenly blocked by the hunched silhouette of the old woman. Curious, Rowena took a step forward, up the aisle that divided the few rows of benches. Andrew abruptly let out a laugh. He reached out his arm and pointed into the dimness. Rowena automatically looked that way.

Someone was kneeling in that first pew. Being closed in on all sides, it hid most of the person. Until he turned.

Rowena felt her heart falter. Lord Stephen looked directly at her.

"Lord Stephen!" the anchoress called out. "I did not know you were here."

If those words had come from anyone else in the village, Stephen would've maneuvered the conversation to discover why that person was lying to him. But Lady Udella was the anchoress, and out of respect, he held his tongue.

But he still knew, without understanding why, that Udella was lying.

He rose and watched Rowena take a step back. Her hand reached up to shield Andrew. As before, the babe's cap sat askew and truly boyish on his curly head.

With lips parted, Rowena dropped her gaze from his eyes to his mouth, then to his chest before dropping to the wide flagstones that were the floor.

Though the babe watched him with bold curiosity, Rowena could not.

Look at me, Stephen thought. *I'm not someone to fear or hate.*

As if hearing his internal words, she dared a glance upward. He tried to snag her gaze, but 'twas like catching a runaway mare by her bridle. He missed, and the loss vexed him.

"Such a beautiful babe!" the anchoress exclaimed. "Bring him closer."

Rowena hesitated. She looked thoroughly mystified. With parted lips, she whispered, "Milord?"

Udella chuckled. "Lord Stephen, we have confused her. You are Rowena, are you not?"

Only you have confused her, Stephen thought. *I have*

scared her. Still, they should explain Udella's strange situation.

Rowena said softly, "I disturbed you, Lord Stephen. I had no idea you were in here."

Now that is the truth, Stephen decided. A far cry from the sly old vixen listening to their conversation. He departed the pew. "I normally pray in the morn. But since the affairs of this village disrupted my routine, I only now had the time for it."

"Bring the child here, Rowena," the anchoress interrupted. "I want to see him."

Still, Rowena didn't move. Finally Stephen nodded. "Take him. Udella will want to bless him." He stepped closer. "She won't steal him, Rowena. Should she not relinquish your son when you say so, I will tear down the cell's wall to free him. *I promise.*"

She toyed with the curls escaping her son's cap, obviously considering his promise. "My lord, this is all so strange. Why have you walled up this woman?"

He shrugged. "'Tis of her own choosing."

Rowena turned to the woman. "But why? Surely the king didn't order it? Is it a punishment you took instead of death?"

Udella shook her head. "Nay. When my son was killed at Senlac, I knew that my home, this manor, would be forfeited to the crown. I asked the king to spare it and the village, in return for my becoming its anchoress."

Rowena gasped. "You just walked up to the king and asked him?"

Udella laughed, obviously enjoying the conversation. "Nay. The king stormed the manor. I would have been a fool and the ruination of this village to fight him. Besides, the Good Lord says to obey those who rule over you."

Rowena glanced over at Stephen, then back to Udella. "How did you manage to convince him, then?"

"I am the daughter of an earl, and my mother's family is from Flanders. They know the queen's family, who are also from there. I introduced myself with enough respect and requested an audience." She paused. "Mayhap I reminded the king of his mother, for we discussed her at some length."

"Then you asked him to wall you up?"

Udella shook her head with a sly smile. "I asked him to spare this village for the promise that I would remain here as anchoress and pray for it. And for him. The king is not so stupid to turn down the prayers of a pious woman who held some sway over her village, even one whose son supported the wrong king."

Rowena studied the woman. "But you're sad. I can tell. Is it because you regret your decision to remain here? Or because you grieve for your son?"

Stephen looked from Rowena to Udella, then back again. Despite Rowena's canniness, 'twas obvious the whole idea of a woman so committed to God she never left a chapel was truly foreign to her.

"'Tis her wish to remain here," Stephen explained. "To take prayer requests and offer advice to all who call on her."

"But your son was killed by Normans, who have taken over your home. How—"

"'Twas in battle, Rowena."

"But King William just ignored that?"

"The king has respect for valiant warriors like himself. But it was Udella's strong faith that impressed him, and he agreed to permit her application to become the anchoress here."

Rowena shook her head. "What *is* an anchoress?"

Stephen looked at the old woman. But when Udella simply watched him, he began, "It's a woman who devotes herself to prayer."

"An anchor is something that secures a ship while it is in port," Udella added.

Rowena said, "I have never seen a ship, so I don't know what an anchor looks like."

"'Tis not important," Stephen answered. Despite her slyness right now, Udella really was an anchor here in Kingstown, listening to those looking for advice, praying for the community.

And shocking Rowena. Stephen felt his jaw tighten, his hackles rise. Udella usually wasn't this jovial. But today, she seemed genuinely excited to see Rowena, setting his teeth practically on edge. He'd like to know why that was.

"Come close, girl," the old woman crooned. "I will not steal your babe."

With a fast glance at Stephen, mayhap to confirm that he would indeed tear down the wall should Udella grab the boy, Rowena slipped past him and along the front pew toward the small door set in the wall beside the altar. Despite the tension, Stephen felt a small smile tug on his lips. Did Rowena really believe that he would tear down the wall for her?

Would he?

Aye, he suddenly realized. He would.

The old woman reached out and tickled the child. Andrew laughed, secure in his faith that he would not be taken from his mother's arms. Then the old woman blessed him.

From where he stood, Stephen could see that even a few days here in the manor had done wonders for the child. He bore a healthy glow, and though obviously a happy child anyway, he now beamed with vigor rather than the languidness that came from near starvation.

All the while, Rowena shyly peered into the anchoress's small home. "Can you not get out? You said you were sick. What if you got so ill that you needed help? Or you got hurt?"

"I have faith that I will not," Udella answered pleasantly. "I'm here to pray for all of us. And I am quite pleased to meet you, Rowena. Is there anything you'd like me to pray for?"

Stephen caught the old woman's cunning tone. He'd prayed aloud here yesterday for wisdom where Rowena was concerned. Though her door was not open, the anchoress must've heard him.

What had he been thinking, coming here? Surely he could have prayed just as effectively in his chamber? 'Twas unlike him to reveal his plans in such a foolish way.

Until a few days ago, he'd been more than comfortable in his role as the king's spymaster and perfectly unquestioning in his own ability to find and arrest those here who would rebel against the king. But something was changing, and it unnerved him. Was it Josane's harsh criticism? Probably 'twas his fool reaction to Rowena. Aye, he admired that she'd taken immediately to wearing a veil, held in place by a simple metal diadem. She'd also tied her two braids together at her nape, so they would not be seen.

Stephen opened his mouth to thank her but shut it again. Not while Udella sat there watching. 'Twould send the wrong message to the crafty old woman. He was interested in Rowena only to force out the would-be enemies of the kingdom.

"I have heard of you, Rowena," Udella said. Sighing, she added, "Oh, I wish I hadn't been sick before now! I could have met you sooner. And met this lovely little boy." With that, she tickled Andrew's chin again. He laughed and turned away, his sparkling eyes meeting Stephen's. The boy held out his hand to him, and suddenly, Stephen felt a smile burst onto his lips. Andrew's toothless grin broadened. His arm stretched out, he pointed at Stephen.

Being almost ten years older than Corvin, Stephen remembered him as a babe. A bright, happy thing like Andrew. His heart squeezed.

Still looking at Udella, Rowena asked, "Are you still unwell? I have some herbs—" She stopped. "Well, I don't know if they survived the fire, but my friend, Clara, taught me which herbs are good for warding off a fever."

Udella's interest flared. She adjusted her wimple as she leaned forward. "I heard of this fire. I will pray that your home is repaired soon. But are you lame, also?"

Stephen bristled. Rowena had not limped the short distance around the front pew to where she now stood. Had Udella already heard of Rowena's injury? Did she know something about the attack? Had someone, in seeking advice, revealed his guilt? Stephen would speak to her later, in private.

"Rowena," he began, "Udella has her duties to complete. Let's leave her to her prayers."

Her expression skeptical, Rowena looked once more at Udella. The anchoress waved to little Andrew, who watched her with big dark eyes. For an instant, Stephen wondered what a child of his might look like, for he was also dark-haired and dark-eyed. Would he resemble Andrew? Or would he show a fairer coloring like Rowena?

Like Rowena? The questions mentally jolted him and

he shoved them aside. "Come. Time to leave," he told Rowena with more gruffness in his voice than he'd intended.

Once they were outside and the arched door shut firmly, Rowena asked, "Were you here when she was walled in? It sounds so frightening."

Stephen tensed. His feelings were mixed about such a practice, but Udella had been adamant. "Aye, but I see to it that the maids care for her. She lacks nothing."

Rowena frowned. "Except her freedom."

"Should she change her mind, I would honor her request. But she won't. Tell me, Rowena, what do you think of Udella?"

He waited for her thoughts. With Rowena's obvious talent for guessing people's character, he wanted to see if he should be looking at Udella as a threat to his work here.

With a slight frown and pursed lips, Rowena stopped. When she looked up at Stephen, her expression was serious. "She has a kind heart. She's also sad and lonely. And a little scared, I think."

"'Tis hard to fathom. She was laughing."

"Only on the outside. But she likes you very much."

"I find her as sly as a vixen."

Rowena laughed. "Oh, she is that. She knew you were in the chapel when she invited me in." She reddened. "Lady Udella did that on purpose, I think. 'Twas because she was curious."

Stephen said nothing. Instead, he watched Rowena. With pink cheeks, she looked away to fuss with Andrew's skewed cap. In such a short span of time, she'd identified Udella's personality amazingly well. Rowena was completely uneducated in the formal sense but spoke more than passable French and knew about people. What a benefit she could be to him, he realized again.

Rowena shot him a furtive look, something that bordered on suspicious. "Don't be harsh with her, milord. She trusts you to protect her."

"And you?" The words fell out of his mouth before he gave them thought.

She looked away. Relief washed through him. He hadn't meant to ask because she'd already told him she would not trust him to protect her.

Good thing, he now realized with shock. He was the last person a simple, persecuted maid should have as a protector. Unlike Udella, who needed only the cook to provide her meals, Rowena needed far more. Nay, he was a failure there.

They crossed the short lawn from the chapel to the main house. Halfway there, Rowena began to choose her steps more carefully. "Oh, I fear I have used my ankle too much. 'Tis starting to ache again."

Stephen, growing tired of the dragging pace after a few steps, stopped her. "'Tis harder for me to walk slowly than 'tis to run. Let me take Andrew, for he's slowing you down further."

Rowena hesitated. "He's no bother."

"Rowena, I won't hurt him. Nor would I separate you two. You trusted me inside the chapel. Can you not trust me on this small matter?"

She stiffened. "Where my son is concerned, 'tis never a small matter." Though, after a few more limping steps, she tugged Andrew free of the sling.

Stephen took the child. The boy was heavier than he looked but did not fuss when lifted from his mother.

Abruptly, the babe reached up and smacked Stephen's mouth. Stephen grimaced with great exaggeration, eliciting a laugh from the child. Satisfied that Andrew would not protest, Rowena began again her hobble toward the manor house. Stephen, still watching the boy closely, followed more slowly.

"A cozy scene," a male voice drawled in English.

Stephen looked over Andrew's head to the chaplain, who stood by the side entrance. The man frowned deeply at them as they approached.

Stephen wondered, *What did he mean by that comment?* "Rowena has met our anchoress," he said.

At the mention of the old woman, the chaplain's frown deepened. "I hope she didn't disturb Lady Udella's prayers."

Stephen straightened. "Nay. Udella is in a happy mood and invited Rowena inside to meet her."

"She is no longer the lady of the manor," the chaplain grumbled. "She has retired from society and should not be so hospitable."

Stephen passed the man, whose long, coarse robe buffeted in the strengthening breeze that swirled around the corner of the manor. Then he turned back. "I would say you need to speak with her, then, for she is far too interested in our daily activities."

The chaplain's eyes narrowed. Stephen felt the sudden rise of the hairs on his neck. 'Twas not too often that he and his chaplain agreed. He knew that the man disapproved of his choice of career, and of being born Norman. The man of God was not the first Saxon priest to rail against the invasion of his land. But to criticize Udella openly, who, until two years ago, had been his lady and patroness? Strange.

Rowena had reached the back door to the manor house, where Ellie now stood holding it open for her. Still feeling suspicious, Stephen bounced Andrew one more time before walking up to the pair and handing him back to his mother.

Rowena quietly thanked him, but her attention remained on the priest, who stood back a few feet. "I'm sorry for speaking with the anchoress, sir. I didn't mean to disturb her. She called to me from a hole behind the roses."

"You've done nothing wrong, Rowena." But still, Stephen clenched his teeth. "Go inside. Ellie, Rowena needs another poultice on her ankle."

When the door closed on the two women, Stephen turned to the older man. "Do not be too harsh with Rowena or the anchoress, Chaplain. 'Twas a chance encounter. An accident I suspect won't happen again."

The priest's mouth tightened into a grimace. "I know what happened to that girl. This town is walking on eggshells. And that girl's wild tale about being a slave doesn't help."

Stephen folded his arms. Although he expected no confession from the man, he asked anyway, "Have you any idea who attacked her?"

"Nay." The chaplain averted his gaze, choosing instead to focus on the grass that brushed against the chapel walls. Sheep were often brought in to graze in the yard when it wasn't required for training. "The people fear the king's wrath."

"As they should, if they choose to defy him. What have you heard about Rowena?"

"She is seen as collaborating with you Normans, my lord. We see the result in that babe of hers."

Frustration swelled in Stephen. "Has it not occurred to anyone here that she may have been an unwilling partner in that?"

"Aye, it has, my lord. But that makes those who mistrust you Normans all the more suspicious. You Normans would use a simple maid, then discard her? Even if she were an unwilling partner, why then would the king grant her freedom? And why would a Norman baron pay her taxes and set her up here? See, 'tis not as simple a situation as it appears. But as you said, there is no reason anyone would want her dead. The girl is nothing, so we're told. Should it happen, her death would be simply a tragic moment in our lives. Nothing would come of it." The chaplain sighed. "And no one is speaking of the attack."

"'Twas a Saxon attack," Stephen confirmed. "The men in this village know something." Stephen drew up to his full height, hoping his stature would intimidate the chaplain. "Should you discover why someone would want her dead, I expect you to tell me."

"And you consider yourself Rowena's protector against her own people? You could not protect your own brother."

"Watch your tongue, Chaplain. I told you that in confidence, and I can throw you in jail just as easily as I could Rowena's attacker."

He spun, tamping down his sudden anger, for he didn't want to argue with the man. And he didn't need the man telling him what he already knew.

The chaplain caught his arm. Irritated, he looked down at the rough, suntanned hand, for the chaplain worked the lands as everyone else did. His gaze moved up the older man's plain brown sleeve to his weather-beaten face.

"What is it?"

"Two things. Be careful how you use Rowena. It will not go unnoticed."

Stephen tightened his jaw. Did the chaplain suspect

his other reason for using Rowena? Stephen had told only Josane and Gilles that he was here in Kingstown to find rebels before they posed a threat to William. "If it serves the king, 'twill be done. What is your other concern?"

The chaplain stood straighter. "Mayhap you're asking the wrong question, my lord, as you seek who attacked Rowena."

"What is the right one?" Stephen asked.

"What would happen should Rowena die? As her baron, you would face judgment for a death you could have prevented. I must ask this because as the chaplain, I must be concerned for all the souls here."

"Her child would be motherless." The babe had few chances for success in life as 'twas, but should Rowena die—the thought fell heavy on his heart for some reason—what hope would the boy have then? None whatsoever.

Stephen yanked his arm free of the chaplain's firm grip and stalked into the manor house.

Chapter Ten

The moment Stephen stepped across the threshold of his home, the sound of galloping hooves reached him. He turned in time to see his courier pull a horse to a halt by the stable and leap down. The man was obviously glad to be home, and considering the danger Normans were in alone in the forests, Stephen couldn't blame him.

The man had taken Stephen's letter to Adrien at Dunmow Keep but had returned the next day, saying Adrien was in London and that the letter would be forwarded along with Lady Ediva's. Stephen hoped that Adrien would dispatch his reply straight from London, using his own courier rather than Stephen's.

Even from this distance, Stephen could see the horse's girth heave with exhaustion, and when it danced fretfully about, he also saw foam at its mouth.

Stephen had a standing order that the horses be kept in good shape, for having a weak mount was as bad as having a poorly conditioned soldier. 'Twas one of the courier's jobs to help with that. He stepped into his home to leave the pair to the required grooming.

Inside the dimness, Stephen drew in his breath. The smell of the next meal, mixed with Josane's herb-and-flower-scented torches, reached him. He strode down the hall, finding the scents of meats and bread increasing with every footstep. At the maids' chamber, he stopped. The tiny door was open, but he hesitated.

Rowena sat at the table mending something. Beside her freshly wrapped ankle was a coil of thin rope and a rope maker's tool, a wooden top similar to a child's toy, only deeply grooved. Draped over a hook above her head were several lengths of fibers.

Stephen recognized the garment she was mending. It was his undertunic. There was a certain intimacy about the moment, with her hands fingering the cloth that had lain next to his skin. He felt uncharacteristic heat flood his face and wished she were wrapping rope instead. He'd ripped that tunic the last time he'd trained with his men. They'd been fighting with maces, and though they were the weapon of choice for clerics, 'twas good practice, for their weight flexed the upper-arm muscles.

Stephen watched Rowena bend forward, squinting at the tiny stitching. She'd have a sore back and eyes like fire in no time.

"I will get you a proper light," he announced.

Rowena jumped. Then, seeing who stood at the door, she stood herself. "Nay, milord. I have a light."

"Not a good one, if your squinting is any indication."

She set down the sewing. "Please do not favor me. The lamp is fine."

"Not when you're sewing my clothes. I cannot believe my sister would cloister you away and have you use good lamp oil when she has a perfectly bright solar upstairs in which a maid can mend."

He studied her reaction. Nay. 'Twas Rowena's private choice not to sew in his sister's solar. Not wanting to risk his sister's caustic personality, he would choose this location, also.

He quickly changed the subject. "For a maid who spent much of her life around animals, you're doing well with the mending. How is that so?"

"When my clothes were torn, who would sew them for me? No one. So one of my sisters taught me."

"Was she your champion? You had a difficult life."

Rowena looked perplexed. When Stephen realized they were speaking in French and that she did not understand his meaning, he switched to English and her expression fell. "Nay, for she was happy to have a small dowry and leave the farm for her marriage."

"Why didn't she take you with her?"

Rowena's gaze slid to her babe as he rocked on his hands and knees. "She started her family immediately. I would have been an extra mouth to feed."

"'Tis a shame she didn't know of your skill at twisting rope."

"Clara taught me rope making. I learned the basics at the farm, using my fingers to wrap and twist the fibers, but Clara gave me this top. When I have the thinner strands done, I will use it to make longer, thicker rope."

She frowned at him. "Is there something I can do for you, my lord? You didn't come to watch me work."

Stephen stepped into the room, the question on his mind demanding an answer. "I have come to ask you if you have someone to care for Andrew should anything happen to you. The midwife, Clara, for instance. Have you arranged for her to adopt him?"

With a stricken look, Rowena sank into the battered chair behind her. "Am I in that much danger? What have you learned?"

"Nothing. I'm only considering what would happen

should you be injured or—" He refused to finish the sentence.

"Killed." Blinking, she looked down at Andrew as he continued his rocking, trying his best to figure out how to crawl. "My child would have nothing. He would be nothing."

"We don't know what his life will be like. The king himself is illegitimate. But his father made him his heir. He had to fight to secure that right, but he was successful. 'Twas what made him the powerful man he is today."

Rowena looked up at Stephen, her eyes wide with horror. "Lord Taurin wanted to make Andrew his heir. That would have allowed Taurin to contest King William for control of Normandy, just on the amount of land he would have owned." She gasped. "Is my son in danger?"

Stephen shook his head as he sat in the other chair. He didn't know for sure what the attacker wanted, but he couldn't worry her. "Nay, he's not. 'Twas a foolish dream and a great risk that Taurin took. He would have been a threat only if he'd been given the lands by his wife's family, which he wasn't. Now he's in disgrace, stripped of all except for one small parcel on which he must farm."

"So no one will be threatened by Andrew? Not even the king himself? How can you be sure?"

"The king has taken measures to stop Taurin or anyone who would use Taurin's bloodline. Andrew is safe."

"Until something happens to me. *I* am his only champion."

Stephen shook his head. "'Tis why I am here. You must find someone to care for the boy should anything happen to you."

"I can't assign anyone that responsibility! What if they take him from me immediately?"

Stephen frowned. "What would that person gain?"

"Mayhap that small parcel of land Lord Taurin has, after they kill him? Who knows its size? Nay, some say this village is small, but to me, 'tis enormous! How do I know someone won't use Andrew the way Lord Taurin wanted to use him?"

"Only a Norman could do that. I was suggesting you ask Clara to take him."

"She will soon have a Norman husband. Aye, she is kind to Andrew and she loves him, but I cannot risk her husband being swayed by the chance of receiving more land."

Stephen sighed. There was no one here, except mayhap Ellie, to care for the child. If Rowena would not trust her Saxon friends, then who would measure up to the responsibility?

Certainly not he.

Stephen stared at Rowena. She would not ask him. He knew that, but for the slimmest of moments, he thought she might.

He stood quickly and ground his heel on the floor, crushing and pulverizing the thresh into the cold flagstones. 'Twould be most unwise to consider him as guardian. He couldn't look after his own brother, let alone a babe.

The memory of the battle rolled over him. The fighting, the cursing, the sounds men made when they fought for their lives. The smell of blood and horseflesh. *The smell of fear.*

His mother's last words to him before he and Corvin left returned to him. *Take care of your brother, Stephen. He is not as strong as you. He needs you and 'tis your duty to ensure his safety.*

Stephen had fended off several Saxons who advanced

on Corvin, whose mount had been injured, forcing him to fight on foot. Stephen had the advantage—a steed well trained in battle and a good, long Norman sword. Corvin's had been dropped, forcing his brother to grab a shorter Saxon blade.

Then, in that moment when an attack came from his other side, Stephen turned.

When he was able, he turned back to find Corvin on the ground, run through with a blade.

One moment of inattention and a life dear to him was gone. He glared at Rowena. "You should consider my suggestion. We do not know how long the Lord gives us. A strong faith does not ensure a long life."

"But one full of peace, though? That's what Clara said."

Rowena saw an odd look come over Stephen's face. He sat down again and drew her fingers into a warm grasp that she strangely ached to cling to. "'Tis not always that simple," he said. "Even a faithful person has days when peace eludes him. But God forgives all."

She shook her head. "You have days like that? If you doubt your faith some days, how can *I* ever find peace?"

She could feel his fingers brush the blisters her rope making had caused. She watched him closely, unable to guess his thoughts, but knowing instinctively he was considering something serious.

"Come to chapel services with me tonight," he finally said. "We will sit together."

Rowena had attended services in the past, listening carefully to the cleric. But it never felt enough. Taurin had rarely gone to services and certainly knew enough not to take her. She was his slave, and the foundation of his argument for buying her was based on her being a pagan. 'Twould not do for her to be seen in a chapel.

So what was Stephen planning? For surely he was doing just that. She yanked back her hands, cringing slightly at the way his calluses scraped over her tender skin. "The front pews are reserved for your family."

"And my guests."

She stiffened. "Will God give me more faith if I sit up there?"

"'Tis not decided by where you sit, Rowena."

"I meant more faith in *you.*"

He seemed to weigh his answer. "He will give you wisdom, and I must ask for more myself."

His eyes were dark and glittering. His hair, short but growing out of that peculiar Norman fashion in which the back of the head was kept shaved, was the color of rich, dark wood, stained with black walnut juice and polished until it gleamed as much as a fancy lady's mirror.

He was so handsome.

Nay! She would not be swayed by such foolishness! Stephen was Norman, and a man, and to add salt to a wound, he was plotting something. She didn't know what. She just knew there was something.

"Rowena, I ask again for your faith that I will find who wants you dead. 'Tis the only thing I ask. I will find who attacked you. That is my promise to you."

"What does that have to do with attending services with you, milord?"

His expression hardened. "Everything." Stephen paused, then worked his jaw as if struggling to sort out something. His voice softened. "Mayhap you can pray for His help in selecting someone to care for your son should anything happen to you."

Her heart pounded heavily in her chest and tears

pricked at her eyes. *Lord, 'tis confusing. Help me to understand.*

Stephen stood. "At evensong time, then," he said before turning and leaving her alone with her son, the reason he'd come to see her in the first place.

He was right. She needed to consider what might happen to Andrew should he be left alone. 'Twas terrifying to imagine, but she must.

Rowena helped Ellie the rest of the day, seeing nothing more of Stephen. Her demeanor cool, Lady Josane directed them to repairing the tapestries in the great hall. At one point, her husband, Master Gilles, walked in. He looked startled to see Rowena.

"Is she well enough to return to her home?" he asked his wife.

Josane glanced over at Rowena and Ellie. "Soon enough" was her only comment.

"I suppose it's just as well. The roof thatching will not start until the morrow." Gilles left shortly after. Rowena's peek over her shoulder met Josane's harsh glare. Then, as if knowing how much she owed Stephen for the repairs and the food she'd eaten, as little as that was, she hurriedly returned to her mending.

Ellie leaned over. "Don't fret, Rowena," she whispered. "Lady Josane is like that with all of us."

"And Master Gilles? He wants me to leave, as well. And he is expected to act as judge should Lord Stephen find whoever burned my home. Can I trust him?"

Ellie shrugged. "Why would he take the side of the Saxon who tried to hurt you? He's Norman."

"You know for sure 'twas a villager?"

Ellie looked away. "I don't know anything," she muttered as she returned to the tapestry. "Only that Lord

Stephen is working the villagers very hard, and some say 'tis because he is punishing them for the attack."

Rowena bit her lip. 'Twas just as she suspected, that the villagers would see Lord Stephen favoring her. 'Twas as if he was provoking them.

She'd promised Lord Stephen she would attend evensong with him. What would that cause? Oh, she was a fool to agree. She'd been swayed by his good looks and the way he'd muddled her thoughts with who would care for Andrew should she die. 'Twas as if he'd thrown that idea out just to distract her from thinking too much about his invitation.

'Twould be wise for her to avoid him completely.

At evensong she entered the chapel gingerly, trying not to limp, but still feeling the extra stress she'd put on her ankle earlier. One of the other maids had offered to mind Andrew, and Rowena had accepted. She found a small space on the far-left bench, offered up to her by a young Saxon man who seemed to be pointedly ignoring his father's scowl. She prepared to sit down, thankful she could attend services and fulfill her promise to Lord Stephen without being near him.

"Nay, Rowena, sit in the front with me."

She looked up to find Stephen standing in the aisle, his arm extended toward her. In the small chapel, all were still standing, waiting for their lord to find his seat.

Silence dropped with a crash around them. Glares slapped her like wet leather. As she reluctantly accepted Stephen's hand and slipped closer to him, she whispered, "I was fine back there."

"I asked you to come to services with me. That means to sit with me, also."

Her heart pounded as she let Stephen help her down the aisle, closer to the altar. He allowed her to enter the closed-in pew first. Despite being grateful for his warm grasp, she whispered, "'Tis not a good idea, milord, for me to have special privileges."

But for all her protests, she couldn't help but dare a glance up at him in the presence of nearly all the village. He stood tall and lean, and she caught the fresh scent of late-season meadowsweet on him, coaxing her to inhale deeply. He opened his mouth to speak, but she quickly finished her words. "Or *to be seen to have* special privileges."

Rowena is quite right, Stephen thought. The villagers would witness her unusual position, but 'twas the only way he would be able to gauge their reactions. Several, including Barrett, scowled when Rowena passed them. As they finally reached the front, he also noticed the anchoress's eyes narrowing as she watched them. The old woman then caught sight of the chaplain's sharp look and lowered her gaze. 'Twas odd that Udella allowed her chaplain to dictate how she should act, when not so long ago she ruled this village.

Josane arrived with Gilles, her displeasure at sharing the family pew with a servant evident on her face. Although he stood to allow them to enter, Stephen mostly ignored her. He'd been subject to her sour attitude all his life and had survived. He would manage just fine now.

On the other hand, poor Rowena dropped her gaze as the couple squeezed past her. He'd fully expected his sister to plop down between them, but judging by the next scathing look, she had no desire to sit near her brother today.

When the service ended, Stephen stood, turned to face the door, but did not depart the pew. As was the custom, the rest of the congregation stood to wait until he and the chaplain left.

Aye, those whom he suspected had tried to stare a hole in the back of his head throughout the service now dropped their gazes. Stephen swept the interior with one broad, challenging stare.

Several men were missing. Barrett, Osgar the Reeve and two others had stood at the beginning but now were nowhere to be seen. They had been remarkably quiet for him not to hear them slip out.

The chaplain strolled down the aisle, nodding to and blessing various parishioners. Halfway down, he stopped and turned, watching Stephen as he cataloged the people. A moment later, a deep frown on his face, he returned to the first pew. "My lord," he said, "you must leave so your villagers can, also."

Stephen looked at the older man. "I see some have already departed."

"I will speak with them later, milord." The man leaned forward and dropped his voice. "But you should not treat one maid better than you treat them."

Stephen lifted his brows. "And are we not all equal in God's eyes?"

"Aye, milord, but Rowena is still your servant."

"She is my guest, Chaplain," he growled.

Josane leaned forward and whispered, "Listen to him, Stephen. He's not criticizing you but pointing out that someone here holds a grudge against Rowena. Flaunting your authority over them by parading her at the front of the chapel will only anger them further."

Then, surprising Stephen, she directed her attention to Rowena. "Do not be offended, Rowena. This is not about your station. 'Tis about your safety, which, believe it or not, *is* my main concern. Stephen is being stubborn and 'twill get you hurt."

Josane stared hard at him. "You cannot fool me. But whoever tried to harm Rowena would be a fool to reveal his guilt at evensong."

Stephen bristled, hating that his intent was as clear as water to his older sister. "I know what I'm doing."

Rowena gasped, but Josane pierced him with another glare. "Do you? I think you're risking Rowena's life to prove you are in charge," she hissed. She shifted her head to hide her mouth from the crowd standing nearby. "We cannot risk causing the villagers to turn against us, not when we have so few soldiers to protect us. And working the villagers to the bone doesn't help, either."

"Tired men don't rebel."

"But they can muster up the strength to plunge a pitchfork into your back, my brother. Then we'll all be dead." She squeezed past both of them before marching down the aisle, her break in protocol as evident as snapping a dry twig.

Stephen turned to Rowena. "You will dine with me."

She looked at him with horror, then shook her head. "Lady Josane is right. This was what you planned all along!"

"That's exactly why I want you in the hall tonight."

"I won't be your bait!"

Stephen tightened his jaw. Like Josane, she saw right through him.

But why shouldn't he do this? 'Twould both find her attacker and fulfill his king's order.

But would it keep her from getting killed? Or keep his family safe? Corvin's face flashed in his mind, and the pain of grief wrenched at his heart.

Stephen said quietly but fiercely, "You said you

wished to help me with my investigation. So here is your chance."

She swallowed. She obviously didn't like being reminded of her own words. He would have allowed a smile to form on his lips had the situation been different. "Come," he told her curtly, suspecting Rowena would refuse his offer if he persisted, "I'm hungry, and though 'tis only a small meal, I want to eat it in the hall with you."

Knowing better than to scoop her up, Stephen allowed her to walk out slowly on her own while he used the time to watch the villagers. But with Osgar and Barrett no longer in the chapel, no villagers met his gaze as they passed.

Chapter Eleven

The following morning, after they'd washed more linen and wool than Rowena had ever seen, Rowena followed Ellie outside to spread out the laundry to dry. She'd offered to help with the other chores to give her eyes and fingers a change from rope making.

The bushes at the far side of the manor's garden, having been stripped of their fruit, were all now covered with an assortment of clothes and linens. Rowena looked down at her hands after spreading the last tunic. They were clean, even wrinkled, as she'd helped to wring out the linens. She had never had clean nails, she marveled to herself.

A short whistling noise caught her attention. She looked around to see the roses by the chapel wall rustle and part. The anchoress peered out at her.

Male voices pulled her attention away and Rowena saw Lord Stephen and Master Gilles walking toward the manor. They were deep in conversation.

The late-autumn sun glinted off Stephen's hair, giving it a warm tone akin to the color of sunburned oak leaves. Yet, surprisingly, Master Gilles's hair showed blonder than ever, as if the waning rays of autumn had still managed to lighten it.

Standing behind the bushes, Rowena watched the men enter the manor house. Neither noticed her, mayhap because of where she stood, or mayhap because she'd begun to cover her head as Lady Josane had ordered.

Oddly, Rowena was now glad for the order. It hid a hair color that had brought nothing but attention.

But still, during each meal that she took in the great hall, she felt eyes on her. Last night's was worse after what had happened in the chapel.

Josane had guessed Stephen's plan to flaunt his authority and use Rowena. Nay, she would not be caught up in some fool idea that Stephen cared for her. He was only using her to find her attacker, to shore up his village's security, because everyone knew King William was due to visit. And Stephen wanted her to put her faith in him?

"Come close, Rowena," a voice beckoned. "We didn't finish our conversation the other day."

Rowena turned. The anchoress still peeked out her tiny hole, an almost silly sight of eyes surrounded by the dying rose blossoms. As Rowena closed the distance, their scent pulled her in. She sat on the bench and dipped her head to spy the older woman.

"I really should be working, my lady."

"The sun is too hot today. Our summer has returned."

"Nay, my lady, it only teases us. The mornings are cool, and we'll have a killing frost soon."

"But I do like summers so, and always hope they will stay."

"The plants need to rest, and without the winter rains, our fields could never be planted in the spring. Our livestock wouldn't breed, either."

"Spoken like a farmer."

Rowena moved back slightly and folded her arms. "I grew up on a farm. Not like the small ones here, but one with oxen and sheep and many fowl."

"Do you enjoy living here, then?"

Rowena paused. She didn't ever want to see her family again, but she wondered if her father had indeed sold her in order to buy back his land. Without land, he and the rest of his family would starve. But enjoy living here? She'd been here only a few weeks and had already lost her home. A farm brought hard work, but good food if the farmer wished to give it. A village offered companions if they liked you. She had neither.

"I have no house here, no life elsewhere. I can't answer your question."

"Poor thing. Caught between the world you grew up in and this one. But surely there can't be much difference."

"There is! My home was a farm away from everything. My parents are pagans who think spirits live in trees and buildings and do all sorts of mischief. That's why my family stays away from towns and villages."

"Pagans? I had no idea those old heresies still existed." Udella made a soft noise before asking, "Did any missionary come your way?"

"There were some men, but my father would chase them away, saying they brought bad luck." The last man to visit did so on horseback with a contingent of Norman soldiers. Taurin had spied Rowena when his horse was taken to the barn to be brushed and groomed.

She shuddered. She didn't want to talk about her family or how her father saw a way to make money quickly. She had never known what a full belly felt like until she'd met Clara and had never broken her fast with warm broth and bread and cheese until she came to this manor house. She liked not being tired for lack of food or being cold for lack of a decent home. She loved that Andrew was finally growing plump and didn't cry for want of milk. But there was much scheming.

A door slammed to her right and she watched as Stephen and Gilles left the manor again. Automatically she stilled, not wanting to be caught idling the day away instead of working as she'd promised she would.

She could hear them speaking in French but was unable to catch any words. As they disappeared down toward the barn that was being thatched, Rowena turned to the anchoress. "Do you mind that the Normans have taken over your home?"

"I could not bring back my son," Udella said softly. "But I could save the people who looked to me for help. Nay, I wasn't bitter, for the Lord gives me peace."

"Peace? How? Every day you see the men who could have killed your son. Doesn't that hurt you?"

Udella paused and leaned forward. "It did for a time, but when I saw Master Gilles, I knew 'twas meant to be."

Rowena frowned. "I don't understand."

Udella's voice dropped. "Gilles is my nephew."

"Nephew? He's Norman."

"Only half-Norman. He's half-Saxon, too. Come closer, for what I will tell you, very few know."

Suspicious, Rowena did not move. "Why, then, tell me?"

"You are searching for the Lord. This may encourage you. And I can see that you keep your own counsel. I know I can trust you. Come, lean closer, so that only you can hear."

After a short hesitation, Rowena leaned forward.

"I saw Gilles when King William passed through

this way two years ago. I recognized him immediately as being my brother's son. You see, long before the battle at Hastings, we were wealthy and 'twas proper for a good family to send a son away for his education. My brother and our cousin went to Normandy to learn French and how to be a proper aristocrat. My cousin returned a few years later, for he missed his family too much. My brother stayed."

"Is he still there?"

"Aye, but buried there. But not before falling for a young woman in the family where he stayed. My cousin said when the family learned that my brother and this woman cared for each other, she was married off to another Norman family. But not before she became pregnant. Gilles is that child."

"How do you know this? Does Gilles know who his father is?"

"I have never discussed it with him, but he bears the same looks as my brother and the same golden hair. And the same ears."

"Ears?"

"Aye, a unique shape to them." Udella peered hard at her. "Don't you believe me that such oddities are born into families?"

Taken aback, Rowena blinked. "Cows give birth to calves that share their colors. I've seen it." She paused. "Why haven't you told Master Gilles that you are his aunt?"

"I can't, though 'tis not an easy decision. When King William came, I saw an opportunity to bring Gilles here to be our baron, as would have been his right. But the king chose Lord Stephen instead, and I feared for Gilles's safety should I ask the king for him and be forced to say why."

"I don't understand."

"What if the king became afraid that Gilles would support his father's family and village? Nay, I could not take that risk. I made the older ones here who remembered Gilles's father take an oath never to mention it. Besides, when Lord Stephen came and brought his family, which included Gilles, I had no need to petition the king anymore. 'Twas an incredible blessing and I would not turn my back on it." She sighed. "I had planned, though, to tell Gilles who he was, for I believed that his mother may never have told him. Mayhap to preserve his life and position because not all men are kind to those who are not their offspring."

Rowena hugged herself. "And you are telling me all of this to show me the Lord?"

"Nay, I can see that you need to learn to forgive. Did the Normans kill someone you love?"

"Nay. But one Norman was brutal to me."

"Ah, 'tis that bitterness I sense. Let it go, lest it eat you alive."

Hadn't Clara said that bitterness caused all manner of illness? Rowena squinted against the sun as she saw Stephen and Gilles in the distance, speaking with a man who carried a huge bundle of thatch. What life would her son have had if Taurin had been successful? A life of privilege, as Gilles experienced? What would she tell her son when he asked about his father? She drew in her breath as she spied several villagers make their way home for the noonday meal. Someone wanted her dead, so 'twas possible she would never get to tell her son the truth.

She thought again of what Stephen had said to her. She needed to get word to Clara to ask if she would raise Andrew should something happen to her.

Because I am bait for Stephen's trap.

She'd told Stephen she would not be used again. Even now, resentment rose in her and she struggled to tamp it down. How could he so coldly use her that way? He'd even mentioned that something could happen to her. So he knew that he planned to risk her life and wanted her to sort out a future adoption.

So cold and unfeeling.

Again, her heart wrenched. Why? Because she could die? Or because he didn't think there was anything wrong with using her? Or because 'twas Stephen who did this?

If she agreed, 'twould put an end to this terror and she could return to her home and be done with Lord Stephen. But she'd have to trust him first.

Put my faith in another Norman.

A few moments of dislike in exchange for a chance to live free. Aye, she would do it. She could draw her attacker into her home.

Rowena looked at Udella. "I must return to my work."

"What are you planning? Is it something I can pray for?"

"Nay. Now that I am healed, I must see to returning to my home."

Udella looked doubtful. But before she could remind her that her home was still without a roof, Rowena stepped away from the wall, out of the circle of rose scent and back to work.

And straight back into danger. She wasn't one who would allow a horse to kick her twice, but in this case, she may need to be.

She would return to her home and act as bait.

Chapter Twelve

Stephen strode into the great hall looking for Gilles, who'd taken several of the soldiers for an unnecessary task. He had far more important work for them than anything Gilles wanted done.

The only person there was Rowena. She was bent over the hearth with a short metal rake and flat pan, cleaning the ashes. He saw Andrew on a mat near her, playing with polished bones.

'Twas a good thing he didn't sit directly on the rushes, for as much as Josane changed them monthly, they harbored ills of every kind.

A cry shot through the room and Stephen spun.

Rowena was dancing around, the hem of her cyrtel smoking as she beat on it with the rake.

With a gasp, Stephen rushed forward, ripping off his cloak as he went. He threw it around her and feverishly patted her down, in his haste shoving her to the floor.

Within a few moments, the smoldering had stopped. Stephen sagged forward next to Rowena, who grabbed him with relief.

"My thanks, milord. I thought the ashes were cold, but there were hot ones deep within."

"Who ordered you to clean this hearth?"

"Lady Josane. I asked for extra chores."

"Have you done it before?"

Rowena hesitated.

"Have you?" he barked.

She looked away. "Only a few times. At my family home, I spent most of my days in the barn. The animals gave off enough heat. When I was hiding from Lord Taurin, I was too scared to light a fire in case it lured someone to investigate."

Feeling his mouth tighten, Stephen said through gritted teeth, "Always stir ashes, even cold ones. And do not refer to Taurin as 'lord.'"

She peered up at him, her pale eyes wide and watery, and tendrils of white-blond hair stuck to the perspiration on her brow. Her lips had parted and she bore a look of compelling innocence. "Aye, my lord," she whispered.

"I do not want you to hurt yourself."

A shadow fell over her face. "Mayhap, but you need to. I have decided to let you use me as bait."

He pulled himself up short. What had he been thinking?

On his knees before Rowena as she, too, knelt, he saw her look of willing expectation that her agreement would be accepted without question.

"My lord," she whispered, "I will help you find my attacker. I want to end this and return home."

He drew back mentally. He'd actually considered setting her as bait for her own attacker? Aye, and he'd felt disappointment earlier when she'd refused. But at this moment, all of his reasons seemed as wispy as the thin lines of dying smoke from the hot coals that lingered in the hearth.

What had changed his mind since he'd made that

addled decision? Nothing. He'd spent the day checking the thatcher's work and seeing about his usual duties. Then as he'd entered his great hall, he'd spied her. She was wearing a wimple that was a tad too big for her, and a veil he recognized as one of Josane's old ones. When he inhaled, carried on the scents of supper was another fainter, softer one of roses. He peered down at Rowena. Had she visited the anchoress today? What had they discussed? Had the woman encouraged Rowena to tell Stephen she had decided to help him with his investigation?

He rose. "Nay, you will not help. I have chosen a tactic of keeping the men so busy that they are exhausted at the end of each day. And watching who might slip away or who complained too much will help me discover who has been staying up at night."

"Many people rise at midnight for services," she countered, standing. "I have heard them. They even visit each other. But whoever attacked me won't bother doing anything suspicious without a reason. So I need to return to my home to be that reason."

"The thatcher will not be starting your home until the morrow, for his work is taking longer than expected. 'Twould be unwise to stay there tonight. Your attacker will see right through the plan."

Deep in thought, she nodded. "On the morrow, and I will spend that time repairing my garden. I need to start that, and 'twould lead my attacker to think I am returning because I need to prepare my land for winter."

"What about your son? Don't tell me he'll join you."

"Ellie will mind him. She can give him barley and water with a spoon."

They stood silently for a moment. Rowena leaned slightly forward. "Please, milord, consider my request. I have done all your bidding here and will leave Andrew in the care of the maids. Surely you have a guard roaming the village. We *must* resolve this. You cannot continue to work the villagers to the bone. That solves nothing."

Rowena was right. So why was he so reluctant? 'Twas not his nature to refuse an opportunity like this. He used soldiers all the time.

"Fine," he muttered. "On the morrow."

Suppertime came and Stephen felt as if Rowena's decision had remained like a bad fever all afternoon. He sank heavily into his chair on the dais. Everyone, including Rowena, had stood as he'd entered. When his eyes snagged hers, he looked away.

He motioned to the cupbearer to offer cider and to the young servant to bring the first flat trenchers of bread, loaded with thick meat stew and sided with slices of firm cheese. Although Rowena had been at the manor a few short weeks, he could already see the difference. Her face no longer looked gaunt, and color had returned to her cheeks. She was finally getting the food she needed.

But she won't get it on the morrow, or the days after. Why had he agreed to allow her to return home? He opened his mouth to speak his change of mind but hesitated. Rowena would refuse, and should they discuss it here in this hall, the wrong ears may hear their plans. He could force her to obey him, but 'twas not completely what he wanted.

What did he want?

Stephen chewed his food as he mulled over possible answers. He wanted to serve his king. 'Twas why the Good Lord gave him life. If it meant Rowena would be in danger, he could minimize that risk easily enough. He would order a guard to watch her during the night and arrest anyone who approached.

When he caught Rowena's cautious look, he felt his

gut tighten. She'd decided in some odd, small way to trust him this once. But fear also lingered in her eyes.

Nay, he amended. The guard *and he* would do their duty the next night.

"My lord?"

Stephen looked toward the doorway. His courier stood with his sword dangling at his side and a rolled missive in his hand. Setting down his cider, Stephen waved him over. When the man reached him, he handed over the parchment.

Unrolling it, Stephen ordered a meal for the courier, for too much travel was hard on a body and soul. The missive was from Adrien.

Stephen frowned. He had not dispatched his courier to collect Adrien's letter, so how had the man known? "Did you come from London or Dunmow?"

"London, milord."

"What is it, Stephen?" Josane asked.

Not wanting to explain too much, Stephen shoved aside the questions and unrolled the parchment. "Just a letter from another baron. 'Tis of no concern." He quickly read the missive.

My friend in Christ,
I greet you in our Savior's name and hope all is well with you. I will answer your questions, but I fear you will not like them. I know of no reason why anyone would want Rowena dead. There are few here who knew her, and those who did were sympathetic. In Colchester, they worried only that the king would punish them for hiding her from Taurin, but since that issue has been resolved, there is no reason for them to be concerned anymore.

Taurin had plotted against the king for control

of Normandy. He had hoped to pass off the Saxon girl's child as his legitimate heir, the son of his wealthy wife, whom he'd planned to murder and thus receive land from his in-laws for giving them a grandson. Now that his plot has been found out, he has had to forfeit his lands both here and in Normandy and remains there in disgrace.

I cannot offer you anything more of use, except that mayhap you should search for a different reason why she has been targeted, for I also wish that she not die. She has suffered enough. Mayhap the child is the target?

'Tis a shame that such strife comes your way, for we both know the real intrigue lies in London.

I wish you well, dear friend, and I have met with a minstrel troupe and dispatched it to you forthwith.
Adrien de Ries

Stephen rolled the parchment again. Aye, intrigue did lie in London. Apart from saying that entertainers were on their way, all Adrien had done was confirm part of Rowena's curious tale. Even his suggestion that 'twas the child who might be the target seemed absurd. Who would profit from the boy's death? Stephen's grip on the missive tightened until he could hear the stiff skin crinkle.

The morrow's night would be the turning point, for surely they would learn the truth then.

Rowena spent the entire next day sifting through her mangled vegetables and finishing the collection of what roots survived the trampling the villagers had given it. As she suspected, precious few remained. She kept on looking, hoping that she'd find something. She felt almost foolish doing this almost-wasted work while Lord Stephen's guard watched from his hidden position.

Then, from the corner of her eye, she spied movement in the long burdocks. Much of that weed had been trampled underfoot like the roots, but some still stood tall. Now they rustled.

A soft cluck and her hen parted the weeds. She peered at Rowena with dark, beady eyes as she pecked the ground. Rowena froze. She'd thought her chicken had not survived the first night's attack, let alone the next one when her hut burned. The hen strutted cautiously around the damaged cage, before jumping up to turn into the nesting area.

Heart pounding, Rowena wanted to kick herself for not checking the battered henhouse. Why, there could be several eggs there!

But she wouldn't peek now and risk disturbing the hen as she mayhap laid an egg.

"What am I going to do?" she whispered to the bird. "You need a decent cage, for I won't risk you running off again." But the door had been ripped from its rope hinges, and someone had taken a knife to one side of the netting. She would need to weave more.

Standing, she searched her yard for suitable material, catching sight of the soldier Lord Stephen had ordered to guard her. Quickly, she averted her eyes so as not to give him away should someone be looking. At the far side, away from where they could bother people, stood the end of the season's nettles. Clara had used them to flavor tea and cheese. She'd also given the leaves to Rowena just before she gave birth to Andrew, for 'twas said to ease the pains and help with feeding.

But Rowena knew of another purpose. With her hands

wrapped around her cyrtel for protection, she pulled on the stalks. She'd watched her mother ret them. This stripping and soaking could be done with a teasel in the old feed trough rammed against the back of her hut. It could take a few days, but Rowena would have strong fibers to weave into rope.

Thankfully, the damp days had half rotted the stalks and they had already split to reveal the short, useless tow fibers inside. Working quickly, Rowena smeared them up the sides of the trough and out of the way. She wanted only the outer fibers.

A fat raindrop hit her arm and she looked up at the darkening sky. Hearing some noises, she peeked around the corner of her hut. The villagers were only now returning from the forest. The men looked exhausted, shuffling heavily toward their individual homes, with only a few, such as Barrett, bothering to glance her way. She thought again of how Stephen had wanted her to be like a morsel in a trap, or a portion of grain at the far end of the pen to lure a stubborn pig inside.

Her heart stalled. Nay, no fear! She needed to end this business.

Another raindrop fell and she sank against the short wall of her hut. Staying inside would be foolhardy and easily seen as the ploy it was. Nay, she would return to the manor.

And to Lord Stephen. She hesitated for a moment. Nay, she would not be so addled to think he would prefer she return tonight. He was a man, and men didn't care what women thought. They were tools, like those the village men carried home. She would not allow herself to think it different.

She slipped free of the eaves and walked over to the

mangled henhouse. The hen was gone, and her breath hitched at the sight of several eggs! She quickly scooped them up so she could hide them away in a far corner of her hut, safe from predators.

Sharp voices reached her. Rowena ducked behind a large bush that sat against her fence, an instinctive action from the years she'd lived on the farm. 'Twas always wise to see who it was before revealing herself.

"He will protect you," a man said.

"Trust a Norman? Are you addled? He sends reports to London."

"Barrett says 'twill be better than what we have."

The second man made a scoffing noise as they passed close to where she hid. "Barrett will say anything for the right coin."

"True, but he wants the same thing we do. He says there's a good reason."

Their tired voices quieted as they walked away. "What is it?"

"I don't know, but I do know he will protect us. And his price is not high."

His voice growing more muffled, the second man asked, "Barrett?"

"Nay…" The voice faded and Rowena couldn't catch the rest of his words.

She looked up, but all she saw were the stooped backs of two men. Who would protect them? What would be better than what they had now?

Rowena shivered. The man they talked of could be bought and his price was not high? Who was that? Barrett? Aye, he was not to be trusted, but did they mean him? She didn't know, for it didn't sound as if they were discussing him.

Several raindrops hit her in succession. A good downpour was coming. If she didn't hurry, she'd be caught in it, and spending the eve in wet clothes wasn't good for the health.

"Milord, Rowena has returned here for the night."

In the armory, Stephen looked up from his work of oiling his mail in preparation for tonight. He usually left the care of his armor to Gaetan, but Josane had asked that the boy run some errands for her, as the courier had been dispatched.

Frowning, he allowed his mind to wander from the guard's quick report. Yesterday, the courier had brought a missive from London, where Lord Adrien was, and he was out again today? He would speak to him, Stephen decided. Traveling too much wasn't good for the stomach. And certainly he should be about Stephen's business, not the business of the person who sent him. He would find that out, also.

He refocused on the soldier. "Rowena did not stay in her hut?"

"Nay, milord. It has begun to rain, and her hut has no roof. Will we still need to guard it?"

The man had no desire to stand out in the wet weather. Stephen paused, silently thanking the Lord for Rowena's good sense as he shoved away unintentional irritability. He turned to the small slit window behind him. "'Tis raining out?"

"Aye, milord. Your squire ran an errand for Lady Josane. He could see rain approaching."

Stephen's mouth twisted. The thatcher preferred drier days and could still work in a light rain, just not a heavy soaking. He looked back at the man. "Where did my squire go?"

"Lady Josane sent him to the next village for some herbs. He told me that some who live to the west have joined the rebels in Ely."

Gaetan should have told him first, Stephen thought. He would correct that later. "Fools! They're addled if they think they can best the king." He stopped. "Herbs? For whom?"

"Master Gilles has need of them."

"What's wrong with him?"

The soldier shook his head. "I don't know, milord."

Stephen narrowed his eyes. "Where is my courier? 'Tis his duty to fetch things."

"He left early this morn, milord. On horseback."

"Headed where?"

"On the road to London, milord. 'Tis all I know. I was beginning my shift when he galloped out."

Obviously, he would not be returning this eve. Only a fool would travel alone at night, for there were still many Saxons who would ambush a Norman soldier alone.

But who had sent the man to London? Stephen felt the hairs on his neck rise. The courier belonged to him. No one should be employing the man except the baron himself. And had the man not brought a missive from London recently? How did he know there was one?

Regardless of those unanswered questions, 'twas more important that Rowena had shown some good sense and returned. But it also meant that whoever had attacked her would see she had not yet decided to return to her home overnight.

Stephen dismissed the guard and rose gingerly from the armory's only bench. He was stiff from the day on horseback, traveling to the various packets of workers he'd employed to erect the palisade per the king's order. Between those times, he'd walked around with Gilles, checking on such tasks as the thatcher's. He and his brother-in-law had also ridden to visit the fields from where the thatch was being cut.

Stephen grimaced. He shouldn't be stiff. And thinking that brought back his sister's harsh words on his going soft.

He wasn't going soft, and to prove it, he would go back out on horseback every day for a month, dragging Gilles with him as they visited each of his holdings here in Cambridgeshire, if necessary.

Stephen stopped. Gilles didn't appear sick today.

He called a young servant over and barked out, "Have you seen Master Gilles?"

"He was in the hall a moment ago, milord."

Ignoring the stiffness, Stephen strode through to the hall. The room was not as large as in some castles, and 'twas not as tall, either, thus was easier to heat. Indeed, 'twas quite warm in the room, with several long torches lit on their mounts and a cheerful fire ablaze in the hearth. Only a light meal had been served tonight, and after that, Josane ordered a few more chores be done before anyone could retire. This was a working manor, he'd heard her say more than once. Any frivolity in the great hall would have to occur on special occasions. His guards had made themselves scarce, he noticed.

Stephen looked again at the lights. Below where the torches sat, someone had brushed aside the rushes usually strewn about the floor and placed a pan under each one, lest a tallow-soaked light drop a burning ember before the chandler could trim it. Not one to see the need for extra light, Stephen looked across the room to the north wall. Rowena was bending over the lower hem of one of the fine tapestries that hung there to block any drafts.

He noticed the burned hem of her cyrtel. She could easily have died yesterday. He glanced over at the hearth, where a strong blaze crackled. He would see to it that only the scullery maid emptied the hearth. She had more experience.

For a moment, he watched Rowena in the bright torch-light. She must have asked for it to finish her mending. 'Twas a simple task, Josane had told him months ago, but to find someone who could weave a finish onto the frayed end, someone with young eyes and a steady hand, was difficult. There was always more work than servants, she'd often complained.

Rowena straightened, then backed up to survey her work. Only then did Stephen notice Andrew at her feet, the edge of the fine tapestry just beyond his reach. He was playing again with polished bones in a toddler's game of making noise. Beside him, the tapestry's edge was almost completely mended.

He walked over to her. "You do good work."

Rowena jumped. Immediately, he stretched out his arm to steady her. "I'm sorry. I thought you heard me."

"My mind was on my task."

"Josane must be grateful for finding you."

"I'm grateful for staying here."

He frowned. "You changed your mind about returning to your hut."

"'Twas starting to rain and my garden work was done."

Crestfallen now for some reason, she lowered her eyes. Had he said something wrong? "You didn't fare as well as you had hoped?"

She shook her head. "Nay."

He grimaced and for a moment as quick as lightning,

he wished the weather had not turned and that Rowena might have stayed there for the night.

He would have been there, also, and caught the filthy cur who wanted her dead. Killed two birds with one stone. An easy task—wasn't it?

Mayhap not so. *You could not save Corvin, a seasoned warrior with his own weapon. How do you expect to save a simple maid?*

He swallowed. He'd asked Rowena for faith in him. Where was his own faith?

As if sensing his mood changing, Rowena dared a glance into his face, searching it. Her hand reached forward, finding his arm and squeezing it. "Milord, nay. Don't think like that."

He crushed his foolishness for not remembering Rowena's intuition. Now her warm hand pressed against his forearm, her pale eyes pleaded, her lips parted as if hoping he might drop a kiss onto them...

He stepped back, Corvin's final expression of shock still in his mind's eye. Shoving it away, Stephen surveyed the tapestry. It held a nice hunting scene, one worthy of a fine manor like this. He looked down at her again. "You said your sister taught you to weave. Is this how you learned to do such a fine finish?" he asked. "'Tis not a farmer's trade."

"I studied how the finish was on the other tapestry. Did you know the weavers in Colchester create different checkering weaves? 'Tis amazing because 'tis not like tapestry, but on the same cloth." She gazed up at him. And immediately his mouth went dry.

"I'm glad you came back tonight," he whispered.

In the warm torchlight, her cheeks stained pink. "'Twould have been a waste of time tonight. But I cannot move on with my life whilst someone wants me dead." With that last word, she quickly dipped her head and returned to her work.

His gut tightened. Aye, someone wanted her dead. He should hurry this investigation along. But at the risk of losing Rowena, should her attacker be successful?

He turned away. 'Twould not happen!

At that moment, Gilles entered the hall, heading straight to the hearth as if not seeing them. Stephen strode over, noticing that his brother-in-law had been outside and 'twas apparently still raining lightly. "Josane needed herbs for you. Are you ill?"

"Nay," Gilles said, glancing up from the fire for just a moment as he warmed his hands. "'Twas a delicate matter, and 'tis healed."

"So, my squire has returned?"

"Some time ago." Gilles peered at Stephen, with only the shortest glance across the room at Rowena. Stephen turned to follow his brother-in-law's gaze, but Rowena remained deep in her work and oblivious to the two men. The light bounced off what hair escaped her maid's dust cap. She had discarded the veil for her meticulous task, and now the pale strands framed her like sunshine. Below her, Andrew gazed with curiosity at the two men, his youthful eyes not missing a thing.

Stephen turned back to Gilles, noticing then that his brother-in-law's hair also caught the lamps' flickering glow. Though not as light, the color was still blond.

"Tell Josane that Gaetan is not her personal servant. Who sent the courier to London?"

Before Gilles could answer, Andrew began banging the polished bones together. Stephen turned to watch Rowena hastily end her work and scoop the babe into his sling. With a shy glance at him, she slipped from the hall. 'Twas obvious that she didn't want to disturb them.

The hairs rose again on Stephen's neck curiously. Gilles snapped, "I will tell Josane what you said, but if you cannot manage your own servants, Stephen, mayhap you need Josane to take on more of the duties."

The man stalked away. Stephen crushed the urge to haul him back and remind him that he ran this manor house quite effectively with Josane as chatelaine.

Nay. 'Twas a tense time for them all. Reports of a growing population of rebels seemed a daily occurrence, and with someone in the village set on murder, everyone was on edge. Though his conversation with Gilles remained unfinished, 'twould have to do for now. Stephen would not act with a foolish outburst of pride. He strode out, spying Rowena at the turn of the corridor. "Rowena!"

She stopped. When he reached her, he guided her away from any unseen ears. With a glance up the stairs in case someone hovered there, he said, "You will stay in this manor until I have found your attacker."

"Nay!" she flared up at him. "The roof will be repaired soon and I need to go home. I have a henhouse to mend, for my hen is alive and has returned."

She was concerned for her hen? "It will be fine. All the rest of the village's poultry are loose."

"'Tis a gift I refuse to squander." Her jaw jutted out. "Besides, milord, did you not want me to help you find this attacker?"

He worked his jaw, hating that his own words were being used against him. "Stay here. I will employ you as a maid."

"As a maid! You have three already. One who works in the scullery at night, plus Ellie, who does the work during the day, and one who assists her. Lady Josane has her own maid, too, so you don't need another!"

"The tapestries need to be repaired."

"They are almost done, and I have already shown Ellie how to finish the edges. I am repaying your generosity. I've already made several long lengths of rope for you." She looked up at him, her expression almost defiant. "Milord, this has to end."

"Rowena, you have more skills than rope making and tapestry mending. You can tell when a person is lying."

"Not all people all the time. Some keep their true feelings well hidden."

"Like who?"

She paused, then answered, "You, milord."

She couldn't read him? She'd guessed he was using her as bait, but not the true reason for it. Nay, she'd guessed only because Josane had hinted at it.

Conviction gripped him, but he refused to acknowledge it. It helped her as much as it helped the king.

"Stay with me. Together, we can help these villagers. We will find your attacker when we question them. Then I can take you to London. You would be a fine asset to the king."

"Nay! I've had my fill of intrigue! Why would I seek out more?"

Stephen's expression softened, though only a jot. "I am offering you a chance to move up from a peasant's life. To know you will eat this winter!"

"Oh, so you ply me with food, as Lord Taurin did to ensure my obedience!"

He pointed to a nearby window. "There is a Saxon out there who wants you dead, woman. Don't be a fool!"

She stared hard at him. "There are many Saxons who know they cannot best the king but would hinder his reign at every turn. Who is to say that this is not the case here? Mayhap someone wants me so scared that I am forced to leave the village."

"Your departure will have no effect on the crown, Rowena. What could possibly happen should you leave?"

Sighing, she shrugged. "What about you? Mayhap someone wants to hinder *your rule* here?"

He had no answer, for he had not considered that line of reasoning. Surely, if 'twere so, that person would have acted before now.

Rowena continued, "Regardless, milord, I refuse to bow to bullying. I have seen enough of it in my life, and my son will not be shamed by a weak mother!" She hefted up the child and her mending kit and tried her best to stand taller. Yet her eyes shone with unshed tears, and the small crease between her brows hinted at fear.

He folded his arms. "You returned here tonight."

"Only because 'twas starting to rain, and 'twould be clear to my attacker that I was only sitting as bait."

Amazed, he just stared at her. A simple girl with the courage of the king and the mind of a tactician. From whom had she learned this ability? He said, "Do the right thing, Rowena. Stay a bit longer."

"Are you saying you will protect me for the rest of my time here? What happened to using me as bait?"

Heat infused his neck. "I'm a soldier used to putting other soldiers in positions that give me a strategic advantage. I realize now that you are not a soldier, despite your courage. I shouldn't have sent you out there alone."

A small smile crept onto her face. "I wasn't alone. You posted a guard on me and you—"

His brows shot up. "You saw him?"

"Don't punish him. He did a good job hiding."

"Not good enough, apparently."

"'Twas very good! But I knew you must have someone nearby, for what would be the point to have me as bait if there wasn't anyone to shut the trapdoor as soon as the animal entered the cage?"

Stephen grimaced. When he began again to speak, she held up her free hand. "Nay, I will return to my hut on the morrow. Surely 'twould not take too long to thatch my small roof." Then, chin lifted, she added, "I will end this fear, milord! Once and for all!"

Aye, they must end it. He'd planned to be there tonight, and he would plan for the same when the sun set on the morrow.

Still, regardless of his decision, indignation pricked him. He would not be bested by a young maid who could think like a skilled warrior.

But he did know one thing. Forcing Rowena to stay here would turn her against him, and oddly, that thought hurt more.

Chapter Thirteen

Her roof was done! Having just arrived despite the late hour, Rowena looked up with immense satisfaction. A thankful smile curled her mouth upward as she murmured a prayer of gratitude to God. She was home again. And as she looked around, she saw the new pallet Ellie had brought, one filled with fresh straw. 'Twasn't as plump as the ones in the maids' chamber, for straw was scarce this time of year. But still, 'twas a gift from Lady Josane, and 'twas thankfully received.

Her smile sagged. Despite her delay at returning home, she knew why she was here. She'd asked Ellie to mind Andrew for one more night. As she sat on her single bench, she strained to hear the world outside. Only the lone call of some distant bird reached her.

She lit both the lamp and a small fire from a spark box she'd found on the mantel.

The bird called again, and the urge to return to the manor house reared up with the unfamiliar sound. She took her lamp and walked outside. The bird repeated its call. 'Twas closer, she was sure, and not a breed she recognized. Rowena rounded the back of her hut, where her retted stalks lay in the trough under the eaves. The past day had been warm and dry, and she noticed the level of water had dropped considerably.

Setting her lamp on the trough's corner, she peered into it. Along the side where she'd smeared the tow fibers up and out of the way was now a layer of something grayish and cloth-like. She carefully peeled it from the wood. 'Twas barely wet, thanks to the dry day.

It looked like bumpy parchment, a sheet of something upon which one would write a missive. Intrigued, and glad for the diversion, Rowena returned to her hut. She smoothed it out on the table and, finding a stick of charcoal from the cool edge of her little fire, drew a line along the driest corner.

Oh, if she only knew her letters, this strange parchment would be perfect. Allowing her mind to wander, she began a simple sketch. Around and up again she drew, wondering if making this parchment could become a source of income. Mayhap she could sell the sheets, with quill-like bits of charcoal, or exchange them for reading and writing lessons for her son.

Rowena stopped her sketching. She'd drawn a profile of a man. *Of Stephen.* Setting it away, she swallowed, then lifted the sheet again. She could draw? Who would have guessed?

A noise sounded outside. She froze. 'Twas not that odd bird she'd heard earlier. Taking her lamp, she eased open her door and peeked out, hoping only an animal had brushed against her hut. Somewhere out in her yard came the quiet clucking of her now-freed hen. Rowena stood still as stone, listening, but her heart thumped so loud she was sure the whole village could hear it. To her left, above the distant manor house, the full moon had risen. 'Twas large and a brilliant yellow and—

At the next noise, she spun, as if her hearing were

connected directly to her body. A man lunged at her. Rowena threw up her arms as the man shoved her hard over her threshold and into her hut. Then he fell on her, his hands wrapping around her wimple and veil and squeezing her throat.

Stephen vaulted over the short fence in one single, sweeping movement and quickly reached the door of the hut. His blade arced downward, but the man shifted suddenly and kicked it from his grasp.

He jumped onto the man, who swung his fist into Stephen's midriff as he turned. Stephen staggered but caught his balance quickly. He plowed into the attacker, knocking him to the ground. In the next movement, he caught the cur's arm and pinned it to his back. While the man cried out, Stephen hauled him up to face Rowena's door.

The guard rushed from around the hut, drawing his sword as he raced closer. But the man was just as quick, bracing himself against Stephen and pumping his legs in and out to connect with the guard's chest. All three men fell, with Stephen losing his grip on the man's arm as he broke their falls.

Catching his balance first, the man sprinted away, loping over the short fence and disappearing into the night.

"After him!" Stephen ordered as he and the guard leaped to their feet. Then he noticed the lamp, knocked from Rowena's hand and still burning near the doorway. Immediately he strode over and ground both the flame and the pottery into the dirt with far more force than necessary.

A groan, soft and weak and gasping, brushed past his ear and he spun. Rowena lay beyond the threshold, propped up on one elbow, touching her head with the other hand. Her wimple and veil were strewn on the dirt floor, obviously torn from her when the man turned to fight off Stephen.

Stephen glanced toward the west, where both men had vanished. His guard was fast, but Stephen knew it would take two of them to catch the culprit.

Collapsing, Rowena moaned again and Stephen immediately abandoned the other option. He dropped to his knees before her. "Stay still. You've had the wind knocked out of you."

Indeed she had. She struggled to inhale. He lifted her up and set her on her pallet. Then, feeling its thinness, he grimaced. "I will carry you back to the manor."

She held up her hand and he waited a moment before she rasped out, "Nay, milord. I'm better now. 'Twas no worse than when a cow once kicked me."

She could talk. 'Twas a good sign. After retrieving his sword, Stephen rose and rekindled the fire, hoping that 'twould light the hut sufficiently, for he'd ground her lamp to pieces in his zeal to prevent another fire.

Leaning small sticks over the flame, he realized his hands were shaking. He set them down on the cold flat stones of the hearth to still them as he turned to face her. "I knew you'd protest my carrying you to the manor anyway."

Her gaze was wide with emotion. "You and your guard were close, weren't you?"

Stephen could not tear his eyes from her. His palms chilling as they lay sealed to the stone, his knees aching from his prayerful position, he could do nothing but stare into her pale eyes.

What had he been thinking, using her as bait? 'Twas

risky enough for a soldier, let alone a woman. His chest felt tight, and a cold wash shivered through him.

"Do you think I would simply leave you alone out here?" he finally whispered, not fully trusting his voice. "You said yourself that only a fool would bait a trap and abandon it."

"But—" She stopped as understanding blossomed on her face. "Those bird calls! From no night bird I had ever heard before. You two? What were you saying?"

"We signaled each other when we were in position." He hastily finished his task, then rose and sat on the bench beside her. The fire grew and warmed her hut. He wanted to promise her that his guard would catch her attacker, but he wasn't sure 'twould happen.

She looked past him into the dark night. "Your guard is wasting his time. 'Twas a Saxon and they are good at disappearing into the woods."

"How did you know he was Saxon? Did you see his face?"

"I saw everything. *He is Saxon*."

"Did you recognize him?"

Rowena shut her eyes, and Stephen knew she was recalling the face. When she opened them again, she shook her head. "Nay."

"He wasn't one of the villagers?" She hadn't been here that long. 'Twas quite possible she had not seen them all yet.

A thought struck him. What if the attacker was a Norman, someone from a nearby holding? Dressed as a Saxon, he could easily skulk around the village unnoticed. This man who'd attacked her was strong, used to fighting, for he employed the tactics of close combat. Stephen kept his own soldiers in as good a condition as possible, and the very way the man fought had been practiced in the yard behind the manor.

He'd been such a fool not to realize how much danger Rowena was in. If he hadn't been here, she would have died.

He needed more soldiers. This cowardly act would not have happened if he had more guards. A good show of force did wonders to deter violence. But to acquire more soldiers meant a trip to London, and that would mean leaving Rowena alone.

"I know what he looks like. His face is burned into my mind," Rowena whispered, touching her throat. "I watched him as he grabbed my neck."

Stephen took her shoulders and turned her toward the growing firelight. His gut clenched. Aye, welts were forming on her neck. "That cur! I should have gone after him myself and throttled him."

Her hand reached to cover his. He could feel it shaking. "I much prefer you here. I saw how he fought you. He could easily lie in ambush to kill you."

"Nay, I'm not that foolish to chase blindly after him, and my guard will be careful, also. But that man needs to pay for his crimes."

"He will." She leaned forward, thankfulness evident on her face as she searched his expression. She gripped his arms. "I'm glad you're here."

She slid her cool hands up to his neck. He felt them shake as they caressed his jaw. He'd chosen a plain, dark tunic to blend into the night. He'd left his cloak back at the manor for ease of travel but now wished he'd brought it to wrap around her.

With the veil and wimple torn from her head, the firelight danced off her hair, giving it unexpected warmth.

He watched her, awed by her maturity. Most villagers

saw her full of folly. He saw something in her he never expected: inner strength.

She was determined to live. *Nay, not just live, but thrive.* It burned in her expression.

Incredibly, she still smelled of those roses beside the chapel. Their scent filled his head, dried his mouth and caused his heart to pound.

She caught and held his gaze. Her voice was as soft as summer rain. "Please don't leave me. I don't want to be alone right now."

She whispered her soft supplication, slurring the words as he strained to hear them. How could he leave her? He didn't want to be alone, either. All his life, he'd been by himself. Even in platoons of soldiers, or halls filled with women vying for his attention, he'd felt keenly alone.

Not tonight, not in this rude hut after that ugly attack. He was sharing a moment like no other with a woman like no other.

Her gaze dipped slightly, glancing off his lips before rising again to his eyes, capturing them and pleading something he wasn't sure he understood. Something he didn't dare to believe for fear it would vanish like morning mist.

He tilted his head to one side and eased toward her, still watching her. Her eyes drifted shut, her lips parted farther, and he was sure her breath, like his, had stalled in her lungs.

They met, lips barely brushing. Stephen wrapped his arms around her, enticing her to close the space between them. Molded around each other, they continued to kiss, deepening the moment of intimacy as they forsook the events that drew them together.

She filled his senses. He could smell those roses, feel

her warmth, see her, taste her. Her fingers plowed into his hair and gripped his curls, for he'd abandoned the Norman fashion of shaving the back of his head. Rowena was as she should be to him—strong, yet all woman, vulnerable, but only to him, trusting that he would be all she needed. Aye, he would be. She needed someone strong to be there for her.

He stalled. That wasn't him. And he couldn't do that. He hadn't even been able to stop the sword that pierced his brother's mail, and look at him tonight. He'd plunked her down as bait because he was a soldier who used people for his own benefit. And he'd failed to capture the man who'd taken that bait. He didn't have just one good reason to prove he wasn't good for Rowena. He had two.

He would not fail again.

You will if you're not careful.

Holding Rowena close, reveling in her kiss like a boy on the cusp of manhood, Stephen was putting them both at risk should that cur backtrack. One swing of a sword could silence them both forever.

He had to pull away. He could not, *nay, should not*, have this moment with Rowena. Hating this, he peeled her from him and set her back, his lips the last to release her.

"What's wrong?" she asked.

"We must focus on the situation," he told her, his voice husky.

"Aye, but there is something more. Something terribly sad."

Ah, that natural sense she had. "I don't want to be distracted. It happened once before."

"Your brother, Corvin? You were fighting for your life."

"I should have been protecting him."

She sat back. "If you continue to blame yourself, 'tis as bad as keeping bitterness in your heart." Her voice dropped. "I know."

He stood, needing to focus on the situation and not on their foolish emotions. "'Tis time to turn the tables and start fighting back."

Chapter Fourteen

"You said his face was burned into your mind. You would know him if you saw him again?" Stephen asked, looking down at her.

Rowena blinked and swallowed as she wet her lips. She struggled to fight the fog that wrapped around her mind the way his arms had wrapped around her body. What did he say? Would she know her attacker if she saw him again? "Aye. I saw him clearly."

She shook off the mists of their intimacy and suddenly straightened. "I can do more than recognize him. I can draw him!"

She faced the table, then gasped. Her drawing of Stephen! It lay between them. Quickly, she flipped the sheet.

"What's that?" Stephen turned over the parchment.

Heat flooded into her cheeks as he tilted the paper to catch the dim light. His eyebrows flew up. "'Tis of me!"

"Nay," she whispered.

He shook his head. "I have not seen my reflection in some time, but I know 'tis me."

"Aye," she recanted.

"Remarkable. 'Tis excellent! I didn't know you could draw."

"I didn't, either, until I picked up the charcoal stick and began."

He flipped the sheet, examining it with his fingertips. "What is this? I've not seen anything like it before."

"'Tis from the tow fibers I smeared on the side of the water trough. They're short and don't make good threads. My mother would soak them in water and feed them to the animals."

He looked at her, compassion warming his expression. "Was she also cruel to you?" he asked.

Rowena's mouth tightened. "She didn't do anything to help me, if that's what you are asking. My sisters would sometimes give me food, but our father would tell them he'd send them out to the barn, too, if he caught them. That would mean no food for them, either." She went silent for a moment. "I suppose he said the same thing to my mother. He was always talking about losing his land to the king, and how he would never have enough coinage to purchase it back because of all the girls my mother gave him." She looked down at her hands. "She felt guilty for it."

She heard Stephen's heavy sigh. "Why were you soaking those plants? You have no animals to feed."

"I was retting stalks to weave a net for my hen's coop."

"I remember. 'Tis like making rope."

"Aye. This parchment is what's left of the inside fibers. 'Tis not fine like vellum, though. You can see bits of the fiber in it."

Stephen studied the parchment, then the sketch it held. "This is truly amazing. 'Tis like looking at myself in Josane's mirror, only better." He smiled at her. "I look ugly in her mirror. What made you think of drawing me?"

Because all she'd done since they met was think of him. Nay, she would not say that, for they matched like oil and water. And he'd broken their kiss as if he'd realized its folly. *'Twas* a folly for her, too. He'd wanted to use her. Taurin and her father had used her, too, even though this time, 'twas for her benefit. Nay, Stephen's main concern was not for her safety. He couldn't be trusted.

Her heart lurched. *What would it feel like to completely trust the man you cared for? And to know he wouldn't put some fool thing like money or power ahead of your life? Or duty.*

She would never know because she would never trust a man. They always hurt her.

Tears stung her eyes as she took back the parchment and flipped it over. Her hands shook as she reached for the charcoal stick she'd left on the table. "I discovered making this parchment by accident. And then I considered making it and offering it to anyone who would be willing to teach Andrew how to read and write when he's ready to learn."

"We will find someone for him, I promise."

She shut her eyes, partly to hide her pleasure and partly to recall her attacker's face. "Give me a moment."

Holding her breath, she pulled free the memory of her attacker. Her heart pounded, and fear clutched her throat as his hands had done. *Nay, I can do this.* She would sketch his face, and they would find him, and stop this madness and fear once and for all.

For if the guard had caught this man, he would have returned by now.

Keep the guard safe, Lord.

Stephen lingered close. She shifted away. "Please, milord, give me some room."

He eased back. "Rowena," he said quietly, his voice dissolving her concentration as warm water dissolved honey. "'Tis time you called me Stephen."

Her eyes flew open and she gaped at him. She could barely breathe. And surely Lor—*Stephen* could hear the thumping of her heart, for it pulsed loud in her own ears.

Don't answer him. Don't let him see how his words weaken you. She looked away and began to sketch with a shaking hand.

Her mind raced. Nay, she could not allow herself to be wooed by Stephen's gentle words. He was a man, and they took more than they gave.

But did he not say he would find someone to teach Andrew his letters? Did she not believe him?

He'd also asked her to find someone to care for Andrew, should she die.

She would have died tonight if not for Stephen.

'Twas not the time for pondering what could have happened. Maybe after the cur was found. Her sketching grew feverish and she focused hard on her vision of the man. His round face and squat nose, his longish hair and tufts of beard that seemed at odds with the bushy brows all grew on the parchment. One of his bulging eyes tilted up and his jaw was too big for his face. She shaded where the bones of his jaw protruded, the play of light and shadows coming to her as naturally as breathing. Finally, she set down the parchment.

Aye, 'twas the man! She'd sketched out broad farmer's shoulders and a cowl that tipped to one side as if sewn by someone half-blind.

Rowena shoved the sketch across the table. "Here," she said quickly, "'Tis he, I'm sure."

Stephen frowned at her expression before lifting the parchment. She held her breath as he stared at it. He still sat close to her, still made her feel foolishly addled and all too warm inside.

Stop it, she ordered herself. She could no more allow this attraction to blossom than she could let her life be ruled by fear.

Stephen shook his head. "I don't recognize him, and I have been working with the villagers building that palisade."

"I haven't seen him here, but—" she paused "—Stephen, he could be one of many Saxons hiding in the forest. I remember my father ordering me to lock the barn doors every night because the men in the forest often came in to steal food."

Stephen looked at her, his eyes dark, yet compassionate. Was that vulnerability she saw in his gaze? Nay, not in him! She fought the urge to slip closer to him. She would not torture herself with this…this growing interest in him. Aye, that moment in his arms felt so right, but 'twas just born of the danger they'd shared. Relief did that to people.

"There are many Saxons hiding in the woods," he was saying. "Adrien de Ries told me his courier was attacked on his way to Colchester last summer."

He stroked his chin as he fell silent. She leaned forward. "What are you thinking?"

Before he could answer, the sound of pounding feet interrupted them. They both looked up, with Stephen quickly drawing his sword and stepping in front of Rowena just as the guard stepped into the circle of light.

"Milord, I'm sorry. I lost him in the woods." The man was still panting.

"Which way did he go?"

"West, milord."

"Awaken the troops. Scour the area." He turned to Rowena. "Were you wearing your veil?"

"Aye. And a wimple, also." She hurried over and picked them up from where they fell. "I'm sorry. I know you want me to wear them at all times, but he must have torn them off."

"Not to worry. Give them to me." When she did, he handed them to the soldier, along with the sketch of the man. "Take the hound from the barn but do not let him smell her wimple until you're in the forest, lest he pick up Rowena's scent around the manor. I want that man caught tonight."

"Aye, milord." The soldier disappeared.

Stephen walked to the door. There he turned, his expression as cold as the winter wind. "Gather your things, Rowena. You will return to the manor with me."

Without thought, she wanted to protest, but his words stopped her. If truth be told, she no longer wanted to stay here. Was it cowardice or wanting to be near Stephen?

Nay, not the latter, for Stephen was bent on only one thing, finding her attacker. 'Twas a purpose that helped her, but men didn't do such things for noble reasons.

She hesitated just outside her home. Stephen wasn't doing this just to help her.

Her heart clenched. Then she took her metal diadem, all that was left of her headdress, and followed him.

His thoughts racing, Stephen threw open his front door, not even allowing the soldier on guard to assist him. He could hear Rowena hurrying to keep up with his long strides, her small feet tapping a swift tattoo since the rushes were not strewn this close to the door, for Josane refused to have them constantly swept outside and lost.

He turned when they reached the area past the armory. Ahead lay the great hall, and across it was the other corridor. "Go to the maids' room, Rowena, and stay there until I send for you. I have something to do."

If she had opened her mouth to protest, he didn't see it. Instead, he strode into the hall, only to find it empty. The guard had roused all the men, his young squire included, to begin the manhunt.

Still seething, he stalked down the far corridor to the short stairs that led to the second floor, to his sister's chamber. He cared not if she had her husband visiting that night, but 'twas unlikely, for his sister's marriage to Gilles had not been a love match. They had long sorted out their differences, aye, and kept the marriage going by turning it into a business partnership, but there was nothing else in it.

Stephen had avoided his parents' trap of an arranged marriage by joining the military full-time. And he was thankful for that. When he married, he wanted it to be a happy arrangement, and not something barely tolerable, like Josane's.

His mother would not arrange a marriage now, unless 'twere to punish him for failing to save Corvin's life. And she knew Stephen could successfully contest such a decision, citing her bitterness and his service to his king.

Jaw tight with displeasure, Stephen reached Josane's door and pounded on it. He had to hear her answer to the questions bursting inside him. "Josane, open up! 'Tis me, Stephen." He drew in his breath to steady his temper. "I will speak with you now!"

Josane opened the door, her other hand gathering the

neckline of her nightshift. "What's wrong? Has something happened to Gilles?"

Stephen barged in and looked around. Spying the only other person there, her maid, on a pallet at the other side of the brazier, he flicked his head at her. "Leave. You may return when I am done speaking with your mistress."

Josane quickly lit her lamp from a hot coal in the chamber's brazier. "What's all this about, Stephen? You can't come barging in here—"

"I can and I will, woman." Josane's position as older sister was firmly entrenched in the pair's relationship, but Stephen's baronage had long since overridden that. "You sent Gaetan to the next village for herbs, did you not?"

"Aye, yesterday. Gilles needed them and we'd run out."

"You sent a letter, also?"

She frowned. "Nay. My instructions were verbal."

"Why my squire?"

"He was the first one I found and he's smart enough to remember my instructions." Josane took her cloak and wrapped it around her.

"What happened to the courier?"

"*You* sent him to London," she snapped back.

"I haven't used him since I sent him to Dunmow, yet he went to London and retrieved a letter from Adrien." Stephen paused. If she didn't send the courier, who did?

Josane interrupted his thoughts. "Stephen, you're scaring me! What has happened?"

"Rowena returned to her home only to be attacked by a man I don't believe lives in this village. You sent my squire to a village west of here, in the same direction that the man fled."

Josane's jaw fell. "You think I paid the man to attack Rowena? Are you addled?" She sank into the chair nearest the lamp she'd lit. Then, with a gasp, she rose again. "Is Rowena hurt? She's not…"

"Nay, I thwarted his attack."

"You thwarted his attack!" She poked him with her finger. "Stephen, did you put that poor thing in harm's way? Did you set her in her home just to lure out her attacker?"

"What would you care if I did?"

Josane slapped the table beside her. "Stephen, I may not want those girls to be my dear friends, but that doesn't mean I don't care for them! These maids can't be treated like handfuls of grain in a trap!"

Stephen looked away.

"Where is she?" Josane snapped.

"Downstairs."

Letting out a frustrated growl, Josane released her cloak before pulling an outer tunic over her night shift. She bustled past her brother, but he caught her elbow. "Josane, who used my courier? Why send for herbs in the next village?"

She rolled her eyes, and Stephen was ready to reprimand her for it, but she quickly added, "We were out of them. There is no intrigue here. Go to London if you want that. Oh, 'twas an unfortunate day when the king gave you this forsaken village and manor. Lady Udella should have asked the king for Gilles to be baron."

Cold sluiced through him. "Why would she ask the king that? When?"

"When he granted her a private audience during his first march north. Later, when I arrived, I went to the chapel to speak with her. She told me that she'd wanted to ask the king to make Gilles baron here. Instead, she asked for the village's safety and in return she would pray for him and it."

Stephen knew nothing about this. Was there more? "Why did she want Gilles to be given this manor?"

"She didn't say and had asked that I not tell anyone about our conversation. She had been the baroness here, daughter of an earl and liked by the king, so I respected her wishes."

"Did she say why she wanted your conversation to be a secret?"

"If she did, I don't remember. She did ask about Gilles's birth. Mayhap she had been hoping for an easy change because Gilles has the look of a Saxon as opposed to our swarthy features." She paused. "But Gilles is not a full-time soldier like you. It makes a difference to the king, I think."

Mayhap. Stephen knew Gilles had the look of his northern Frankish roots, for hadn't his mother once said her people came from where a great Rhein river meets the North Sea? But all Gilles knew was Norman. Stephen threw up his hands. "Josane, you would still have had to come here."

At the door, Josane smoothed her tunic and tipped up her chin. "But not required to stay. I would have employed a chatelaine, as you have done with me. As lady of the manor, I'd have had more freedom." Her tone softened with hurt.

Hurt?

"Did you ever tell Gilles this?"

"Nay. What could he do? He became your bailiff. Our families expect a wife to stay with her husband. If he'd been made the baron, I would have convinced him to return to Normandy. He dislikes it here as much as I do." Her expression clouded. "Now, if you will pardon me, *my lord*, I will check on Rowena. I doubt you would know how to ensure she is well."

She left Stephen standing in her bedchamber. Did she really resent being here? When he heard his sister's maid return, he stepped back into the narrow upstairs corridor.

Udella had wanted to ask for Gilles instead? When King William marched through here two years ago, both Stephen and Gilles were with him. Stephen knew Lady Udella had met her new sovereign, but he'd not been privy to their conversation. He knew nothing of Josane's first conversation with Udella, either.

Did Gilles know any of this? Stephen remembered the day his own service, and Corvin's, also, had been rewarded with this village. Stephen had made Gilles the bailiff and Gilles had accepted the position with gratitude. He hadn't seemed disappointed, and even now he didn't appear to know anything of Udella's request. In fact, Gilles seemed to like his position. And why not? It came with much power. Among other duties, Gilles decided sentencing in civil cases. That brought with it a lot of influence.

Stephen made his way downstairs. He could hear Josane's murmurings to Rowena, but the words were muffled by the closed door. He strode down to the hall, and as before, 'twas still empty, with pallets and blankets strewn on the tables. These trestle tables functioned also as beds and had been circled around the hearth, as if waiting for the men to return.

Lord, bring me Rowena's attacker.

No answer. No wash of satisfaction as he'd felt when serving his king. He'd always believed he'd been doing the Lord's work, but today, it did not feel so comfortable. Instead, disappointment blossomed on his tongue. He folded his arms and glared into the dying fire.

"Stephen?"

The word was so soft, 'twas as if it were carried on a draft that wafted in when a door was opened. Stephen looked up.

Rowena stood in the doorway, another borrowed veil pushed back slightly to reveal the wisps of white-blond hair that framed her delicate face.

His heart leaped as he recalled their kiss. "Come in," he said briskly. "Did my sister find you?"

"Aye. But I am unhurt and milady has returned to her bed. 'Twas no reason for her to hover over me."

"I doubt she would have done that. But 'tis good that she cares." He paused as she walked up to stand next to him in front of the fire. "I asked you to remain in the maids' chamber," he reminded her.

"Forgive me. I just wanted to—"

"To what?"

She swallowed and he knew instantly she was battling some inner decision. She blinked, wet her lips and then steeled her spine. Whatever trouble haunted her, she had conquered it.

"I want you to be Andrew's guardian should anything happen to me."

He felt his eyebrow shoot up. "Me?"

"Aye. 'Twould be easier for you than Clara to arrange for Andrew to learn his letters and numbers." She paused. "I nearly died tonight and would have left Andrew an orphan, for his real father is long gone and I know he cares little for the boy now."

"I am a soldier, Rowena, not a nanny."

"But you can arrange for his care. Ellie would gladly do it, and I will start immediately making many sheets of parchment and enough lengths of rope to last this manor for many years. I will pay in advance for Andrew's care."

"So this isn't about trusting me to be a good guardian for the boy. 'Tis about me being able to provide for him effectively."

Rowena glanced at her feet. He watched her swallow and purse her lips.

"Is there no trust in your heart at all, Rowena?"

"Do not ask me that, Stephen. What have men done for me?"

"Naught but sinned against you." He felt a similar edginess to her own. "Someday, you will have to forgive them. You'll never see them again, but this bitterness will eat you from the inside out."

She peeked into his eyes and he saw a hollow fear in her expression. Her spine might be straight as a fresh arrow, and her jaw like steel, but she couldn't mask the fear that lingered within.

Still, he recognized a certain practicality here. Nay, 'twasn't complete trust, but 'twas the closest thing to it.

Slowly she whispered, "And you, Stephen, when will you do some forgiving of your own? Don't you deserve peace, too?"

"Nay. I allowed a beloved son and brother to die. 'Twas an unforgivable sin, not in God's eyes, but in my own. And that is the reason I must decline your request."

Then he strode from the hall.

Chapter Fifteen

Rowena squinted as she stepped out the kitchen door to attend morning services the next day. She had Andrew with her, knowing she would probably sit in the back, near the door. Should he begin to fuss, she could slip outside.

But being close to the door also meant that Stephen would see her more easily than if she sat hidden in the darker recesses.

'Twas with sadness that she'd watched him stalk from the great hall last night. How could he say that his sin of accidentally letting his brother die was unforgivable? Hadn't Clara said no sin was unforgivable? Her heart ached for him. It shouldn't, but it did.

The men of the manor had returned empty-handed late last night, and now some of them, bleary-eyed and tired, were here and no doubt thankful for the dark of the chapel.

Stephen entered with his sister and her husband. With the rest, Rowena stood as he entered, and was glad that a tall man had come in a few moments after her to block Stephen's view of her. She peeked around the man's barrel chest to see Stephen's gaze search the chapel. Quickly, she straightened again and lowered her head.

Last night, his bitterness had splintered their conversation. But what did she expect? She had asked him to care for Andrew not because she trusted him, but because she had hoped to purchase his guardianship. She didn't trust Stephen any more than his family forgave him. In fact, she was much like them. She refused to forgive *all* men, Stephen included.

Lord in Heaven, how can I stop this?

She wished Clara were here, for her wisdom and strength of faith were invaluable. Rowena blinked away fresh tears. Would she always be this foolish and naive? She knew so little and could hardly understand the words of the hymns sung or the paintings in the little frames that sat around the pulpit. Long-bearded men and gentle-faced women worshiped Jesus. Clara said He'd risen from the dead to give them life. Rowena could hardly fathom the notion, but she knew He was real because He felt real in her heart. 'Twas the only way she could explain it.

Across the chapel, Udella scraped open her small door and sat by it to listen to the service. If she saw Rowena, she gave no indication.

Ahead, Stephen allowed Lady Josane to enter the front pew first. Rowena remembered how it felt to sit on the wool-filled cushions and have the enclosed pew block the cold drafts from the door. Gilles entered next, rearranging his cushion before he sat beside his wife. Stephen entered last. With the rest, Rowena dropped to one of the cold, hard benches, feeling oddly alone despite the crowd. 'Twas a sad, unexpected emotion. She'd been alone since she was ten, sleeping in the barn, hiding from the men when they'd shown up for their chores.

This very moment hurt more than all the nights she'd curled up with the dog to exploit his body heat.

When the service was over, after Stephen had followed the priest out, Rowena lingered behind two larger women who dawdled in their departures. She hadn't even looked up for fear she'd meet Stephen's gaze.

Was she afraid of him? Nay. She knew her own heart. She was ashamed that she thought she could barter for Andrew's guardianship instead of trusting him. Even his own family did not trust him anymore. She slipped from the crude pew, in the process getting shoved hard. If she hadn't caught the bench to steady herself, she'd have fallen to the floor on top of Andrew. Spinning, she faced the other person. 'Twas the old man Barrett. His filthy glare bored into her.

"Say you're sorry," he growled.

Indignation flared in her. "Nay, you shoved me! Hard, too!"

The group around them stopped. For a terrifying moment, she regretted her outburst. 'Twas foolhardy to argue with the man who had much influence in the village and with Gilles. She'd seen Barrett speak with Gilles on several occasions.

"You would dare to talk to me like that, fool woman—"

Her feet with a mind of their own, she stepped forward and straightened up as much as she could. "I would dare, because you deliberately shoved me! I have done nothing wrong, not here nor in the past."

"That brat tells us otherwise."

Automatically, she touched Andrew's cap as he still slumbered in his sling. "Nay, he tells you nothing. But *I will.*"

Suddenly, she was sick of the rumors that she knew were whispered about her. "I was sold into slavery by my own family to a baron who wanted a son so he could gain power in Normandy."

Standing in the aisle, Barrett folded his arms, his coarsely woven sleeves getting shoved away from his filthy, callused hands. "Sold by your own family? Slavery has been abolished. Who are these fool people? You tell wild tales about them."

"My father isn't a Christian, as I am, and the Norman who bought me knew he could argue that point in his favor."

That surprised the man. Indeed, those lingering in the chapel fell silent. From the corner of her eye, Rowena spied Udella leaning out her small door to eavesdrop. "Your family isn't Christian?" Barrett glared. "Where are you from? Surely not from England."

"They farm to the west, near the villages of Cambridge and Grantchester."

She was less than ten miles away from her family, she'd been told once by Clara. Both villages were primitive, backwater places whose only benefit came from the bridges built there. "Foolish lies!" Barrett spat out. "Why haven't you been recaptured?"

Rowena tightened her jaw. Barrett, and indeed this village, didn't need to know her business, but she couldn't stop the words. "The king himself freed me after the Norman baron was sent home in disgrace."

"A Norman king with no right to be here!"

She stepped closer. "I did not betray my people!"

She turned on her heel to face the crowd. "In what way could I betray anyone? I was kept in a room at a manor house until I escaped. I gave birth in Colchester, protected by a midwife there. How could I, a child of a farmer, know anything of interest to the Normans?"

Emboldened by the gaping looks on the faces of the

crowd, Rowena shouted, "Who here wants me dead? Whoever you are, do it now! But look me in the eye as you kill me."

Nothing happened. All who stared at her fell silent. "Nay, you're a coward," Rowena continued, "whoever you are, listening to foolish lies that someone has spread about me, without even asking me for the truth. Am I the only girl you've met who's suffered under a Norman? Wouldn't it be more obvious that I had no choice?"

The crowd shrank away from her appeal. Women dropped their gazes to their feet, and one man pulled his family out of the chapel. Suddenly, the villagers parted from the outside inward. Stephen stepped into the circle she'd created.

"Go home, all of you," he ordered the crowd.

The people melted away like a dollop of fat thrown into a hot fry pan. Within a few breaths, there was no one there.

When he glared at Rowena, her bravado also dissolved.

Oh, dear Lord in Heaven, what have I done? She had disgraced Stephen in his own manor, shouting like a madwoman. He would surely send her packing now. Indeed, his scowl suggested as much.

When the crowd was gone, she dared a peek into his face. His expression had not changed. "I was shoved and I was tired of these people thinking so ill of me," she said in her defense.

"So you risked your life to prove your point."

"Nay."

"Aye, you did. I heard you challenge someone to kill you."

She blinked at the memory of her foolishness. Her

heart pounded in her chest as she realized the full extent of the danger in which she'd put herself and her son. "'Twere only foolish words spoken in haste."

"Aye, they were. You think that someone wouldn't thrust a knife through you while you're standing in this chapel? Worse things have happened in God's house." Stephen sighed and closed the gap between them. She could see his gaze softening as he lifted her chin with his finger. Or was it the unshed tears in her eyes? She'd disappointed Stephen, and it cut her to the quick.

"Do not do it again, Rowena," he said quietly. "These people are not thinking wisely, and I have yet to discover which one of them wants you dead, or even why."

She shut her eyes, hating that she wanted more than just his attention. She wanted him to hold her tight. Then, wrapping her fingers around his wrist, she tugged down his arm. "I won't. I was shoved and I flared up. Even now, I don't know why I did it."

"Because you have been hurt. Turn the other cheek, Rowena." He frowned. "Did you notice anyone with enough hatred to want you dead? Did you feel anyone here hated you that much?"

"Nay. But sometimes when I am angry or scared, I cannot guess anyone's emotions."

"Then trust me. Have I not sheltered you here? I will find your attacker."

"Do you think he was here today?"

He stepped back. "I searched the crowd but saw no one who looked like your sketch."

So her bravado was for naught? She sagged. "I'm not very good help, am I?"

He smiled briefly. "Nay, you're not. And I'm not very good at finding your attacker, either." He paused. "But we will get better."

With every bone in her body, she wanted to walk into his arms. But here in the chapel? And with Stephen stepping away from her as if he regretted he'd touched her in the first place? Nay, seeking comfort in his embrace would not be wise at all.

As if to confirm that, Stephen muttered, "Rowena, your roof is finished, but I will ask you to stay here at the manor. 'Tis safer."

She peered into his dark eyes. Aye, 'twould be safer, indeed. At her hut, she'd risked her life. But here at his manor house, what would she risk? All her life she'd known that men could not be trusted. Would she risk learning 'twas not so? That even Stephen, however embittered and hurt by his family that he was, was trustworthy?

She wasn't sure she wanted to learn that.

Stephen took another step away from her, for he was certain if he stood close to her any longer, he would pull her into his arms and kiss her fear and sadness away.

With her assailant somewhere near? One of the first rules of soldiering was never to show a weakness. You would surely be dead should the enemy see your vulnerability.

From afar, the lilting strains of flutes drifted in. Thankful for the distraction, Stephen stalked outside and over to the corner of his large home. Rowena followed with Andrew. A band of minstrels was marching into the village from the road to London. Several acrobats wheeled on their hands or leaped gracefully on another's back, only to whirl away and land on their feet again. A drummer kept the beat with almost military precision. Trained dogs pirouetted around their masters.

Several children broke away from their families to run over to watch.

'Twas the minstrel troupe Stephen had asked for. Though 'twas late in the season, they'd been willing to come. As Stephen watched them greet the children, a plan blossomed in his mind.

One older man broke from the crowd and walked toward him. 'Twas obvious to Stephen that the man noted his clothing and stance and guessed he was the baron here.

Immediately, a guard stepped between the newcomer and Stephen. The man bowed. Stephen dismissed the guard, deciding he would defuse the tensions created today with a celebration of sorts. 'Twas no holy day or feast, but the troupe could entertain well enough in the great hall.

And fulfill his plan.

A short while later, after arrangements were made and payment of the troupe agreed upon, Stephen turned.

Rowena had come close and now stared wide-eyed and open-jawed at the brightly clad visitors. He walked over to her, leaving the leader to inform his troupe. "I took your suggestion on getting the villagers to trust me more. Have you ever seen a troupe of entertainers before?"

She shook her head. "I've only heard of them. These people would never come to a small farm so far from a village."

"What was your closest village's name?"

"We lived between Cambridge and Grantchester. When the family I traveled with said they were headed to Colchester, I remembered my father mentioning the town, for Baron Eudo holds it as well as several villages near Cambridge. I traveled with them because I thought it was far enough away that Taurin would not find me."

Colchester, where Eudo, Adrien's brother, held the town. Stephen grimaced, keenly wishing for more information. But the courier was gone again, he suddenly realized, and Stephen would not send a pair of guards when they were needed here.

Frustration rose in him. *Why seek more about her? You don't need it to fulfill the king's order. Your plan today does not hinge on what Rowena did before she came here. The king needs a calculating man, not one who goes soft when a woman speaks to him.*

Lord God, am I not allowed to enjoy any of this life's pleasures?

Hating the lack of a decent answer, he straightened. "You will join me tonight to watch this troupe."

Rowena's eyes widened farther as she looked from Stephen to the troupe's leader. Her throat bobbed as she met his eyes, as if searching for something. From the sadness in her expression, he knew she didn't find what she'd hoped was there. "Stephen, are you asking me to sit with you as these people entertain us?"

"Aye. Is there a problem? The most danger you will suffer is a foul look from my sister. Trust me, you will survive that. I have received them for years and remain quite healthy." His voice dropped. "Sometimes I long for a normal life. Won't you give me permission to have one for just a single eve?"

Rowena studied his expression, and he was glad she had admitted she could not read him as well as she read others.

Finally, though wary, she nodded.

For all that, no satisfaction flowed into him. *You've manipulated her. You've used all your skills against her.*

Before those words could convict him further, he nodded to her and said, "Tonight, in the hall, we will share a good meal before the troupe performs." Then he left her.

Chapter Sixteen

The evening was lively and exciting, and Rowena felt as though she couldn't open her eyes wide enough to take it all in. Before the performance, she and Stephen had shared a trencher of meat and roots, savored with onions and herbs. It had been a satisfying meal, finished off with fresh cider and cheese and fine sweetmeat pastries that glistened with honeyed nuts, made complete with cups of custard for dipping.

And she had survived Lady Josane's scathing looks. Thankfully, the woman chose to ignore her after the trenchers were filled. Master Gilles glared once at her before turning his attention to the chaplain, as he often did.

The hall filled with the villagers soon after supper. The troupe began entertaining with songs and music that danced delightfully around Rowena's senses. She tapped her foot to the drumbeat and swayed gently to the flute music. One young man plucked a stringed instrument, sometimes several of the strings at once, to produce a sound as lovely as the birds when they returned in springtime.

She glanced at Stephen and found him watching her.

A smile hovered over his features. His dark eyes were soft and as delicious looking as the dark sweetmeat that filled the pastry she'd just eaten.

He'd wanted one normal moment in his life. Oh, how she knew exactly what he longed for! For this brief evening, she could be a woman with few cares. A woman who wasn't hunted for something she hadn't done.

Aye, 'twas a good eve.

The acrobats began, and a young man snatched apples from the head table to juggle, so many of them in the air at once, Rowena couldn't keep them separated. Supple young women dressed in men's clothing danced and hopped on top of men's shoulders to jump and twirl away as everyone around them gasped.

Then an old man with a long beard stepped forward, twirled his hand and produced a puff of smoke from his palm. Rowena gasped. He stepped closer, pulling from her ear a coin, before twisting his wrist to toss it away. Suddenly it became a dove and the bird fluttered off.

Startled, Rowena jumped back. Stephen laughed. "How did he do that?" she asked.

"'Tis *leger de main.* Sleight of hand. You never know what a person has up his sleeves."

Feigning shock at the accusation, the man pulled up his long, billowing sleeves. Then, leaning forward again, he found another coin in her ear.

Rowena touched the side of her head. "I don't understand. He had nothing up his sleeves, yet you say he did!"

Stephen leaned closer, his soft whisper tickling her ear. "Ah. Nothing is as it seems."

A shiver rippled through her. What did he mean by that? Was he referring to their earlier conversation outside? That he may look like a normal man enjoying life, but was never to be one?

Such was her life, also. She must devote herself to her babe, for no man would want her as his wife. She leaned back thoughtfully. Little Andrew and several other babes were cloistered in the maids' room, cared for by Ellie, who had volunteered for the task. Rowena was grateful to her.

The old man performed another trick, all the while smiling at her. Again, Stephen whispered, "Do you notice that 'tis always the young, beautiful women who attract the most attention at this performance? Be careful, Rowena, or he will lure you out to the center and make you disappear. Can you not tell that he is tricking you?"

She glanced quickly at Stephen but found his brows lifted up in a jovial warning. For that heartbeat, she could imagine what it would be like to be a part of his life. "Nay. He must be well trained in hiding his feelings." A shiver ran through her. She could not read Stephen. Was he hiding something, too?

Several people at the entrance to the great hall began to clap, and Rowena moved her gaze toward them.

Ellie stood clapping with obvious pleasure.

Rowena went cold. Who was caring for Andrew?

Nothing is what it seems.

She turned to Stephen. "I must leave! Ellie's there at the door. She was supposed to look after Andrew!" Her voice grew. "I need to check on him!"

She scraped back her chair and fled the dais table. She heard Stephen call out, but thrust herself through the crowd toward Ellie.

"What are you doing here? Where's Andrew?" she demanded of her friend. Not waiting for an answer, she raced down the narrow corridor. The maids' chamber door was closed. With a hard shove on the door, Rowena rushed inside.

Another maid lay beside Andrew, who slept soundly on one of the pallets. Two other babes shared another pallet. The maid looked up at her.

Ellie burst inside. "Rowena!"

Rowena sagged as she turned. "I thought you'd left him alone."

"Nay, I would never do that! Matild has a headache and came to lie down. She offered to watch the babes so I could see the performers."

"I'm so sorry. I thought that…" She pressed her hand against her pounding heart.

Ellie hugged her. "Nay, I would never shirk my promise to you, Rowena."

"All is well, then," someone called from the threshold.

Rowena turned to see Stephen standing with his arms folded. Her heart sank as she realized she'd probably embarrassed him.

"I'm sorry. I thought Ellie had left Andrew alone." Her face heated. "I'm a fool, but your words scared me."

"My words?"

"Aye, when you said 'Nothing is what it seems.'"

"I meant the old man. They use the art of diversion to create what seems like an impossible feat."

"I was scared." Rowena let out a nervous laugh as she looked at her friend. "I'm sorry, Ellie. I should have trusted you."

Ellie gripped Rowena's hands. "'Tis all right! I understand."

"Nay, 'tis not all right," she answered as she shook her head. "I acted unwisely, not even letting you say anything. I…I—"

Footfalls pounded down the plank floor toward the maids' chamber. Gilles burst in. "What's wrong?"

"A mistake, 'tis all," Stephen said, his eyes like dark

ice as he stared at Gilles. Really stared at him, as if seeing him for the first time.

Swallowing, Rowena prepared to offer Stephen another apology, but shouting noises rolled down the corridor to stop her.

Stephen stepped out of the chamber. Gilles, then Rowena, followed. A young man, the courier, pushed through the curious onlookers and staggered to a halt. "Master Gilles, your missive."

Crimson flooded Gilles's face as he snatched the rolled parchment.

Rowena moved her gaze from Gilles to the courier. Was the young man drunk?

Nay! His face pale, his mouth hanging open, he swayed as he stood. Rowena could see the sheen of perspiration on his forehead and upper lip. The courier spoke again, a garbled, drooling word, before coughing loudly. He wasn't drunk. He was ill.

The gathered crowd shrank back. Then the courier fell to the planks and rushes beneath him.

Chapter Seventeen

Several ladies fled. The men drew their sleeves up to their faces to protect themselves as they backed away. No one wanted to touch the man, who was surely deathly sick.

Rowena gaped at them. How could they not help? Immediately, she surged forward and dropped to her knees, finding herself bumping into Lord Stephen as he did the same.

"Stay back, Rowena," he said sharply as he tried to push her away. "He's very ill, and should it be a fever, 'twill spread quickly through the manor. I will take him outside."

She stopped his hands. "Outside! He needs to be cared for, not discarded!"

"I wasn't going to discard him." He hefted up the man.

Josane shoved several men out of her way. "Stephen, are you addled? You'll get sick, too. Put him down!"

"And let him suffer in our corridor? Nay. Get some healing herbs and hot broth ready for him. I will take him out to the hospice room."

Rowena followed Stephen as he carried the young

man outside to a small, lone hut beyond the kitchens. She'd seen it when she'd first met the anchoress, but assumed 'twas just a storehouse for foods and grains.

Stephen glanced back at her. "Run ahead and open the door, Rowena."

She hurried in front and pushed open the door. The odor of stale dust rolled out to her. "I thought this was a storeroom."

"Nay, 'tis a hospice hut for the sick. No one comes in here for fear he will become ill himself."

Moonlight spilled in. The small room held only a pallet and a fur, a chair and table. Stephen set the man gently on the pallet. Dust from the room's disuse puffed out from underneath the courier.

Stephen turned to Rowena. "Thank you. You're the only one who wants to help."

Rowena peered outside to see they were alone. When she looked back, she found Stephen covering the man with an old fur. "Do you know what's wrong with him?"

He shook his head. "I've seen plenty of illnesses, but 'tis too early to say what this may be. He made several trips to London, and traveling can sicken a man." He looked up at her. "You should return to the manor. I don't want you ill, as well."

"I've never been sick. I haven't even had a fever before."

Stephen frowned. "Have others in your family?"

"Aye, relatives have died from a fever, but I didn't catch it."

"Your life on a farm away from villages has strengthened you. They say milkmaids are always healthy."

She tipped her head to one side. "Then I *should* be helping you."

"What about Andrew?"

"He's safe. Ellie stayed in our chamber. She'll take care of him. I see that now." She glanced at the man who lay at their feet, his face slack. "I want to be here, Stephen. You shouldn't care for him alone."

A slow smile lifted the corners of his mouth to warm her soul. It felt good to be at his side.

"Good," Stephen said. "Because I'll need you. Go see where those herbs and broth are."

A few minutes later, Rowena returned with a few small pouches of herbs and a pot of meat broth, all with instructions from Josane on what to do with them.

"Milady says to mix these into the broth to stop him from sweating." After measuring some herbs, Rowena handed Stephen a small cup and filled it halfway with the broth. "She says he must be cut to let out the bad blood."

"Nay. I have seen many a soldier cut up in battles, and losing blood kills them more than it saves them."

"I'm glad you think that way. I dislike the sight of blood. Clara says I should never become a healer, and I think I agree."

"'Tis all right. Not everyone has the stomach for it. Did Josane say anything else?"

Rowena nodded. "Aye, we are to burn these other herbs in the brazier. Their smoke will clean his breath." She looked around. "But first we need a brazier."

"And more furs," Stephen added. Rowena left and returned a few minutes later with a lamp and glowing brazier. After disappearing again, she returned with another fur. She reached around Stephen to cover the man.

"Thank you."

With a shy glance up at Stephen, she nodded. "'Tis the least I can do." She paused. "You aren't afraid of him, like the others. Why?"

"Someone needs to care for him and he is in my employ. I could order one of the servants, but they will not do it properly for fear he will make them sick, as well." He looked at her and in the lamplight, he smiled grimly. "'Tis the Christian thing to do. Even though we don't always like our responsibilities, we must complete them."

"He was delivering a missive to Master Gilles, not you."

He frowned. "Aye."

"What's wrong?" she asked. "Do you want Master Gilles to care for him?"

"Nay, he would surely lock him in here and ignore him for fear he'd get sick, also. I merely wondered why Gilles needed the courier."

"Go ask him, then. I'll stay here. I can spoon-feed him the broth. I've started to do the same to Andrew."

Stephen considered her words, then nodded. "Thank you. I do need to speak with Gilles on that matter." He glanced over her shoulder to the brazier. "I'll bring back more hot coals, too."

At the door, he paused. "Rowena, you are either very brave or completely addled to tend a sick person you don't even know. But either way, 'tis good to have you here."

She smiled, the heat of his compliment warming her more than the nearby brazier. "Clara would agree with you, that helping the sick is part and parcel of Christian charity. But I'm sure you would get along well without me."

"Would I?" The small smile on Stephen's face dropped as his brows knit together. He opened his mouth, but shut it again.

What was he thinking? He had disagreed with her comment, and indeed, her heart surged at the thought, but he said no more after that. Instead, his dark gaze lingered on her. Immediately, she recalled his kiss, and heat rose anew into her cheeks. Despite the serious circumstances, she could think of nothing she'd like to do more than to work alongside Stephen, caring for this Norman stranger.

She had no idea what he'd thought at that moment she offered him a small smile of her own. All she knew was that indecision flickered over his face as he turned on his heel and left.

It took some time to find Gilles, for the minstrels had hastily finished their performances and everyone had retired for the night. 'Twas in Stephen's own private office that he found his brother-in-law. The man spun as Stephen shoved open the door.

"Gilles, why are you here?"

The pale light from the desk's oil lamp lit a small circle around them. Stephen saw only shadows on Gilles's face as the man answered, "I'm returning the parchment. I don't need it anymore."

On the desk lay the missive that had just arrived. Stephen strode over and picked it up. 'Twas a table of numbers and lists. "This is what you used my courier for? Ledger notes?"

"I consulted my counterpart in London on a system to organize the collection of monies other than rent. I didn't care for the way I was doing it before."

Stephen dropped the missive. It seemed an insignificant reason to sicken a man, for they both knew too much traveling sickened everyone. "You will inform me if you wish to use my courier, Gilles. I may have need of him."

"Fine." he said curtly. "How is he?"

"'Tis too early to tell. I left Rowena with him." He paused. "Gilles, do you ever speak with the anchoress?"

Gilles's brows shot up. He was obviously taken aback by the question. "Rarely. Why should I?"

Stephen wanted to ask if he knew what the older woman had wanted to ask of the king, but held back. Then he thought of the anchoress's recent illness. His heart chilled. Was the fever spreading through the village? "The anchoress was ill and saw no one," he finally told Gilles.

"She shouldn't be talking to anyone except the chaplain. I thought she requested a life of solitude and prayer and was allowed to stay here only if she did just that. Obviously she has forgotten her promise."

"She also requested you be made baron here."

Gilles's expression darkened. Stephen waited patiently for him to reveal more, but all his brother-in-law did was shake his head. "She's old and addled. Ask Josane. She chats with her. I'll tell the chaplain to keep her quiet." He rolled up the parchment ledger and set it in the box that held the other parchments, then departed quickly.

Stephen remained, his thoughts straying to the box that still sat open on his desk. Nothing Gilles said was unexpected, but there lingered a feeling that something was amiss. Was it Josane? Was Gilles protecting her?

No answer came. Stephen remembered his sister's warning. Was he going soft and losing his ability to know when someone was lying? He grimaced. He was missing something important, but he couldn't even guess what it might be. If it concerned Rowena, he had better get it sorted out.

She had been the only one to follow him as he carried the sick courier out to the hospice room. She was risking her own life and that of her son's by tending the man. What would happen if she died from the fever this man had?

Stephen swallowed. She had asked him to be Andrew's guardian, but only out of practicality. There was no trust involved.

It left a bad taste in his mouth. Did he actually want her to ask out of trust, when he was quite willing to lay her out as bait? He'd be a hypocrite if he did.

Still, cold washed through him at the thought of what he'd done. And even though he'd questioned the wisdom of putting her at risk, it wasn't until she was attacked that it truly affected him.

He reached out to close the parchment box. Each rolled missive sat there, some waiting to be cleaned of their ink for reuse. All of them had seen plenty of wear. The sheet of nettle parchment on which Rowena had sketched her attacker may be a good substitute, but 'twould not stand up to the scrubbings skin parchments suffered. Her hope of selling them may be for naught, and so would be her hope to see Andrew educated.

A thought struck him: someone in the manor might recognize her attacker from the sketch she'd drawn. Shutting the box of parchments, Stephen turned and left his office. After finding his guard, he ordered him to query each person in the manor about the man in the sketch.

Then, with more coals and herbs, he returned to the hospice room.

Rowena was washing the man's face when he entered. She'd abandoned her veil but had tied her hair back with a leather thong. Wisps of white blond shone around her face in the lamplight. "'Tis good you remembered the coals," she whispered. "This man is chilled to the bone from his own sweat. And coughing terribly."

"We will have this room warm enough before long." He stooped down beside her. "Thank you, Rowena. 'Tis good you are here. But you will need to rest soon."

"I'm fine for now." She looked across at him. "But you shouldn't be here. You're the lord of this manor, not a servant or healer. You shouldn't have to do this."

"Fevers scare others, but not me. They are afraid this man's sin will spread to them."

"His sin?" She shook her head, and a lock of her pale hair danced free onto her forehead.

"Aye, 'tis often thought a man's sin sickens him."

"Do you think that?"

"Nay. Many sinful men don't get sick at all."

"True. My father and Lord Taurin both stayed healthy." She let out a small gasp.

"What is it?"

She leaned forward and sniffed. "I think I smelled this odor on my attacker. He may have been ill, too. 'Tis an odd, sickly smell."

He tucked the lock of hair over her ear, his hand straying downward to brush her neck. Her expression softened as he spoke. "I'm truly sorry for what happened to you. And yet, had it not happened, I would not have met you."

She frowned as he dropped his hand. "I hadn't thought of that. Do you suppose God allowed my suffering so we could meet?"

He swallowed. Why? To fulfill the king's order? For he knew that someday he would be expected to marry a noblewoman from his own land, a marriage that would align loyalties in Normandy. His friend Adrien and other knights had been ordered to marry Saxon women of influence to secure loyalties here, but there were only so many high-born Saxon maids.

The only reason Stephen had avoided the marriage fate was because he'd been needed for a single purpose— to seek out rebels or who might endanger the king's hold. The villagers needed to see that 'twould be more beneficial to swear fealty to William than to risk his wrath.

So how *did* Rowena fit in all of this? To torment him until the time came that William would assign him a wife? 'Twas not God's way to torment. Mayhap Rowena was here to show the villagers that if their baron cared for even the least of them, their king deserved their loyalty, too. Had it not already happened to Lord Eudo, and later, his brother, Lord Adrien? They had both earned the loyalty of the Saxons under their rule. If so, then was Rowena's time in his life to be fleeting? His heart stalled at the thought.

"I don't know why God allows us to suffer," he finally said. "But I know that suffering makes us stronger and better able to deal with future difficulties."

"I don't want any future difficulties."

Her words pierced him with their quiet, pained tone. He felt the urge to pull her into his arms. The feel of her lips on his still lingered in his mind. She was a remarkable woman, trying her best in a cruel world. For a moment as quick as a coal popping, he had one desire. If 'twere at all possible, he would take her far from the intrigues of this village and shelter her as she deserved to be sheltered.

But 'twas an addled dream, and he was foolish to think it. He belonged to his king, and any attraction between himself and Rowena would be in vain. The king would never waste a marriage that could secure alliances and strengthen his kingdom. "My thanks, Rowena. And my promise stands. I will find who attacked you. I have employed an unusual method to locate him."

"What is it?"

He hesitated, not wanting her to expect success that might not come. After all, who had ever distributed a sketch of a criminal in order to locate him? "I won't say yet, but I will do my best to find him, I promise."

"I know you will try, but 'tis sad. Thus far nothing has worked." She drew in a sharp breath. "I'm sorry. I shouldn't have said that."

"Nay. 'Tis true." He wished he could promise her that he would find this man, but his investigation had been thwarted at every turn. Too many distractions.

When her gaze dropped to his lips, he immediately guessed her thoughts and steeled himself against yet another distraction.

Sharing a kiss here in the hospice room was inappropriate and 'twould not teach her to trust him. With strength he pulled from deep within, something he didn't realize he had, he shifted away.

Still, he felt the loss keenly.

Chapter Eighteen

Rowena awoke with a start. She looked around the small room. Daylight squeezed through the thin cracks around where the door met its frame. The young courier moaned, and she saw 'twas he who'd roused her.

They were alone. She sat up from her makeshift bed. She'd been in this hospice hut two days. She'd spent all yesterday tending the sick man, recalling as much as she could from her time with Clara, suggesting different herbs and washes that could help the man. Only last night, when she felt the man was showing improvement, did she make herself a bed and sleep.

Stephen had left yesterday, no doubt to see to the normal routines of the day. She wished she could go, also, for she needed to nurse Andrew.

The courier's eyes fluttered open, and after Rowena checked his forehead, she stood to relight the lamp from the dying coals of the brazier. That done, she looked back at him. His color had returned and his face no longer shone with cold sweat.

Last night, as she'd curled up on the thresh she'd gathered, she prayed for healing and now thanked the Lord for it.

Though she must not give up her duty yet. The young man needed more broth and herbs and warm water to bathe away the sick odors. She leaned forward and pressed her hand on his shoulder. "I'll get some more food for you. Do not move."

Outside, Rowena shielded her eyes against the bright sunlight. She spied Stephen and two servants crossing the short distance to the hospice hut. As they closed in on her, Rowena caught the tempting scents of rich broth and baked bread from a large tray one servant carried. The other hefted up a bucket of steaming water.

"'Tis for the courier," Stephen explained.

"That 'twill be much appreciated, I'm sure, milord," Rowena said as she looked at the sun high above her. "'Tis late."

"Aye. You tended the man for two days and refused my order to rest and take nourishment."

"I did?"

Stephen laughed. "You don't remember? Working too hard does that to a mind." He pulled a small piece of straw from her hair. "But I see you finally slept. How is our courier?"

Self-conscious, for she'd set aside her veil, Rowena smoothed her hair. "His fever is gone."

"Good. Now that you're willing to take a break from your duties, I will see to his care. Go tend to your ablutions. I'll send broth and hot water to your chamber. Oh, and I believe I heard Andrew screaming earlier."

She flushed at the thought of her child's growing temper. "'Twill be good to see him. Thank you."

"Nay, Rowena. Thank *you*. Your ministrations have saved my courier's life." He smiled. "Go, and when you're done, join me for the evening meal. I have something to tell you." He walked away.

Her traitorous stomach growled. Was it wise to eat with Stephen? Aye, they'd done well caring for the courier, but now?

She made her way with plodding steps toward the maids' chamber. After thanking Ellie for caring for Andrew, she set about her ablutions and feeding him. The broth Stephen had promised arrived, but only when her stomach again protested its emptiness did she think about eating.

After she took it, she rocked Andrew as much to comfort herself as to keep him asleep. Her situation had not changed, and yet as she looked down at her son, she thought of when she'd asked Stephen to care for him should she die.

It hadn't been based on trust, but it should have been. And after all they'd done these past few days, she should have learned to trust Stephen.

She did. So why did the notion of eating with him scare her?

Because she knew someone out there still wanted to kill her. She knew that Stephen would still use her as bait.

Trust. She must simply trust Stephen, the man who had done her so much good.

Abruptly, Ellie threw open the door. "Rowena, milord is asking for you in the hall. No one can eat until you're there. Don't you know 'tis time to sup?"

She hesitated. Already? "I don't know…"

"Don't be silly. The soldiers were very impressed by your courage in looking after the courier. I heard them speaking." Deftly, she took Andrew and laid him on the pallet.

"I should check on the man."

"Nay. He's much better. Lord Stephen saw that he ate

and bathed." Ellie smiled broadly. "I'm so proud of you. I would be terrified I'd get sick, but you didn't even think of yourself!" She grabbed Rowena's hand and pulled her nearer to the door. "Come!"

"What about Andrew? I should stay with him."

"He's fine! I'll look after him. You know you can count on me."

Rowena stalled. "Why are you so anxious to have me go to the hall? Surely others think I will pass the illness on to them."

"Nay, they won't. They'd dare not say anything if they did think that way, for Lord Stephen attended the man with you and he's already in the hall waiting!" Ellie smiled secretively as she lowered her voice and said, "I want you to go because it annoys Lady Josane. Oh, she's been terribly harsh on all of us maids these last few days. 'Twould be nice to see her squirm in her seat, for she dare not say a thing in front of milord."

"I don't believe that. She's his older sister and I've heard her speak her mind. Besides, you shouldn't talk like that. 'Tis not Christian."

"True. But she's been so mean lately, and I overheard Lord Stephen tell her that he was lord, not her, and 'twill come a time when she must hand over her keys to his wife, so she may as well get used to the idea that this manor doesn't belong to her."

Rowena gasped. "His wife! Is Lord Stephen pledged to someone?"

"Not that I've heard, but 'twill be his duty someday, and that high-and-mighty Lady Josane better realize that. Now go!" She shoved Rowena toward the door.

Rowena grabbed the doorjambs. "'Tis wrong to be a party to hurting someone, Ellie. I don't want to upset Lady Josane!"

Ellie sighed. "She won't be as upset as Lord Stephen will be if you don't go. Please, Rowena. He sent me to get you! You wouldn't want me to get into trouble, would you?"

With those last words, Ellie gave Rowena another gentle shove down the corridor. Rowena tripped lightly forward. After she found her footing again, she looked up to see Stephen watching her from where the corridor turned.

He held out his hand to her. "Come, Rowena. You've rested long enough. I want to eat this meal with you."

She swallowed. He'd changed his clothes, opting for a long tunic of forest green, with pale embroidery and a snug belt keeping it secure over his undertunic. Leather thongs crisscrossed his strong calves, keeping his leggings in place. He looked every bit the lord of the manor, tall and strong, feet firmly planted shoulder width apart.

She looked down at her borrowed tunic, one discarded by Lady Josane, and cut for a more rounded figure. If only she'd had time to tailor this dress to her own shape. It had shorter draping sleeves and a deep, embroidered collar. The undertunic was lighter in color than the outer tunic, but showed only at the sleeves and neckline. Thankfully, she'd donned a clean veil. A plain metal diadem she'd found among the clothing kept it from slipping off her fine hair. She was able to take its length and drape it around her neck for extra modesty.

'Twas the best she could do, and she was grateful that the pale blue color matched her skin well. With a deep breath to embolden her, she stepped toward the splendidly dressed Stephen. He took her work-roughened hand and, after a short moment, kissed it. Her knees went foolishly weak, betraying her growing affection for this wonderful man. 'Twas as if he saw beyond her outward appearance. As though he saw something within her short, thin frame and hurting manner.

"You had promised you would sup with me," he said after lowering her hand. "I saw in your eyes that you wanted to. What changed?"

She *had* promised, but in the time she'd spent rocking her babe, her courage had waned. "I…" Her voice dwindled away. She could not lie to him and say she was too tired or not hungry, but nor could she tell him the truth. "I shouldn't come…"

"Nonsense. Why would you think that?"

Oh, 'twas so silly, she told herself sternly. "There is no reason," she said as he set her hand onto his forearm. With her other hand lifting the long, dragging hem of her cyrtel, for Lady Josane was taller, Rowena allowed Stephen to lead her down the corridor.

The evening meal was a far less festive affair than the night the minstrels visited. But the meal was sumptuous. Meats, cut and glazed with buttered herbs, were spread on one platter, while roasted roots and onions, each drizzled with a dark gravy, filled another. Pastry-sealed birds filled yet another large platter. Rowena spied a thick creamy pottage steaming in a tureen, and round buns dusted with fine flour encircled it.

"You have a feast here!"

He laughed. "Our cook received fresh provisions and was pleased to show off her talents. And we have news worthy of a celebration. First, though, let's eat. I can't bear to look at this food anymore without tasting it, and everyone is waiting for us."

News? The health of the courier? Stephen was indeed kind to use such a simple event as an excuse to offer a celebration. The chaplain said grace, and Rowena silently gave extra thanks to God for saving the young courier's life. She shared a trencher with Stephen. He ordered it filled with tastes of everything. And then he ordered only one goblet filled. One for them to share.

Rowena lifted her gaze and it bumped Josane's. The older woman glared hard, forcing Rowena to drop her eyes to her hands. "I shouldn't be at this table," she whispered.

"I disagree. You have saved my courier's life and are under my protection."

She studied him, for as time went on, she could see subtle changes in his expression. He looked proud today.

"Where else should you be?" he asked.

Anywhere but here, she thought. But as quickly as those words blossomed, they faded. For Stephen smiled at her as he said softly, "We have more cause to celebrate. I wanted to tell you earlier, but you looked like you needed rest first." His voice dropped further. "Someone has given me the name of your attacker. I have sent troops to the next village to arrest him."

She gasped. "You've found him!"

"Shh. Not everyone knows yet, for I'm unsure of what the response will be here and there are still many questions to be answered." He added quickly, "Your sketch did him justice. 'Twas a good likeness. His name is Hundar."

She didn't know anyone by that name. "What are you going to do now? Do you just hand him over to Master Gilles? This man has tried to kill me."

"'Tis more complicated than that, Rowena. Yours is a civil case because you are a *villein* and it could be argued that 'tis just an assault, not attempted murder. We don't want this cur to go free, so we must follow the law. A manorial court would be convened, and Gilles will be in charge of it. A jury of men will decide his guilt or innocence and Gilles will decide his fate.

"But first, after he is brought here, I will interrogate him, and if I am satisfied he is your attacker, aye, he will go before the Gilles."

He continued to look pleased. "There is more to this, isn't there?" she asked softly.

Stephen's expression faltered slightly. She leaned closer. "What is it?"

"Nothing you need know."

Rowena wasn't so sure. "What will Master Gilles do then?" she whispered lest he hear her.

"Decide his punishment, most likely. By then, I'm sure I will have proved his guilt."

"Will he be punished here?"

"For attacking you, aye."

"Is there more?"

"I may take him to London after."

"Why?"

"Because he could be organizing a rebellion against the king. That is beyond my jurisdiction."

"Even if Master Gilles sympathizes with him?"

"Why should he?"

She leaned forward to whisper, "Because Master Gilles is half-Saxon."

Stephen froze, his morsel of venison stalled halfway to his mouth. His voice dropped to a mere breath. "Where did you— Who told you that?"

Chapter Nineteen

"The anchor—" Rowena lifted her arm to indicate the direction of the chapel, only to have Stephen swiftly close his left hand over hers and lower it. He leaned forward and whispered harshly, "Say nothing. Do nothing!"

Her throat dry, Rowena resisted the urge to swallow and show her fear, trying instead to obey Stephen's order completely. Still, she peeked up at him. Those dark eyes, usually as rich as the polished wood beneath their clasped hands, demanded her obedience with a stare so icy, she shivered.

Then, his expression turning calm, Stephen slipped his hand from hers. With his other hand, he brought his food to his mouth.

Any appetite she had was suddenly gone, leaving in its wake a stomach so knotted she could barely breathe. Aye, she would try to eat, but the fierceness in his tone scared her.

"Eat, all of you. 'Tis good fare and our cook worked hard for us," he ordered, much more loudly than his words before. To prove his sudden nonchalance, he cut into his meat again and ate with gusto. Around them, the noise level grew as several soldiers at a far table began to laugh and speak in ever-increasing volume.

She dared another glance at Stephen, who watched the men with narrowed eyes. His lips pursed tightly together, and a crease at one corner formed as he chewed. She leaned over. "Stephen, what I said was important—"

"I know," he ground out. "But 'tis not the time for it. After we eat, we will speak."

"Milord!"

Both Stephen and Rowena looked up. A young soldier stood in front of them, his expression agitated. He still wore his thick leather armor, and Rowena noticed heavy splatters of mud and dirt on it. Hearing a sharp sound, she looked back at the rest of the table. Josane glared, clearly more concerned with the dirt he carried in than with anything else. Gilles's brow furrowed deeply, and the chaplain wet his lips nervously at the youth standing before the head table.

"What is it?" Stephen asked.

"Milord, Hundar, the Saxon you ordered to be arrested, has fled. His family refuses to say where he might have gone." The man swiped the back of his hand across his cut and swollen cheek, leaving a smear of drying blood. He had not given up Hundar willingly.

"Did you arrest his family?"

"Nay, milord. They are only a sick, aged mother who is blind and half-deaf, and a young daughter. Hundar's wife died two years ago when King William marched through here, leaving only a toddler girl. His father also died in the battle. We did post a guard near his hut, should he return."

Cold washed through Rowena. This Hundar had lost so much already. Was he angry at the Normans? At her? A bitter man would hate any Saxon seen as a traitor.

Stephen waved the man away, his expression darkening. He glanced at Rowena, then dropped his attention to his meal. "Eat. We will deal with this situation later."

The rest of the meal dragged on, with Rowena forcing herself to swallow the fine courses. Never before had she eaten sweetmeats alongside the various savory dishes, as was the Norman style. Like the tumult around her, they scrambled her senses, but she took some food in her attempt to act as if naught was wrong.

When the meal ended, Stephen rose, and seeing him do so, the people in the hall rose with him. "Continue with your meal. Rowena and I will see the courier one last time tonight."

Barely reaching Stephen's shoulder, Rowena kept her gaze down, only once peeking through her borrowed veil to see Josane and Gilles watch with suspicious interest as Stephen led her off the dais and out of the hall. Rowena noticed that the young squire immediately jumped up to follow.

As they walked toward the front door, Rowena stopped Stephen. "Ellie says the courier is fine. We don't need to visit him again."

"That may be so, but where else can we speak in private?"

He continued, as if thinking aloud, "If what you said about Gilles is true, I need to know what he has been doing. Mayhap the courier knows, for Gilles has used him. I will question him. But first, was it the anchoress who told you this?"

"Aye. She would not lie to me." Rowena shivered, thinking of the poor courier just regaining his strength only to face an interrogation. "Mayhap the courier doesn't fit into it at all. Gilles could have simply had need of him."

Stephen opened the door and led them out. "He hasn't needed him before now," he muttered.

Rowena had no argument. Nor was she sure of how Hundar fit in. If Stephen knew, he was saying nothing of it. Outside, the crisp air was far colder than any night so far this season. The dew had already fallen and frosted the grass, and Rowena rubbed her arms as her breath streamed from her lips.

"A cloak for Rowena," Stephen ordered from his squire, who tarried behind them.

She turned to watch Gaetan hurry away. "Your squire is always behind you?"

"Only when Josane has no use for him, which hasn't been too often lately," he answered as they crunched across the yard. "He is the youngest son of Adrien's oldest brother, sent to me to train him. I fear that Josane has done more of that. The boy will make an excellent handmaid if I don't soon correct his instruction."

Rowena shook her head. Stephen may be making light of that situation, but she knew things were more serious. She turned as the boy hurried inside. He was a small, silent lad. She rubbed her arms again.

"The courier will be well soon enough and can take back his duties, leaving your squire to his training." She stopped. "But we didn't come here only to discuss him, did we?"

"Nay."

Gaetan returned with Rowena's cloak, a battered and threadbare thing, but not so poor that it didn't keep out the frosty night. She thanked him and asked how her son was. The lad reported that Ellie was giving him morsels of mashed food.

Rowena wrapped her cloak around her, and they continued on toward the hospice hut. There, they roused the dozing courier, and once the lamp was lit, they could see the man was growing steadily better.

Stephen pulled out the chair from the little table and indicated for Rowena to sit.

"Master Gilles gave you a missive to take to London," he stated, towering over both Rowena and the man. "Whom did you see there?"

The man sat up. "I gave it to the palace bailiff, milord. At first."

"At first? Then who did you give it to?"

"The bailiff used me to deliver it and another message to Baron Aubrey de Vere."

"What kind of message?"

"A short note, milord. The bailiff wrote it in front of me."

Rowena glanced up at Stephen. By the set of his mouth, 'twas obvious that he did not care for his courier to be used so indiscriminately, but he said nothing of it. 'Twould be pointless to ask what was in that message, as the courier could not read.

Rowena leaned forward. "What did Baron de Vere do after reading the note?"

The man answered, "He ordered a servant to ask for an audience with the king."

"Then what did you do?"

"I was sent back to the bailiff. He gave me a new missive, which I brought here."

His tone curt, Stephen told the man to get some rest. Rowena turned down the lamp, stirred the coals in the brazier and then followed him from the hospice hut.

"What does all that mean?" she asked when the door was closed.

"Baron Aubrey has the king's ear. He has only to ask for an audience and is granted it."

"Who is he?"

"An adviser to the king."

"What would he advise him of here?"

"I don't know. The last thing he counseled the king on was for many of William's knights to be married off to Saxon ladies of influence."

"Like Lady Ediva?"

"Aye." He tilted his head. "Do you know her well?"

"Not well, but she helped Clara provide for me. She has a kind heart."

"'Twas Aubrey de Vere who arranged her marriage. I was in London at that time. I remember her, for she was furious at being forced to wed again. I think she would have been happy to remain a widow."

"She seems happy with Baron Adrien. They have a son now."

Stephen kept walking, not offering his opinion. Rowena bit her lip. "You were not married off?"

"Nay, I was useful in London at the time, and they'd run out of Saxon royalty by then. I was fortunate, for some of those marriages are in name only and are difficult to maintain."

Rowena swallowed. *They'd "run out of Saxon royalty by then"?* What if they found more, or suddenly maids from families of wealth needed husbands?

"But more important," Stephen said as they walked away from the hospice hut, "Gilles told me his note was merely inquiring how to do ledgers."

"You don't believe him?"

"Aye, what he said was true. The missive that was returned had ledger notes on it. But 'tis odd that the bailiff of London needed to send a note to Aubrey de Vere. I wonder if Gilles's missive said more."

"Mayhap the second note was not related."

"That could be." Stephen thought a moment. "But Aubrey de Vere has holdings on the road to Ely. He likes the country there and says 'tis mild enough for him to re-create his home in Normandy. Having the king's ear makes him influential enough to get what he wants."

"Wouldn't it be normal to want a piece of a beloved home while away from it?"

Stephen shrugged. "I suppose. But not even the king has brought over vines and winemakers. De Vere thinks highly of himself."

"Can he be trusted?"

"I trust no one in London," he muttered. "'Tis my duty to suspect all of usurping the king."

"Would Aubrey de Vere do that?"

"Nay, I don't think he'd be so foolish, but I have heard that he and his wife took possession of more land than they are entitled to. Land near here. The king cares not for the fenland around Ely, so he ignores it, but we both know what happens when men try to take more land for the purpose of threatening the crown."

She shivered and drew her cloak closer. Mayhap she should have agreed to aid Stephen with his duties. She could help him read people like this Aubrey de Vere.

It could save his life.

Nay, he was far better at dealing with the intrigues of London. All she could do was listen as Stephen worked it out in his mind. She looked at him. "But the fens are useless lands, so Aubrey de Vere would be wasting his time. You can't graze sheep on them, nor do they have any peat for fuel."

"True." Stephen walked on slowly, still deep in thought. "I see no reason why Gilles would have anything to do with de Vere, either. Mayhap 'tis as you say and there is no connection and the bailiff used my courier for another matter."

"Do you believe that?"

"Nay. Coincidences rarely happen where the seat of power is concerned. But there is nothing to connect Gilles to de Vere and his illegal seizure of land so close to us. And what would it have to do with Hundar, a disgruntled Saxon from another village who carries a grudge against you? Nothing makes sense, which means I don't have all of the information."

Rowena wanted to ask him about what other plans he seemed to have, but suddenly, they didn't seem as important. "But it may make sense. Master Gilles is half-Saxon."

Stephen stalled and turned. In the light from the moon, a knowing expression dawned on his face. "*Aye*! You said that at the table! How would the anchoress know that? Did Gilles tell her?"

"Nay, she said that she recognized him as being her brother's son. Udella's brother and his cousin had been sent to Normandy to be schooled there. When her brother fell in love with a wealthy Norman noblewoman, she was married off to another Norman. But Udella's brother and that woman were lovers and she became pregnant. The cousin returned to England and told Udella all of this."

"Udella knows who Gilles is just by looking at him?"

Rowena could hear the skepticism in his voice. She shrugged. "By the shape of his ears, and his looks. She says he is the spit of his father."

"Ears? Aye, Gilles had an odd shape to his ears. I have not yet seen Udella's ears, but now that 'tis mentioned, I can see a resemblance between him and Udella." He paused. "Josane said that Udella asked her about Gilles's birth, so she must have been confirming what she suspected. What else did she say? Did she tell Gilles?"

"Nay. She feared for his life. She wanted to ask the king if Master Gilles could be given this estate but didn't want the king to ask why."

Stephen nodded. "Gilles and I fought at William's side, though Gilles is not a full-time soldier. Udella was here when we marched through. Did she tell anyone else?"

"Nay. The only persons who knew who Gilles really was were some of the older villagers, whom Udella swore to secrecy. Then you returned as baron with Master Gilles as part of your family. She got what she wanted, to have Gilles close."

"And since Gilles was married and I am not, there is a good chance that he would have sons long before me. Mayhap she was hoping that Gilles has a son who will inherit this holding."

Remembering more, Rowena caught Stephen's arm. "Udella said that she had planned to tell Gilles who he was, but changed her mind. What if his mother felt keeping her son's sire a secret would preserve his life and position? I know that when I learned that Taurin wanted to lie about Andrew's parentage, my babe's life was at risk because all of Normandy would have seen him as heir to a vast area of land."

At Taurin's name, Stephen's scowl deepened. "Speak no more of that vile man. The only good he did was bring you here with your babe."

She felt her face heat and, afraid Stephen would see her reaction, dropped her hand.

"Nay, Rowena, look at me."

She looked up into his eyes. She could see the partially full moon reflected in them. They stood near the chapel, and after a glance around him, Stephen drew her into its shadows. Off toward the center of the surrounds of buildings, the squire stood. He was small and skinny, not yet filled out, but looking the other way, in the direction of the manor house.

"You asked me to be Andrew's guardian should anything happen to you."

"You declined."

"Because 'twas not born of trust."

She said nothing.

"Do you trust me now, Rowena?"

She swallowed, afraid of what he might ask if she said yes.

"Mayhap I should put it this way. I will see to your son's care should anything happen to you."

"But that is not born of real care for Andrew."

He chuckled softly. "We're a fine pair, aren't we?"

She agreed, but held her tongue on the matter. Thinking quickly, she whispered, "Please don't approach Udella. She told me about Gilles in confidence. Only what has happened has forced me to say something."

He didn't answer right away. But finally, he nodded. "Nay, I will say nothing of this and neither should you. 'Tis unlikely Gilles knows anything, if the village's elderly kept their promise. And they would, for surely they would see him as much a Norman as I am. Your child is hated and he is only half-Norman.

"As for what went on in London, it makes no sense for Aubrey de Vere to concern himself with the borrowing of ledgers between bailiffs. I'm unsure of the connection, but we will soon capture Hundar, as he's likely to return home. Then we'll have our answers."

Rowena pressed her hand to Stephen's warm chest.

"Thank you so much for all of this. Where would I be without your kindness?"

He took her hand and kissed it. Then, drawing her close, he released her hand to curl his around her neck, under her veil.

Then he lowered his lips to touch hers, a soft brush like the first time, but suddenly 'twas bursting forth like wildflowers after a night's rain. She gripped him back, allowing herself to follow the sweep of emotion and longing.

He answered her kiss further. They clung to each other, tasting supper on each other's lips, the lingering honey from the sweetmeats and the cool, tangy cider. She wanted, nay, needed, his embrace, and emboldened by the strength of her emotions, she kissed him with far more abandon than she thought possible.

He lifted his head. "Do you trust me now, Rowena?"

She backed away. And she nearly ached with yearning to stay in his arms. There, she felt protected, sheltered. But this was her life and she had to think of Andrew. He still needed her, in spite of Stephen's assurance he would be cared for.

You trust God, and you know nothing of Him. You know Stephen.

Stephen stepped back, but Rowena could still feel his gaze heavy upon her. She dared to peek up at him. Finally, she whispered, "I trust God and I know Him not, so I should trust you, or I'll be nothing but a hypocrite. I know you'll do your best for Andrew."

Stephen's brows shot up. "I am not worthy to be compared to our Savior. But I accept that you are trying to trust. We have to start somewhere."

"Milord?"

Stephen turned toward the lawn, where his squire stood.

"Someone is coming," the boy whispered.

Immediately voices rang out from the manor house as a stream of people advanced. Stephen pushed Rowena deeper into the shadows and stood next to his squire.

She peered into the crowd. Josane strode ahead of the rest. "Stephen, this Saxon demands to see you."

A short, stocky man stepped from the curious crowd. "Milord, please forgive this late hour," he began in a scratchy voice. "I have been traveling for many days, desperate to find my beloved daughter—"

Rowena gasped in horrible recognition.

Her father had found her.

Chapter Twenty

"Nay!"

At the sound of Rowena's soft word, her father peered into the darkened shadows. Still as stone, she fought the urge to flee.

No more fear, she told herself. No begging for food, nor cowering when the men came into the barn. She was worth more than the small sack of coins that had been tossed at her father's feet as Taurin had grabbed her arm. She knew this now.

It may have been Taurin who treated her the most cruelly, but her father had pushed her onto that path. Her fists curled, her jaw tightened. That man would never hurt her again!

Rowena flew from her sheltered spot. In the next breath, she reached her father and drilled her fists in a rapid tattoo against his chest. "Go back to your filthy farm!"

Someone grabbed her from behind and pulled her off her father. She wrenched herself free. From the direction of the manor, a guard rushed, carrying a long torch.

Rowena turned to glare at the man who'd dared to pull her from beating her father. She gasped. 'Twas Stephen! Nay, did he not remember all she'd told him about this man?

"Rowena? Why did you hit me?" The man peered through the flickering light at her face.

"Why! Are you addled?" She lunged at him again.

"Stop!" Stephen pulled her hard toward him before pinning her hands behind her back. She struggled with all she had, feeling her mind spinning out of control like a child's toy. The yard and people around her blurred as her heart raced faster and faster. With a deft movement, Stephen wrapped his arms around her and yanked her close. She felt his tight grip and shut her eyes.

"Rowena! Stop!" His harsh whisper brushed past her ear. "You'll only hurt yourself!"

She stilled, her breathing fast and short, her head spinning and dizziness threatening to drop her like a stone. After a moment of shocked silence, Rowena felt her heart slow, her breath ease.

"'Tis not the place." He looked at Rowena's father. "What is your name?"

"I am Alfred, son of Althen. I'm a poor man, milord, but a free one. I own my own hide of land."

"Well, Althenson." Stephen gave him a last name. Rowena had never heard of one in their family, only among those who came from Normandy. "We will go into the hall," Stephen told everyone.

Still wrapped in his arms, Rowena shook her head. "I won't stand in the same room as that man!"

"Rowena, why?" Her father looked up at Stephen, his expression gaping. "My lord, I don't understand this. My daughter, my flesh and blood! She ran away over a year ago, but I have found her safe in your fine care! Blessings to you, milord! Blessings!"

Rowena glared. "Whose blessings?"

"My own, Rowena. I heard where you were and I left immediately to come for you."

She stiffened. Turning her head slightly, she said to Stephen, "You can release me, milord. I will not shame you with my behavior anymore."

Slowly, Stephen let her go. She stood resolute and in control, as tall as she could make herself. "I did not run away. You sold me to Lord Taurin. Have you forgotten your vile actions?"

Althenson stared blankly at her, then at Stephen, his expression showing shock. In the dancing light of the torch as it buffeted about in the breeze, he shook his head. Oh, how she wished she could read his true emotions, but her own had built a wall against him so high, she could never reach over it.

"Lord Taurin came to us, but I refused his offer," her father said. "He threatened to beat me, but I refused him still. Only when he saw he was outnumbered, for our kin was close at hand, did he finally leave!"

Rowena snapped her stare to Stephen, but with his expression inscrutable, he said nothing. "Nay, Lord Stephen, do not believe him!"

He held up his hand. "'Tis not a matter to discuss outside. We will take it into the hall, where I will listen to it."

When the crowd moved away, Gilles stepped forward into the light. "I should be deciding this case, Stephen."

"Nay, 'tis not your jurisdiction. The king granted her freedom, personally, so we shouldn't treat this matter in a simple manorial court, not with the chance of William visiting this winter and learning of it. Come inside, all of you."

He strode past Rowena without as much as another glance her way. She felt as though her life were dissolving, but she somehow managed to follow him. All the while, so many eyes seemed glued to her like insects caught in tree sap.

Inside, Stephen was the first to speak. "Come, Rowena, up here."

She remained rooted by the door, refusing her seat on the dais and hating how her father's brows shot up. Did he think she possessed some authority, some power within the manor? Gaetan found her a stool, and with a small thank-you to the sympathetic boy, she accepted it, ignoring Stephen completely.

"Milord," Althenson began, "Rowena knows nothing of my dealings with Lord Taurin. Oh, he threatened me greatly, but I would not give up my child! I thought she'd run away, but from her protests, I can see that she had been kidnapped by Lord Taurin. I only wish I could take my complaint to London, but I am a poor farmer and can only rejoice that my lost child has been found."

Rowena peeked up from beneath her veil. *Nay!* Her heart cried out. *Do not believe him!*

Beside Stephen sat Josane, a truly satisfied look upon her face, as if she'd finally heard a truth she'd known all along. Beside her, Gilles wore a dark, stressed look, probably nervous from the tension in the room. Rowena's eyes went automatically to his ears. Aye! They stuck out from his longish hair.

She bit her lip, discarding such inconsequential nonsense. Would she have to present her case before Stephen, as if he had not heard a single word she'd said all the time she'd been here? 'Twould be useless, with her father denying all that had happened. She knew her words would be wasted even before they could be formed.

Tears blurred her vision and she had to bite her lip to stop herself from sobbing.

"What we need is a full night's sleep and to hear the whole tale again on the morrow," Stephen decided. "Then, Althenson, you may state what you wish to come of this. After I hear your case, I will retire to decide what to do. But I will not hurry through this process, Saxon. For remember, as a *villein*, Rowena is bound to this estate and cannot leave unless I give her permission. Do you understand what this means?"

"Aye, milord. For I was once bound, also, but earned enough for my freedom."

Stephen's mouth tightened. "Nor will you speak with your daughter."

The Saxon bobbed his head, then shook it in obedience. Rowena quivered all over. Her father wasn't the simpleton he pretended to be. Nay, he feigned innocence as easily as she changed Andrew. She glanced over at Stephen, hoping for some of the compassion he'd begun to show her.

But not once did he look at her. Again, Rowena's heart cried out in silent pain, but she said nothing aloud. 'Twas as if her throat was choking on unshed tears.

But what could be expected? She was nothing, a traitor in the eyes of this village and someone Stephen could not trust. Oh, he was like all other men, thinking of his own business and not caring for anyone else's! An inconvenience she was, a nothing, a girl attacked by a man she didn't even know.

Attacked by a man she didn't even know?

That thought struck her hard. How was that possible? Why would some stranger attack her? Unless that man was paid by someone. Such as her father, who stood nearby, his cap in hand and cloak removed, looking earnest and mayhap hoping to get her back. Why? So that he might sell her again?

She pressed her lips tightly together, hating the memories of his ordering her to stay in the barn, that unless she proved herself useful, her food would be what the dog rejected.

Did her father have her attacked so he might offer to take her home? He was as sly as a fox. But should she cause division, mayhap Stephen would be glad to be rid of her.

Tears stung her eyes anew as she listened to her father again thank Stephen for saving his precious daughter's life, bobbing and bowing and displaying to all how humble and sincere he was.

Nay, she could not listen to the lies anymore! Standing, she pivoted on her heel so hard, she was sure she'd gouged the fine wood of the floor.

"Rowena, stay!"

She stopped. Stephen's tone was too hard to read and she refused to turn to see his expression. He had been kind to her, but had she become so tiresome that he'd be willing to listen to her father and then release her to his care? After all, he'd ended their kiss early.

She burst out, "Nay, milord. I have to see to my—" She clamped shut her mouth. She would not reveal to her father that she had a son. Who knew what he would demand then? "I am needed elsewhere."

She kept her back to the people and the despicable scene unfolding. "As you said, we will finish this on the morrow." With that, she rushed from the hall.

Stephen felt his heart plummet as Rowena dashed away. But he held up his hand to stop the guard from pursuing her. She needed to be alone, to pull together her strength, for surely 'twas a shock to see her father.

'Twas for him, also. He had fought with William on many occasions, the greatest at Senlac for the English crown. He'd known 'twas his duty to his liege and he would do it again in a single breath, but never did he hate his work as he did at this moment.

The man who had caused Rowena such pain stood before him, and it took all Stephen's willpower not to order him tied up in the stocks that stood in the center of the village.

He glanced surreptitiously around the hall. While the majority of the people here were Norman, there were a few prominent Saxons—the priest, Alfred the Barrett, Osgar the Reeve and several others with their wives.

'Twould be unwise to accuse Rowena's Saxon father of lying. With few troops around, the slightest reproof of a Saxon could send the rest rebelling.

Stephen wasn't afraid to fight, but he was no fool. Blood would be shed if he angered the villagers to the point of revolt, and the blood would include innocent women and children. Then the situation could easily bring King William's wrath upon this village.

Nay, he would listen to this cur and then remind him that Rowena was under his protection. The man would have to prove that what Rowena had said was false, that he had not taken money for selling her.

But even if Althenson had sold her, there was the matter that neither he nor Rowena was Christian. Though the spirit of the law could be argued, and King William had expected all of England to be Christian, the letter of the law allowed Althenson to sell his own flesh and blood.

Why wouldn't he?

Money. As in London, power and money motivated

people. Stephen stood, anxious to do the one thing that might prove Rowena's story.

"I will retire now. Josane, see that Rowena's father has a *safe* place to sleep."

Josane opened her mouth, but when he shot her a lethal look, she shut it again. Aye, she was the chatelaine, and 'twas hardly her place to see to a Saxon serf, but she read in Stephen's eyes, as he'd hoped she would, that she needed to obey. She was quick-witted enough to know without asking that this Saxon cur would not only get his own chamber, but his own guard, as well. 'Twas not for Althenson's comfort, but to keep him segregated from other Saxons, even from the one who had brought him here, whoever that was.

Josane nodded, calling upon a guard and a maid to assist her. As she swept past Rowena's father, she snapped, "Follow me. You may sleep where the minstrels slept."

He followed her, wide-eyed but bowing repeatedly as he left.

Only then did Stephen exit the hall. He called for his squire and demanded half a dozen men.

In his private chamber, he wrote out three missives, divided his men into three groups and then gave them strict instructions.

Money motivated Saxons and Normans alike. And where there was money, there was often a trail of proof as clear as the road to London. One pair of soldiers would go to the seat of Taurin's holdings. A soldier named Kenneth, promoted to knight for his bravery exposing Taurin's plans to usurp the king, had been granted the man's holdings. He may have a ledger proving Rowena's purchase.

To London, Stephen sent another group. For if Rowena's father had purchased back his land from William, there would be a record of it there. And there would be a record of Taurin's misdeeds, also.

He paused. Had Gilles sent the courier there for such a reason and, having discovered nothing of use, declined to mention it to Stephen?

He would find out soon enough.

The last pair were to go to Rowena's home. If Althenson had purchased back his land, he'd keep a record of it, regardless of whether he could read the deed or not. And surely someone would know something that could prove Rowena had not lied.

Did that mean he suspected she *had* lied? Nay, he told himself fiercely. Common sense told him that Rowena had had no motive to lie before her father arrived. Even if she'd deceived people for sympathy, she hadn't known Stephen well enough to assume she could garner influence. She didn't even care a jot for him then.

Did she care for him now? His heart lurched. Oh, how she must hate him for housing her vile father in the manor and for even being willing to listen to his tale! But she didn't understand Stephen's position here. With few soldiers, he needed to tread carefully.

The guards and missives dispatched, he strode out and down the corridor. His manor had fallen quiet, as if the whole of the estate were holding its breath and waiting. The uneasy feeling crawled over his skin.

Behind him, Stephen heard men quietly preparing for the night. Abruptly, a thump of something dropped chilled the men into complete silence, before someone dared to shift on a trestle table again.

Stephen reached the maids' chamber and he rapped swiftly on the door. A scurry of muffled footfalls could be heard before the door swung open.

Ellie stood in the open doorway, her expression stricken. "Milord?"

Stephen stooped and strode inside. 'Twas not proper for him to barge into these women's private quarters, but Ellie had pulled the door wide open, anyway.

She was alone. He hadn't expected the cook's maid to be there, because she would bake most of the night for the next day's meals. And the other maid was probably assisting Josane as she saw to Althenson. But Rowena should have been there.

"Where is Rowena? And her babe?"

Ellie shook her head. "I don't know. When I returned a short time ago, she wasn't here. And her cloak and the babe's things are also gone."

"Did you search the manor for her?"

"Nay, I had to help prepare a room for Rowena's father. I only just returned." She pursed her lips, but looked as though she was bursting to speak.

He stopped her. "You don't know where she went?"

"Nay, milord! I thought she may have gone to the chapel to pray, but I just checked there and 'tis empty!"

She burst into tears and rushed forward to grab Stephen's arm. "I fear she is gone for good, milord! She had a terribly sad look on her face in the hall. What have we done to her, milord? What have we done?"

Chapter Twenty-One

Rowena hefted Andrew to shift his weight. He was sleeping soundly, probably having been up late playing with Ellie, who loved to dote on him.

'Twas just as well, for Rowena needed him silent as she stole from the village. She'd paused as she passed the lane that led to her hut. Nay, there was nothing in it she could use. She'd borrowed a skin of cider and a quarter of cheese from the kitchen without anyone seeing, promising herself silently that once she reached Dunmow Keep, she would ask Lady Ediva to replace them in exchange for Rowena's working there.

Dunmow was the only place she could go. Clara would still be there, for she had yet to marry her beloved Kenneth, who had gone to accept his new holdings. Clara had promised Lady Ediva she would stay on as healer until someone suitable, such as their cook, could manage the distribution of the healing herbs.

Dunmow was to the east, toward where the sun rose, while her birthplace, and Taurin's estates, were to the west and London to the south. The east was the only place to offer any security.

The night had chilled further, but as she moved, her

own body provided heat for her babe. She hiked up her cloak and tucked the hem in around Andrew. Aye, she could walk that much faster now.

But soon, her ankle began to ache again. She should have taken a pony, but 'twould have been too hard to slip one from the stables unnoticed. All she could do was walk as far as she could tonight, her feet fueled by churning emotions and her mind forcing away the pain in her ankle. Though she knew she wouldn't be able to sleep when Andrew awoke, she needed to put a great distance between her and Kingstown.

Away from Stephen. A sob caught in her throat and she nearly choked as she shoved it back down. Aye, she could have stayed to fight her case, but she couldn't risk her father learning of Andrew. She wasn't sure what he might do, but she wouldn't take the chance. He'd sold his own child into slavery. He could easily sell his grand-child. And she could not stand to hear him tell that filthy lie of never selling her, or ever mistreating her.

She would never go home again!

Rowena paused and shifted Andrew again, taking time to catch her breath and ease the weight on her ankle. Those few moments in the manor's great hall returned to her. Stephen had said she was bound to his estate, but he said nothing about wanting her close to him, no mention in his words or hint in his tone of how he felt. Had the kisses they'd shared meant nothing?

Could it be that he was merely dallying with her until the king ordered him to marry? After all, had Stephen ever told her that he loved her? Nay, and worse, he'd mentioned he knew his duty could lead him to marry someone King William chose for him.

Aye, though they'd shared kisses and those moments in her hut had been sweet, she'd seen men turn from kind to cruel in the blink of an eye. As much as her heart might yearn for someone who cared for her, she was lucky to get free, she told herself. She might never get the chance again.

Then why did it hurt to leave him? Why had she not risked seeing Stephen listen to her father, and mayhap believe him? She swallowed, refusing to answer her own questions.

Moonlight filtered through the trees, and Rowena forced more determination into her limping steps. And she did her best to ignore the ever-tightening ache in her heart.

Stephen ordered the village searched immediately. He wanted more done, but all his men were now employed in other tasks, while his staff were busy searching the manor and outbuildings.

The anchoress had been awakened, but she could offer no clue to where Rowena went, for she had not even known she was missing. Stephen wanted to ask her so much more, but with Gilles standing beside him, he could not. And Rowena's immediate safety was far more important.

'Twas deep into the night, almost to the point where the east would soon begin its soft glow of dawn, when the last of his staff returned from their searches. Rowena was nowhere in the village, nor in the forest to the north where the palisade was being built and small shelters had been erected to house the foreman and his office. Her hut was also undisturbed.

Stephen could order some men and horses to the various roads, but he hesitated. They were sorely taxed with half of his guards already dispatched with missives and the other half, minus one on a roaming picket, needing to sleep. He needed his men fresh, for that cur Hundar remained at large, and that sly old fox Althenson was still here. Either could easily rally Saxons to attack. Such was unlikely, but Stephen would not take that chance. 'Twas bad enough that he had been forced to take the guard he'd placed on Althenson.

"Milord?"

Now in his office, for he had ordered the remaining soldiers to go to ground in the great hall, he looked up from the table on which he'd spread his maps. The other maid whom Ellie had helped prepare Althenson's chamber, a girl whose name he couldn't recall at this moment, stood holding a tray of hot broth and sliced cheese.

Stephen returned his attention to his maps. "Take it away. I'm not hungry."

"Milord, Lady Josane said you must eat. And—" she glanced behind her to the empty doorway "—I think I have something of interest."

His head shot up. "What is it?"

"When I was ordered to bring you this fare, the cook's maid was telling the cook that a skin of cider and a quarter of cheese were missing. Cook always has her count the provisions each night before she begins her baking, for she fears the guards may slip in and steal food and ale."

She was probably right, Stephen thought drily. But 'twas beside the point right now. "Only those two things were stolen? No ale?"

"Nay." She hesitated. "I don't want to place blame, milord, but I saw Rowena leaving the kitchen shortly before the count. And now—"

She snapped her attention to her left as a noise interrupted her. Immediately, her gaze fell to the floor as she shut her mouth.

Rowena's father stood in the open doorway. "Is there something wrong, milord? Can I help?"

'Twas too bad he'd taken the man's guard. He would have stayed out of Stephen's way. "Nay, return to your pallet. 'Tis of no concern to you."

Immediately Stephen could feel the young maid's strong stare return to his face, as hot and riveting as the sun in July. Her back was to Althenson and 'twas as if she was trying to tell Stephen something without words.

Althenson took a step forward. "What has happened to my daughter, milord?"

"Nothing." Stephen paused. "She has left the manor and I have men out searching for her."

The older man came closer. "She has run away? In all her days with me, she never ran away! She loved her home."

Stephen felt the hairs on his neck tingle. "'Twas just a farm, wasn't it? A place of smelly animals and hard work. Did she love animals so much that she'd never want to leave?"

"Aye, milord. She was always wanting to stay in the barn. We wanted her in the house, but nay, she insisted on staying with the beasts."

Stephen's frown deepened. Was this man saying he had no choice but to relent to his daughter's childish wishes? His lips pursed. Nay. This was a lie, he was sure. And that part of running away? "Say that again."

Althenson looked bewildered. "Say what again, milord?"

"All the days she was with you, she did not run away?"

"Aye, milord."

'Twas a slight contradiction to what this man had said earlier. He'd said he'd thought Rowena had run away, but now he saw that she'd been kidnapped by Lord Taurin. In fact, twice he had said she'd run away. He sounded as though he'd never considered she might have done so. "Milord, is it true that she has a child?"

"Where did you hear that?"

"Lady Josane told me, milord."

Stephen stared at the man, whose throat bobbed once. The maid nearby hardened her glare. *Nay*, Stephen told himself. Josane wasn't given to chattiness with anyone. She may not like the girls under her care, but she would not gossip about them. Besides, she'd caught Stephen's fierce look when he'd ordered her to see to Althenson's comfort. She would give as little information as possible, because she would see this man as beneath her station and not worthy of conversation beyond what was barely necessary.

This man had just lied to him twice in the span of a few breaths. Stephen was sure of it, even without Rowena's careful observations. He had made a career of reading situations, and if this man was trying to deceive him right now, what else had he lied about?

The whole fabricated tale of Rowena's being kidnapped? On the morrow, he was to listen to this man's sorry story of losing his beloved daughter. 'Twould be full of more lies, he was sure.

Still feeling the maid's harsh stare on his face, Stephen took the tray from her and set it on the dais. He quickly dismissed the young woman. He would talk with her later. Right now, he had more important things to do. To Rowena's father, he snapped, "Return to your pallet. We will speak later."

As the man left without an answer to his question, Stephen grimaced and returned to his maps. The men had searched the surrounds. Would Rowena go to the west, to confront the man who'd attacked her?

Nay, not with Andrew. She would go to where she felt safe—

"What have you found out?"

Stephen looked over as his sister swept into the room. "I have discovered that Rowena's father is not what he seems," he said tersely.

Josane rolled her eyes. "I could have told you that!"

Stephen tipped his head. "Why the sudden turn-around? You looked surprisingly smug when he wanted to present his story."

Josane frowned. Stephen knew contrition when he saw it, though 'Twas a surprise to see it on Josane's face. "'Tis true. I wanted Rowena to be the liar, because she has wrapped you around her finger." She sighed as if life was easing from her like air from old bellows. "But 'tis wrong to think that way. And watching her father has changed my mind."

"How so?"

"When you left him in my care, *he* was the one who looked quite smug." She walked over to the table and tilted her head to peer at the maps. "I gave him a small chamber down the corridor, and when my maid and I returned with a blanket, I noticed the drinking flask I had left was missing. I ordered my maid to search his things whilst I distracted him. She found it tucked in a secret pocket in his cloak. He's a thief, Stephen."

Ah, so that was the other thing the maid had wanted to say, Stephen thought. He should have had her tell him while he had the chance.

"And," his sister went on, "he did not once ask to see Rowena. He did not even ask a thing about her. Does that sound like a loving father to you?"

It appeared Josane had inherited the same reasoning skills as he. But it did not explain how he knew Rowena had a child. "He lied twice to me. First, he said that Rowena had never run away, the opposite of what he'd said earlier. And he said you told him about Andrew. Did you volunteer that information?"

Josane took Stephen's cup and poured hot broth into it. As she handed it to him, she lifted her brows haughtily. "Do I look as if I would chat with him?"

He accepted the cup. "Nay."

"Then I did not." She pursed her lips as she shook her head. "Stephen, I know I warned you about growing soft away from London, but you must forgive me for that. I fear I have not wanted to stay here for a long time, and 'tis making me bitter."

"Where do you want to go? London?"

"Nay. I want to return to Gilles's estate in Normandy. I am homesick for it. It has been my home for years."

Gilles. As Stephen drank, he pondered Udella's claim about Gilles's parentage. But 'twas of no import now that Rowena was missing.

"Why all this fuss over a girl, Stephen?"

He did not look up from his drink. "Because I pledged to protect her and now she's gone."

Josane took his cup and refilled it. "Well, consider this, Stephen. In Rowena's eyes, you have failed to protect her. So she has returned to the only place she feels safe. Where did she run to before?"

"Colchester, but the townsfolk didn't want her. The only reason she chose that 'twas because a group of merchants were traveling that way."

"Think, Stephen. That midwife who came with her to settle her here, and who protected her after she came from that area, is the one she's gone to. She has returned to the woman, not the town."

He mulled it over. "Aye, I know where she would go. Where she knows she will be safe." He called out to his squire, demanding any male servants available to come immediately. A stable boy and the thatcher arrived.

The thatcher? Stephen grimaced at how someone, Gilles probably, had brought in the villagers to assist in the search. But neither male in front of him was suitable for the task.

Again, Josane took the cup from his hand. "Go after her, Stephen," she said softly. "Wherever this place is, 'tis where your heart is now." She smiled. "You say you only want to protect her because she is bound to your estate, but 'tis not the whole truth, is it?"

He glared at her. His foul expression rolling off her like water off a duck's wing, she continued, "And forgive me for not approving of anything you've done lately. I have ached for Normandy and for something special in my marriage. Gilles and I have no children, and 'tis only because there is no love between us. Our marriage wasn't that kind, and I fear it has worsened. Gilles is different now, more secretive and spending far too much time on his work with the Saxons. But you have a chance for happiness." She paused. "And I…I didn't want you to have something I didn't have. 'Twas petty of me to think that way, and I'm sorry for it. And I am sorry for blaming you for Corvin's death. I've thought long of it these last few days, mayhap because the babe has been here and I remember Corvin as a child. I could have also lost you as we lost Corvin. That was not because you did something wrong. Nay, 'twas a Saxon sword that killed him, not you. And the more I thought of that, the more

I knew I wanted to go home to Normandy and not face these people anymore."

Josane drew a restorative breath. "But that is my life, not yours. So, go, find Rowena. I will manage the manor in your absence."

His heart thumped in his chest. "Thank you. And when I come back with Rowena, we will discuss your return to Normandy. Our parents would like to see you again."

"And I could help our *mama* understand why 'tis wrong to blame you. Now go!"

Stephen pressed his lips to his sister's warm cheek before striding out.

After retrieving his sword, he went straight to the stable, where Gaetan was already preparing Stephen's courser. The saddle he chose was a lightweight one, and the bridle was already secured on the stallion's large head. The animal stamped his feet impatiently. When Stephen leaped onto his mount, his weight agitated the beast further. Stephen steadied him by circling the boy, who fearfully eyed the huge animal he didn't completely trust.

"I will head east toward Colchester, stopping at Dunmow Keep on my way," he said, accepting a dagger from the boy. "Should Rowena be found, I want someone to catch up with me immediately." He then galloped out of the stable.

Rowena crept forward, hugging her son close in case he awoke. The flickering campfire had attracted her from afar, and she made her way stealthily through the forest toward it. She accidentally snapped a twig and froze, with her head down and body hidden, until she was sure the men in front of her had not heard her over the crackling fire.

Still hidden in the trees, she lifted her head and watched three men as they sat around the fire. One man, whose back was to her, coughed loudly. Though their words were spoken in low tones, they rang clearly through the night. They were Saxons, discussing the division of some money. One, the man who coughed too much, held the purse strings, she thought, for the others were asking when their shares would come.

They leaned toward each other, heads close, and their voices lowered until she could no longer hear them. Finally, two of the men stood and wandered into the woods for a moment. One returned to sit on a mossy log and pick up the conversation.

The third was cooking a rabbit over the fire, turning it on a makeshift spit. The alluring scent of seared meat reached through the trees to fill Rowena's nostrils. Poaching game was forbidden in the forests, but Rowena knew 'twas done more often than not. King William's forests were too vast to be successfully guarded all the time. The other man began to scrape the rabbit's hide with his knife.

Rowena shifted to ease a stiff muscle in her back. She peered hard at the pair, trying to identify them, but with the flickering firelight, their faces were nothing but distorted expressions.

All she wanted was to know which way, if any, they planned to go. 'Twould decide her own route. But they said nothing of their journey. Only one thing was certain. They would not be traveling tonight, which meant she could mayhap put another mile of road in before resting again.

She eased back as quietly as possible. Time to move on.

Then she turned.

A hand clamped over her mouth as an arm swung around to pin the slumbering Andrew to her.

She'd been caught.

Chapter Twenty-Two

Stephen galloped his mount for the first quarter mile, then reined him in. 'Twas hard on the beast, and he could easily roar right past Rowena and not even know it.

He gritted his teeth. Something about her made him lose all sensibility. In London, he prided himself on remaining cool and detached from all emotion, focusing only on the king's safety. What was it about that tender, pale woman that made him such an addled fool?

Was Josane right, though she didn't say the word? Did he love her? Aye, he knew he was beginning to care for Rowena, but was he even capable of loving? He'd long since closed off his heart. How could he expect himself to love when he'd been responsible for his beloved brother's death?

Was he? His heart squeezed as he considered Josane's words. She had decided not to blame him anymore.

So, could he also stop blaming himself? His heart squeezed. He just couldn't.

Stephen's thoughts wandered back to his sister. Her marriage was unraveling like a poorly sewn chemise giving in at the slightest pull and tug. Gilles was spending more and more time dealing with Saxons and less at home, where he should be.

Ahead, the sparse trees thickened, and in the full moon's light, as it began to set, he spied a simple signpost, the whitewashed letters practically aglow. When he pulled his horse to a halt, he saw the sign read, Hainghe-ham 20 miles, Colcestra 30 miles, Melforda 15 miles.

He had forgotten about this fork in the road. Heding-ham and Colchester, he translated from the ancient Saxon language. They were on the same sliver of a road. Long Melford was to the left, a road much better to walk along.

Stephen hesitated. Rowena had Andrew, and because of him, several days' travel ahead to get to Dunmow, which lay before Colchester. But the road was barely a dirt path and the forest thick and dangerous, harder to walk with a babe. Melford was closer and the road better traveled.

Which would she take?

His courser anxious to move again, Stephen gripped the reins. He had to decide, *and quickly*, for he didn't want to waste time. Should he take the Colchester route, Rowena could easily reach Melford before he realized she was not on that road. If he took the way to Melford, she could become lost in the difficult path that was supposed to be the way to Colchester.

Yet, she'd have had to come that way to Kingstown. 'Twould be more familiar to her.

His horse turned toward Melford, preferring the wider route.

Lord, give me wisdom.

Stephen shut his eyes, then after a moment's breath of time, he swung his horse to the right. Rowena would go to her friend and a dangerous path would not stop her. She was not one to shirk a difficult task or take the road better traveled.

* * *

Rowena fought off her assailant, awakening Andrew, who screamed his own protest.

"Silence, woman, or I will slice off your head!"

She stilled immediately and found herself being dragged through the trees until her captor reached the campfire. There, he tossed her onto the ground.

Rowena threw out her hands to prevent falling on Andrew. His screams rent the night air.

"'Tis a woman?" one man called out as he stood. "We're being followed by a woman and her brat?"

Her captor hauled her up and yanked off the hood of her cloak, revealing her pale hair. "Nay, not any woman, but the one I told you of. Rowena."

She spun at his voice and gasped. Her attacker! The man she'd drawn on the parchment for Stephen! The one Stephen had searched for and who had escaped.

Lord in Heaven, protect me! Stephen, find me!

Andrew screamed even louder. She huddled down, trying to soothe him, shaking all over and knowing he would sense her fear and continue his screams.

"This is that woman? Why is she following us?"

Hundar prodded her with his foot. "Why did you follow us?"

"I–I didn't. I have run away from Kingstown."

"Going where?"

"To Dunmow Keep. I have friends there." She continued to bob Andrew in a vain attempt to soothe him.

"Why are you running away? You would have a good life at the manor."

"Why did you attack me?"

Leaning forward, Hundar pressed a knifepoint to her throat. "Answer me!"

"I would not have a good life at the manor! My father has come for me, and I don't wish to return to my home. He sold me before."

Hundar scoffed as he grimaced as if in pain. "Sold you? 'Tis an unlikely story."

"'Tis true!" She eased away from his blade as she looked him up and down. "You're injured."

"A little stiff, but no Norman soldier will ever best me in a good fight. I was ready for him."

She gasped. "You escaped Lord Stephen's men as if you knew they were coming!"

The man laughed, then fell into a fit of phlegm-filled coughing again. Sweat beaded on his face as he spat. When he was finished, he said, "Like Lord Stephen, I have my spies."

With Andrew settling, Rowena peered up at Hundar. He sweated so much. Was he ill? "I don't understand. I don't know you. Why did you attack me?"

"For the coins. I have been well paid."

"*We* have been well paid, Hundar," one of the men corrected him. "Remember we helped you."

"You've done nothing!" he snapped at the other two. "Be thankful for what I give you!"

"I want it now," one growled.

"You'll get it when I see fit to give it to you. Look, we have more than coins now. We have the woman."

The one cooking the rabbit stood. "And what would we do with her? You hired us to hide you and swear to your innocence if necessary. I won't kidnap anyone."

"You'll do as I say!"

The cook threw down the poker he held. "Nay! You'll not change the agreement."

"Think, Hundar!" the other man said. "We cannot just kidnap her and then let her go so she can finger us. And I won't be killing my own kind. She's a Saxon, and by the looks of that babe, she's had enough problems with Normans. We should leave her be."

"You'll both do as I say!"

"Then pay us now and be done with us," the first man said. "I won't have anyone's blood on my hands. And I won't have you holding the purse strings like a Norman overlord."

Hundar grabbed Rowena's arm to yank her closer. The man's sweat and filth overpowered her, and she gasped at the stench. His arms were thin but sinewy, like the ancient vines that covered the south side of the chapel. He continued to cough in her ear. "You'll do as I say, or this woman's death will be on your heads, do you understand? I'll swear you killed her, not me! See what Lord Stephen does then!"

Rowena wrenched free and drove the heel of her palm hard into his nose. He cried out and dropped his dagger. The two others leaped on him to scramble for his sack of coins, but in the dirt and darkness, they struggled to find it.

Abruptly, a loud whinny cut the air, and through the brush and trees sprang a huge horse. Rowena lunged out of the way as a long Norman sword arced downward to slice into one man's side. He screamed, then turned and staggered painfully into the forest. Hundar still hunkered down, his hands covering his face. The cook backed up. The rider turned his mount and the animal kicked the cook hard. The man landed on the outer edge of the fire, singeing his back.

Rowena peered up at the rider. "Stephen!"

He dismounted, grabbing a length of thong from his belt. Then he tied up the cook as the man fought back with the intent to kill. Rowena glanced over at Hundar, who seemed to be squatting with his hands covering his face.

Seems to be. Nothing is as it seems. Hundar was too tense, his fingers spread open too much. He pulled in his breath, and Rowena knew what was coming. "Stephen, watch out!"

Immediately Stephen spun, released his dagger and pinned the man to the downed log. Something clattered to a rock beneath them. Rowena kicked it far. It was another dagger, one that Hundar had had hidden away.

Shooting Rowena a thankful nod, Stephen bound Hundar, as well. The man coughed and spat at his feet, then swore at Rowena.

Disgusted, she turned away to peer into the forest for the third man. "There's another man!"

"He won't be back," Stephen said. "He's injured and he would have to face his friends' anger for leaving should he return. Are you unhurt?"

She checked Andrew, who was screaming again. "I'm fine, but Andrew is more than upset."

"A ride on a horse will calm him." Stephen bent and grabbed the coin purse. With a frown and a soft mutter, he pocketed the delicate leather pouch and then mounted his horse again. Bending forward, he wrapped his arm around Rowena's back. She stiffened.

"Nay, Rowena. Relax. Trust me."

She held her breath. Trust him? Stephen was surely going to turn her over to her father again. With Kingstown on edge, she would be sacrificed to find and arrest rebels, or even to keep the peace. Or she would be called a liar, for punishing her father would incite the villagers, who'd see it as Norman oppression yet again.

But Stephen had found her, and 'twas what she'd

prayed for. Was her belief so weak that a babe's was stronger?

Lord, strengthen my faith.

Rowena looked up at him, eyes watering, watching him as he blurred before her. He'd come for her, and her heart nearly leaped from her chest at the thought.

With a swallow, she battled the doubts that flared within her foolish heart. And hadn't she just seen the subtle language Hundar's body spoke and had warned Stephen of it? She'd worked alongside him as he'd once asked her to. *Trust him.* She took a deep breath and reached for him.

He swung her up onto his lap. She clasped Andrew with one hand, though his sling stayed firm, and with the other, she gripped Stephen.

"Thank you," she whispered.

He leaned forward and kissed her soundly on the lips. Oh, to have him hold her again! The feel of his strong arms around her, the warmth of his lips on hers, battled any doubts within. She shut her eyes while cushioning Andrew's head as it lay against Stephen's hard chest.

But when he broke the kiss, she saw his expression had turned grim. "Do not thank me, yet, Rowena. This matter is not finished, I've just realized. It has taken a difficult turn, I fear."

He then swung the horse around and, shielding her and Andrew with his strong arm, he drove the animal through the brush toward the narrow road some distance away. Rowena felt her heart pound in her throat at his cryptic warning, but dared not ask him to explain.

Chapter Twenty-Three

Stephen kept the horse at a canter, hoping the gentle bobbing would soothe Andrew. His crying eased, thankfully, but in its stead came a silence as weighty as a woman heavy with child.

There were so many unspoken issues that needed to be sorted out. Finally, unable to stand it any longer, he drew his horse to a halt. "You ran away, Rowena. You stole some food like a child, too."

She didn't answer immediately, but rather clung to him with her head down. Finally, she whispered, "I would have replaced it. I was planning to ask Lady Ediva to send some back here, and I would have worked for the cost."

He made a soft noise and hoped it didn't sound disapproving. He cared not for the lost provisions. Rather, he needed to start this conversation with something.

Rowena added, "What are you going to do with those two? You can't leave them tied up there."

"Nay, I won't. I will dispatch a pair of guards to bring them in. The third man is too injured to return to help them. I will send the dog to find him."

They dropped into silence again. Stephen wondered if

he should urge the horse to walk. As if the stallion knew his master, the beast stamped his foot in answer. To ease the edginess, he turned it in a wide circle.

They had not finished this conversation, but he could see no way to segue back to what needed to be said. He finally said firmly, "You need to explain your actions."

Rowena tipped her head to one side and pressed her cheek against Andrew's soft curls. He waited.

Did Stephen want her to defend herself? Aye. He could engage that, but not this heavy silence.

Were you planning to argue your point? What was your point? How you forced her decision to run away? How you were justified to treat her father so kindly?

He wasn't. But he did not want a rebellion. Or was it just the way he preferred to work?

Slyly, hoping those who opposed you would slip up and make a mistake, so you could justify an arrest? Or accusingly, like Josane, until the truth of your actions slapped you in the face?

Stephen tightened his grip on the reins. 'Twas easier to fight on his own terms than to risk the unknown. Aye, and 'twas easier to do what he wanted than to trust that God had His own plan.

What about his plans? Such as the ones he'd implemented using Rowena as bait. In his quest to find her, he'd set aside the fact he'd used her for the safety of the kingdom, but now, holding her, he could not go further until he admitted it to her.

"Rowena, I need to confess something."

She looked up at him.

"I used you as bait to find your attacker, but not because you were attacked. Not completely, anyway, but rather, 'twas part of an order from the king."

"What order?"

"I was to find any rebels who might plot against the king. I was to arrest them and take them to London to be questioned and punished. King William cannot put whole platoons in each village, for his men fight the Welsh and up north. So he must use people like me to remove any threat to his sovereignty. I guessed that who-ever would hurt you would also rebel against the king, and that is the real reason I used you as bait. For that, I am sorry. 'Twas wrong of me."

Rowena was silent for a moment. "Why are you tell-ing me this now?"

"Because I trust you. I didn't completely before, and we both know you can't demand another's faith when you don't trust people yourself. Do you forgive me?"

As he looked down at her, her expression changed. "If you trust me with this, Stephen, then will you trust me with something else?"

"What is that?"

"To know fully in your heart that you are not to blame for your brother's death. I have watched you and heard what is said about how you feel about it. But 'tisn't true, Stephen. Corvin was killed in battle. Don't believe any-one who says 'twas your fault. Can you trust *me* with that truth?"

Blinking and tightening his jaw, Stephen urged the horse forward. They rode for some time, with him mull-ing over Rowena's words.

In a moment back at the campsite, he realized, his attention on fighting the cook, he hadn't seen Hundar prepare to attack him. Rowena saved his life.

He could have died, and then where would Rowena be?

He'd been looking in another direction that day at

Hastings. Corvin had also been fighting while Stephen's attention was diverted by that one Saxon. 'Twas a tragic accident.

"I know I am not to blame for Corvin's death." The words slipped from his lips before he could stop them. But they were true.

Rowena did not look up. Shouldn't she say something? All she offered him was a small sniffle and a tightened grip. And what did she mean by her soft crying? He hated being so unsure.

She sniffled again and he pursed his lips. The only thing he was sure of right this very moment was how he felt. But did he dare risk this softened heart of his, when more danger lay ahead?

Could he say *I love you* when he didn't know how the day would turn out? He spurred the horse back to a canter, and they remained silent all the way into the village.

When they reached Kingstown, he'd spotted the pair of guards returning from the west, from Taurin's estate. He ordered them to where he'd left Hundar. When they returned, they were to tell him what they'd discovered on their trip.

Stephen halted the horse in front of the small church, with its door shut tight and nary a soul around. 'Twas still too early, even for the priest, who rose early to pray and prepare for morning services. But not for long. Dawn was close at hand. "Go into the chapel, Rowena. And do not leave until I come for you."

Stephen eased her onto the frosty ground, and looking down at her, he knew his sister had seen the truth in him long before he had. He was truly in love.

Rowena looked up at him in the waning moonlight, her pale eyes wide. Hurt blossomed there.

Have I lost your love, Rowena? Oh, how I know so little of it, having shut away my heart for so long.

And her child, that sweet boy with warm, dark eyes full of watchfulness, that little round nose, and mouth open in constant awe, stared also up at her.

Regardless, Stephen would protect them both. He wanted to hold them close and keep them there, but the chapel was safer than being with him, considering the task that lay ahead.

"Where are you going?" she whispered.

"Hundar has no reason to bear a grudge against you. He was paid. And I intend to confront the person who paid him. Now go into the chapel and stay there."

Stephen swung his horse around and looked over his shoulder at the pair watching warily. "And, dear Rowena, pray for me. I have been betrayed and my task is a distasteful one."

He spurred on his horse toward the stables. Aye, distasteful and surprising. He'd arrested many a man for conspiring against the crown. He'd fought at Senlac and battled fools who'd tried to assault the king. And although William was a powerful man in his own right, battle-hardened from years of fighting to be the successor to his father, Duke Robert, Stephen was his chief bodyguard and well trained for it.

Until today, he was one who cared little that he hurt people. He'd long ago reconciled with that warrior side of him. He was a soldier as King David had been, and 'twas all the justification he needed.

He wasn't as cold as that anymore. He knew the sin of it.

But now he was afraid he wasn't up to the battle that lay ahead.

* * *

Rowena watched him ride off, fear gripping her. Not just from what could happen, but also from what had happened back on the road. She'd accepted Stephen's confession without so much as a blink of the eye. He'd used her for his own gain, just as her father and Taurin had done.

And it didn't matter. She not only trusted him, but more. She loved him.

God in heaven, protect him.

She pulled hard on the chapel door, for it, like the manor's main door, opened outward on loud, unwilling hinges. 'Twas for safety, she presumed, for opening the door took effort and an unarmed hand, thus detracting from an easy invasion.

Andrew wriggled and called out in his usual gibberish, though the tone was fast becoming whiny and hungry.

"Hush," she told her son softly, though he ignored her as he squirmed. Having recovered from his ordeal by the campfire and been lulled to sleep on Stephen's mount for a time, he wanted to be out of the sling and moving around. She wondered if she should let him crawl in the chapel.

She pulled the door shut behind her. No expensive candles were lit. After feeling her way to the spark box, she opened it, and the draft made the piece of bone glow brighter.

Putting Andrew on the floor, for she now feared he would reach for things he shouldn't, she quickly lit the lamp beside the spark box.

The wick was too short, but the small flame did much to drive away the penetrating darkness. Rowena set down the lamp and sat on the closest pew, leaving its short door open. Feeling a bit uneasy, she only perched on the bench's edge. Andrew held up his hands. Typical of a child, he'd changed his mind about being free.

Mayhap he hated the darkness as much as she did. All those years living in the barn, hearing the sounds of vermin and livestock but not seeing them, had taught her to hate a world with only noise. Lamps and torches were too dangerous to be left lit in stables, so she'd endured many black nights.

Rowena pulled Andrew into her arms, and as she hugged him, she prayed. Then after taking a break, she prayed again. Each time for Stephen's safety, followed by a plea to teach her to forgive.

How was it possible to love a man and not forgive him? She truly loved Stephen, yet she knew he could never return that love, nor would he see any reason to disbelieve her lying father's filthy tale. Stephen had found her only to keep his promise to shelter her, and should that include her return to her family, so be it. No doubt he'd be glad to release her, for she had brought nothing but trouble.

Lord, help me to understand everything. Help me to forgive. If You can help with unbelief, You can help with unforgiveness.

Time rolled by, and when Andrew nuzzled her, Rowena fed him. He let out a loud burp before settling down against her bosom. Without any windows, she couldn't say if dawn had started already.

Then a harsh scrape ripped through the chapel.

Stephen strode into the manor, finding the expected quiet of the predawn. Only the cook and her maid were up, but already the scents of fresh bread and warming broth had begun to waft through the downstairs. New lights lit the corridor, and he was grateful for them.

He went straight to his office, stopping only to awaken Gaetan and hand him his sword and dagger and order a light breakfast. He wanted to send a meal to the chapel, but 'twas best that no one know where Rowena was. He would act as if all were normal until he found the proof he sought.

In his office, he lit the lamp and drew out the financial ledger. Before he opened it, he freed the delicate, embroidered purse he'd confiscated from Hundar and counted the silver coins. A considerable sum, and one not readily available to most men.

Gaetan returned with the kitchen maid, appearing to hope he would offer good news, but Stephen stayed silent. She served his food, dipped her head and with the squire left quietly.

Setting the purse with its counted coins aside, Stephen opened the ledger. Comparing it with the coins in his strongbox, he began to pore over the record of the manor's logistics, half hoping he would not find what he eventually found.

'Twas as he suspected. The money to pay Hundar came from within the manor for 'twas the exact amount missing. Silver coins only a manor would have.

And so, he thought, looking again at the small feminine purse he'd scooped up at Hundar's feet, 'twas time to force an answer, though his heart ached at the task.

Nay, Rowena deserved the truth.

Even from you. Tell her the truth about how you feel. Risk your heart, even though you now know how you've sinned.

He discarded that reminder. Not yet. After locking up his proof, he went straight to Josane's room. There, after pounding on her door loudly enough to awaken the entire manor, he shifted impatiently. There was only one rush lit upstairs, and it was nearly out.

Josane's personal maid opened the door a crack, and Stephen, accepting the invitation boldly, strode into his sister's chamber.

She sat up in bed, her braids hanging from her night-cap as she pulled up on her bedclothes. "Stephen! What is it now? You are worse than a child!"

"I want answers, Josane."

"At this hour? What's wrong? Where is Rowena? Has something happened? Have you been up all night?"

"Aye. And I find it interesting that you retired earlier, then bounced out of bed to ask after Rowena, especially since you told me to look for her on a road on which I could easily be ambushed."

"What are you talking about?" Josane accepted a cloak from her maid, tossing him a scowl as she pulled the garment over her shoulders. "Of course I told you to search for her. What else could I do? I couldn't ride out into the night myself, nor could I—"

"Never mind. I need to know where a quarter of the manor's coinage has gone to."

The maid lit the lamp as Josane fastened her cloak. Both women gasped. "Are you addled? Rowena is miss-ing and you decide 'tis time to count the manor's silver? If those coins aren't in the strongbox in your office, I have no idea where they are!"

"Where is your purse?"

She looked blankly at him. "My purse? 'Tis with my things. My maid takes them for the night. But 'tis nearly always empty. I'd be a fool to prance around this village with coins jingling."

"Where are your keys to the strongbox?" he barked.

Josane stiffened and he knew she would not crumble under his harsh tone. "I will assume Rowena is safe, for surely you would not be asking this nonsense if she weren't." She looked through the dim room to her maid. "Get my belt, my purse and my keys."

The maid hesitated. She glanced at Stephen, then at the door, then at her mistress.

In a sudden, surprising burst, she fled past Stephen and into the hall.

Chapter Twenty-Four

Rowena spun at the harsh noise. The tiny door to the right of the altar scraped open, and still unused to the odd arrangement, she waited, her breath held fast.

Udella peered out, her own lamp already lit. "Rowena! I thought 'twas too early for our chaplain to come for services." She looked more intently. "What has brought you here, child?"

Rowena bit her lip. She had put her faith in Stephen, and so she must also believe in Udella and her sincerity. Or could she? Stephen had said he'd been betrayed. But if he suspected Udella, he wouldn't have asked Rowena to stay here so close to her. "I ran away tonight, but Stephen found me and brought me here," she blurted out.

"Why did he bring you to the chapel?"

Rowena paused. Stephen must have thought 'twas the safest place. But did that mean he trusted Udella and the chaplain, who would arrive at any moment?

"I don't know. We found the man who attacked me, but Stephen said this business was not over yet."

"Who was it?"

"A man from a village west of here. Oh, Udella, 'tis so complicated!" Rowena cried. "Stephen took a purse from the man, but before that, my father arrived here. 'Twas why I ran away, for he's telling such a tale, I am sure no one will ever believe me! But I didn't lie! My father sold me to Lord Taurin, and now he's saying I was kidnapped!"

"Hush, dear. Start again."

Rowena told her the whole set of events, all garbled and backward and upside down, and she could only hope the old woman followed her words. "And then Stephen took the man's purse and we returned," she finished.

"The man had a purse? Was it heavy with coin?"

Rowena frowned at the anchoress. "Aye. And 'twas not a man's purse, but a fine lady's one. Why are you focusing on that? More important, I am sure my father will insist I return with him. I fear Stephen will be tired of all the trouble I have caused. I cannot go back, for my father will probably sell me again, or worse, sell Andrew. That was why I ran away!"

"Trust in Lord Stephen's good judgment, Rowena." The words were comforting, but the tone bore a curious edge to it. Rowena peered at the woman, but in the dimness, with only two small lamps lit, Udella's expression was hard to read. Was she worried?

"Rowena, there is something you should know. I didn't tell you the complete truth with Gilles. He and I spoke—"

Andrew chose that moment to gurgle and coo and stare at Udella with unabashed interest. Rowena waited for the woman to continue to speak, but tears now streamed down her wrinkled face, and she seemed to choke on her words. Finally, she whispered, "I am such a sinner, Rowena. And look at you, fresh with new faith, trying so hard. And your babe is such a sweet child! Makes me long for when I had—" She stopped, then gripped the wall beneath her small door. "Did you hear that?"

Rowena spun, straining to hear beyond the dim chapel, but only the sound of her pounding heart reached her ears. "Nay."

"I know each sound this estate makes. 'Tis too early for the priest..." Udella gasped, then turned to Rowena, her face a mask of deep concern as she held out her arms. "Quick, Rowena, give me the child."

Rowena frowned. "Why?"

"For his safety. Hurry!"

She hesitated. Then Andrew perked up, pushing himself to standing as he peered over her shoulder.

Rowena froze. For far too long she'd lived in a stable and learned to rely on the animals' keen hearing. Andrew's youthful hearing was also fine. Taking a fast breath, Rowena surged toward the small door and over to Udella. But still, she could not relinquish her child.

"Now, Rowena! Trust me. Oh, my dear, not even my own flesh and blood could force me to hurt a babe!"

Another curious moment. But after kissing him, Rowena quickly handed over her only child. In a single fluid movement, Udella took him and shut the small door as quickly and quietly as she could.

A noise grated behind Rowena and she pivoted sharply. A draft winked out the lamp.

Then a sound she'd heard before. *The unsheathing of a sword.*

Stephen tore after the maid and easily caught her at the end of the narrow corridor, directly in front of Gilles's chamber. The girl cried out as she struggled, "Master Gilles! Please, help me!"

Stephen made short work of subduing her. He spun

her and pinned her to the floor with one hand, tearing off his belt to bind her wrists with the other. Finally, the maid dropped to the planks and sobbed quietly.

Footfalls approached and Stephen glanced over his shoulder to see his sister as she hurried close with her lamp. She quickly lit the unlit rush torch nearest Gilles's door and peered at her brother. "Stephen! Release her!"

"Nay. She bolted and I want to know why. Do you have your keys?"

"Aye." Josane held up her belt, then examined the set dangling there. She gasped. "Nay, not all of them. One is missing."

Stephen stood and hauled up the maid by her crooked arm. "I would wager that 'tis the key to my strongbox, isn't it? And you took your lady's purse, too. Where is the key? Why did you steal it?"

The girl hung her head. "'Twas not me, milord. I was ordered to. It came with a promise of safety!"

"Who ordered you?"

"Master Gilles! Gilles, my love, come out!"

Josane gasped. "Nay!"

Stephen dropped the girl and she threw herself against Gilles's door. It remained closed.

Cold anger washed through Stephen and he lifted the latch, but it held fast.

Lord, ease my temper. I need to be as clearheaded as I am in London.

As I am in London? Nay, I need wisdom, Lord.

"'Tis locked from the inside," Josane whispered.

"Not for long." Stephen hauled the girl away and stepped back. He drew up his leg and drove it forward. Splinters flew as the door slammed inward to bang against the wall. Grabbing Josane's lamp, Stephen marched in over the broken wood. "Gilles!"

A sniffle reached them from deep in the chamber. Stephen held the lamp forward. Gilles's young page, a boy of less than eight years, cowered in the corner. "Nay, milord. He is gone," he whimpered.

"Where?"

The boy shrugged.

"When?"

"Shortly after you arrived downstairs. I heard you order food and drink. He left then."

"How long had he been here?"

"He came up here only for a moment in order to take his sword. I was to stay here and open the door only to him."

Gilles had been downstairs when he arrived? Stephen had delivered Rowena to the chapel because 'twas the best place for her to hide in a hurry. He'd turned his mount toward the stable and noticed the lights behind the shuttered windows on the manor's main floor. He'd assumed the cook and her maid to be up, and had found them so. But in the kitchen, not near the shuttered windows. Fresh rush lights had lit the corridor outside his office.

The cook would never waste the torches. She lit only the kitchen, for she had no need to roam about the manor.

Gilles had been downstairs... 'Twas wholly possible he'd seen them arrive at the chapel.

He pivoted to face his sister. "Order a guard to watch your maid, Josane, and I want all others in the hall guarded."

"All others?"

"Aye, especially Rowena's father. I have not yet dealt with him, but I will." He grabbed the freshly lit torch and roared down the stairs.

* * *

Master Gilles! The breath of time before the lamp winked out gave Rowena a single glimpse of him.

But it also gave him the same of her.

Rowena dropped to the wide stones below and crawled past the enclosed front pew before trying to squeeze herself under the next one. She could hear Gilles stride up the aisle. He knew this chapel far better than she did, and when he stopped at the altar and faced right, she guessed he knew exactly where to go.

She wasn't able to crawl under the family pew, so she chose the second one. She banged into it, and the sound bounced around the small chapel, betraying her location. She scurried under the next one, then the fourth one.

The scrape of metal on stone ruptured the tight silence that followed. Another scrape, then another.

Not knowing where she was, Gilles was plunging his weapon repeatedly under the open pews, hoping to stab her.

Rowena shuffled back, horrified to find she'd reached the end of the pew. She froze.

He was only an arm's length from her as he prepared to step forward and thrust again. Rowena shut her eyes tight.

"Gilles!"

She threw open her eyes at the sound of the male voice. Torchlight filled the chapel, and from her hiding place she saw Gilles spin away. He growled out a filthy Norman word and moved forcibly to the center aisle.

Rowena lifted her head and gasped. Stephen stood in the doorway unarmed, carrying only the rush torch.

"Leave her alone, Gilles!"

"Nay! She will die, and all in the village will think 'twas by your hand."

Stephen stepped closer. "And you will see to it that her father will blame me, and dissent will follow. And with an inadequate number of guards here, I will be unable to defend myself."

Gilles stalked toward him. Rowena slipped free of the bench pew. "It matters little to me if you die or not. I will not mourn you, brother-in-law."

Stephen held the torch like a sword. "If that is true, then all of this finally makes sense. You wanted only to stir up the villagers against me, right?"

Gilles lunged at him, but Stephen jumped nimbly back.

"I was to hold this estate, not you! 'Twould have been mine if William had not succeeded at Senlac! I am the true heir to Kingstown, not some palace bodyguard! The blood in my veins is far more royal than anything you carry. Royal to Saxons and Normans alike."

"'Tis my duty and my honor to guard the king and stop dissent in the palace. You should be so lucky to have such a task."

"Instead I am but a foolish bailiff, forced to pander to your whims."

He lunged again, and this time, Stephen swung the torch down and then up, dangerously close to the lethal weapon.

The burning end of the rush light scorched Gilles's hand. He yelped and dropped his sword. Stephen quickly changed hands before he lunged again with the torch held forward. Gilles jumped back, abandoning his sword. Stephen snatched it and immediately swung it up to slice through Gilles' tunic. He cried out, and with a stumble, tripped backward and fell, cracking his head on the stone floor.

He didn't move.

Rowena rushed toward him, and Stephen handed her the torch before he rolled his brother-in-law over. The man groaned, and immediately Rowena breathed a sigh of relief. He was alive.

Stephen leaned over him. "Who told you that you were the heir to Kingstown? How do you know this is your father's birthplace?"

Gilles's eyes fluttered, then stayed shut. "Barrett. He heard his parents speak of it last year. They disliked that you became their baron."

"The Barretts dislike too many things!" Stephen growled. "They would also dislike having a coward like you as baron."

"I would make a finer baron than you!"

"Because you are half-Saxon?"

Gilles winced, probably at the pain in his head. "Aye. Saxon or Norman, I am higher born than you are!"

Rowena glanced over at Udella's small door, but it remained shut. Was this what she'd wanted to say, that Gilles knew about his heritage? But Gilles had learned it from Bar—

Stephen scowled. "And should I argue that with you, you would remind me that our king is in similar stead as you."

"I am the true heir of Kingstown, not you, not even the king. And," Gilles spat out, "I am not one to spy on people like some snake in the grass!"

Stephen leaned closer. "But I would not steal my own wife's keys and purse to incriminate her!"

Rowena gasped. "He did that?"

"Aye. He wooed her maid and had her do his filthy work for him."

"Josane isn't happy here anyway!" Gilles said, the

strength in his voice waning. "Whatever the outcome, you would have had mercy on her and sent her home."

The guards barreled in, and Stephen dragged his groggy brother-in-law to standing and ordered him be taken to the hospice hut and guarded. When they left, Rowena rushed up to him. "Was he the one who paid Hundar to attack me?"

"Aye. They had been close enough to each other to pass along the fever Udella had had. She gave it to Gilles, though I know not when."

"She says she spoke to him and had lied about it. She was deeply sorry."

"Gilles suffered only lightly with the fever, but he'd passed it to the courier who took the report of my affairs to Aubrey. Gilles also passed the fever on to Hundar."

"Hundar's illness lingers in him."

Stephen nodded. "I believe Udella knew who would hurt you."

Immediately, Rowena spun to face the small, tightly closed door that led to her cell. "She has Andrew!"

Chapter Twenty-Five

Rowena raced to the cell door and smacked it hard. "Udella! Open this door!"

Stephen rushed up beside her. "Udella! Now!" He turned and sheathed Gilles's sword.

"Where are you going?" she asked him.

He strode to the chapel door. "Remember I promised I would tear down the wall if she refused to hand over your babe? *I will.*"

Rowena gasped.

The anchoress's small door scraped open. Udella, babe in her arms, peered out. "I'm so sorry, Rowena," she said softly. "I dared not open the door while the fight ensued for fear Gilles would use it to his advantage. Especially if he thought he could grab Andrew. Oh, I have misjudged him terribly! I only wanted to see my family here again. I'm so sorry! Milord, can you forgive me?" She leaned over with the babe.

Stephen looked grim. "Indeed, I can, for we all misjudged Gilles. And I have not been free of sin, either."

Spotting his mother, Andrew cried and held his hands out. Rowena took him and gripped him tight. "I don't understand. Why me?"

"He hoped to create dissent in the village. Gilles was sending reports to Aubrey de Vere on how I was failing our king and not finding the rebels. By paying Hundar to attack you using my money, he could make it appear that the rebels here were trying to push me to fight back. I wouldn't be surprised if Gilles had promised he would shield them from prosecution. But as bailiff, he heard only civil cases. I would send the criminal cases to London, if they affected the king's sovereignty. There, Gilles has no jurisdiction. He knew that, but hoped that the locals and especially Hundar wouldn't be aware of it."

"Why attack me?"

"He guessed I would use you to lure out any trouble-makers. Gilles knew what the king had ordered me to do. You were a stranger here with no one to confirm your story that you had been abused by Taurin. He then suggested to the villagers that I protected you because you were aligned with us Normans and had betrayed your people. I suspect he paid Barrett handsomely to help him with rumormongering. 'Twas well conceived because no matter which way I acted, I was condemned in the villagers' eyes. Gilles also needed a person from outside the village to attack you because you may have recognized one of the people here. Who first heard Gilles approaching?"

Rowena spoke. "Udella did."

The older woman nodded. "I know each sound this estate makes and each footfall on the yard beyond." She looked contrite. "I spoke to Gilles last week, after I had recovered from my fever. I had been afraid that I would die this time, and thought about telling Gilles who he really was. I asked for him, but when he came, he was different somehow. Smug and cruel. Though I hesitated to tell him who he was, I did so, but it turned out he already knew. Barrett would have said it to curry favor." She looked at Rowena. "I allowed you to think that I did not speak with him, but 'twas a lie. When I heard someone approach this chapel, I knew who it would be, for I realized what was happening."

Stephen nodded. "He must have watched me bring you here, and whilst I checked my ledger and found there was money missing, he crept upstairs for his sword."

Rowena bit her lip. "Was he planning to kill me?"

"I think so. I had sent him off to find you earlier, but he must have returned some time ago." His look softened. "We have much to discuss."

With a nod, she started to walk toward him. He stopped her. "But it should be alone. Allow Udella to care for Andrew a bit longer. There is still one matter I need to see to, and you must also witness it."

Rowena hesitated. She didn't want Andrew to fuss too much for the older woman.

"Please, 'tis of great importance that you come with me."

She looked at Udella. "Is it all right if I leave him with you?" She had no idea what would happen, but… aye, she trusted the older woman. And she trusted Stephen. No matter what might happen, she knew he would always protect her.

But would he love her? Aye, there was trust in their hearts, but was there also love?

Udella beamed. "I would love nothing else than to care for him."

Stephen led Rowena from the chapel. Once in the manor, he ordered Hundar and his accomplice be brought in. With hands bound and feet tied so close that they could only shuffle, the men arrived in the hall, several guards behind them.

Stephen took Rowena to the dais, where they both sat. She barely perched on her seat as she listened to Stephen order everyone to enter the hall.

She held her breath when her father came in, followed by two guards. Was he also under arrest?

One of the guards forced the defiant Hundar and his friend to their knees. Stephen addressed her father. "Do you know these men?"

Rowena peered hard at Althenson. Looking only briefly at them before staring at Stephen again, he shook his head. "I know neither of them, my lord."

Stephen stepped off the dais and in one long stride, reached her father. Much shorter, Althenson was fairly quaking in his old, flat boots as Stephen glared hard at him. "Finally, you've spoken the truth."

Then he ordered Gilles to be brought into the hall. After he was led in, bound and still dazed from his head having smacked the stone floor earlier, he dropped to the floor beside Hundar. The Saxon spat on him.

Rowena held her breath. What was Stephen doing? Her father quivered openly and refused to look upon the bound men at his feet.

"Althenson, do you know this man?" Stephen asked.

Again, her father shook his head. "Nay, milord. I know none of these men. Though I met this third man last night."

"Then tell me how you learned that Rowena was here."

Sweat beaded on Althenson's forehead. "I don't re-member. A minstrel troupe passed my way. I think it was they who mentioned her. My wife has similar hair."

Stephen's expression darkened. "Nay. The minstrels would not have had the time to reach you from here. Nor would they visit a lonely farm."

"Nay, milord, 'tis true." His gaze darted about. "But I saw them in the village nearest my home!"

"You are lying again, Saxon."

"I'm not, milord. I swear it openly! How would I know about the minstrels being here if they had not met me?"

A slow, mirthless smile grew on Stephen's face. "Lady Josane said she would put you where the minstrels slept when I told her last night to find a place for you."

Blood rushed into Althenson's face, and Rowena knew Stephen had caught him in his lie. But she still held her breath.

Stephen pierced her father with a glare. "'Twill not be hard to discover who went to your farm. I suspect we will find out soon. I have also sent for the records of finance from Lord Taurin's estate, for he would record the purchase of a slave, because Rowena was not a Christian then and he considered it legal to buy her.

"And from London, I will receive proof that you have purchased back your land from the king, for there will be a record of it, also. In the meantime, you can give me another lie about where you were able to acquire the funds to buy many hides of land."

"Nay, milord, I had only enough for one hide of land. 'Tis many acres and—"

"Another lie! In this county, land is divided in multiples of five hides. You would need only one hide to support your family, and even with that, you would not be able to afford its purchase. But to buy all of your land? Where would you get the coins for that?"

Rowena's heart swelled. Her father's breathing quickened as his throat bobbed and his nervous gaze darted about. "I sold—"

"A woman, your own flesh and blood, to be a slave

to your enemy? Know this, Saxon—I will compare the monies missing from Taurin's estate with the amount given to the king. I will scour your estate for the receipt of purchase of your land back from the crown, for even a fool Saxon as you are would not dare to destroy the proof that you own your land."

Althenson's shaking increased. "Milord, have mercy on me!"

Stephen turned away, gesturing to the guards. "Arrest this man for assisting to overthrow my estates. We'll let Picot, the sheriff of Cambridge, decide your fate. I hear he is a crafty old fox who nurses a hatred for all Saxons."

The guards grabbed Althenson as he cried out, "Nay! Milord, nay, I have done nothing wrong! I have been tricked by Master Gilles to come here!"

"Stephen!"

Stephen turned to Rowena. She shook her head. "My lord, there is no love lost between my father and me, but I ask you not to hurt these men. Please ask the king for mercy. Send them all away. Fine them, also, for an empty purse hurts more than a lashing. But to have them flogged or worse…"

Stephen shook his head in disbelief. "He has wronged you all your life, Rowena."

"Aye, he has. But Udella, whose son was killed at Senlac, forgives all. And haven't you also told me to trust that God forgives and I must forgive, also?"

She drew a long breath. "I…I am trying to forgive my father for what he did to me. I cannot move forward in my life until I close this part of it. Take his lands again and his plow oxen. 'Twill make him have to work harder if he must plow his small plot by hand. Mayhap he will be too tired for any more trickery."

Stephen stared at Rowena until a slow, smooth smile

grew on his lips. He nodded as he took her hand. "Very well. But I reserve the right to banish them all. The king will trust me on this matter and order them never to enter this village again."

To the guards, he gave instructions to detain the men until the charges were recorded and read to them. Then he ordered the remaining people to the chapel for morning services.

When they were alone, Stephen drew Rowena into his arms and kissed her soundly. After he'd lifted his head, he tipped it to one side. "You are a wise young woman."

"Not always wise."

"I disagree. You showed me how to forgive myself for Corvin's death."

"I only said what was true, my lord."

"Please, call me Stephen. I want to…" He drew a breath. "Rowena, my life is not complete without you. I think you will teach me something new each day. Will you stay with me here?"

"In this manor?" Her heart squeezed as she whispered. "As what?"

"As the lady. Josane wishes to return to Normandy, and I will send her husband there, as well. 'Twill be difficult for her, but I think she wishes for a happy marriage and is willing to work on hers to make it so."

"With Master Gilles, after all he's done?"

"None of us is perfect, Rowena. But in time, mayhap Gilles will see his wrongs."

"He nearly fooled us completely."

"He has watched how I work for many years and could hide his feelings."

"How did you know 'twas Master Gilles who conspired to kill me?"

"A number of things hinted at this. I began to realize

I must not ask why your attacker chose you, but rather what would happen if you died. If something happened to you, Gilles would see that King William learned that I have not been able to find any rebels who would plot against the crown. He could easily take this holding from me and give it to someone else. But who would be the most likely person to receive the manor? Gilles, of course, since he had been sending missives to London, and I will find out what they say soon enough."

"How?"

"Aubrey de Vere may have considerable influence, but I am not the captain of the King's Guard for no reason. I also have the king's ear, and de Vere knows this. He will deny conspiring to remove me, but it matters not. He will not cross me again."

"Why would he conspire with Master Gilles to remove you?"

"Most likely de Vere was interested in holding this village, as well. It lies between London and Ely, and could become influential."

Rowena shook her head in awe. "How did you guess this?"

"Aubrey de Vere would not be informed if the missives were only queries on the financial logistics, but he would be informed if they held something that would affect him or the king."

"'Tis all so hard to believe." Rowena looked up at Stephen shyly. Her breath left her again as he smiled down on her. A smile so filled with love, she found herself returning it. "As is the idea that you want me to be the lady here," she whispered.

"'Twill take some time for you to learn how to run a manor and to be the lady for the villagers, but Udella and Josane will help you. I know the villagers will accept you in time, especially once they learn the truth and see that Udella is on your side."

"But how will I become the lady?"

Stephen laughed. "So many questions! By virtue of marrying me, because I love you with all my heart and soul." He lifted up her hand as he bowed on one knee. "Rowena, will you marry me?"

Tears sprang into her eyes. "Aye, Stephen, I will marry you. I put my love and my faith in you forever."

He stood and leaned forward to kiss her again, this time deeper, stronger and so filled with love she knew that she would be sheltered in his arms always.

* * * * *

Dear Reader,

When I began this story, all I had was a very simple premise. What if someone asked you to trust him when all your experiences told you that you shouldn't?

Rowena was introduced in my previous story as a woman who had suffered under one Norman soldier. Now another Norman was asking her for trust. Naturally, it would be hard to give.

So often we have to relearn our own trust in God, especially after suffering. Trust is something that is earned, yes, but consider this: while one who trusts must take a leap of faith, when this kind of faith is given to us, we should not take it lightly. Are you doing that?

I hope I have delivered a heartwarming story of faith, responsibility and, of course, love.

Blessings,

Barbara Phinney

WOULD-BE WILDERNESS WIFE
Frontier Bachelors
by Regina Scott

Nurse Catherine Stanway is kidnapped by Drew Wallin's brother to help their ailing mother...but she soon realizes that she's also been chosen by Drew's family to be his bride!

HILL COUNTRY COURTSHIP
Brides of Simpson Creek
by Laurie Kingery

Maude Harkey is tired of waiting for love. But then an orphan baby is suddenly put in her care, and the generosity of her handsome rancher employer offers a chance at the new beginning she's always wanted...

THE TEXAN'S INHERITED FAMILY
Bachelor List Matches
by Noelle Marchand

When four orphaned nieces and nephews arrive on his doorstep, Quinn Tucker knows they'll need a mother. Could marrying schoolteacher Helen McKenna be the most convenient solution?

THE DADDY LIST
by DeWanna Pace

Despite their rocky history, Daisy Trumbo agrees to nurse injured Bass Parker back to health. Bass hopes standing in as father figure to Daisy's daughter might put them all on a new path together...as a family.

REQUEST YOUR FREE BOOKS!

2 FREE INSPIRATIONAL NOVELS
PLUS 2
FREE
MYSTERY GIFTS

Love Inspired.
HISTORICAL
INSPIRATIONAL HISTORICAL ROMANCE

YES! Please send me 2 FREE Love Inspired® Historical novels and my 2 FREE mystery gifts (gifts are worth about $10). After receiving them, if I don't wish to receive any more books, I can return the shipping statement marked "cancel." If I don't cancel, I will receive 4 brand-new novels every month and be billed just $4.74 per book in the U.S. or $5.24 per book in Canada. That's a saving of at least 21% off the cover price. It's quite a bargain! Shipping and handling is just 50¢ per book in the U.S. and 75¢ per book in Canada.* I understand that accepting the 2 free books and gifts places me under no obligation to buy anything. I can always return a shipment and cancel at any time. Even if I never buy another book, the two free books and gifts are mine to keep forever.

102/302 IDN F5CN

Name _____ (PLEASE PRINT)

Address _____ Apt. #

City _____ State/Prov. _____ Zip/Postal Code

Signature (if under 18, a parent or guardian must sign)

Mail to the Harlequin® Reader Service:
IN U.S.A.: P.O. Box 1867, Buffalo, NY 14240-1867
IN CANADA: P.O. Box 609, Fort Erie, Ontario L2A 5X3

Want to try two free books from another series?
Call 1-800-873-8635 or visit www.ReaderService.com.

---

* Terms and prices subject to change without notice. Prices do not include applicable taxes. Sales tax applicable in N.Y. Canadian residents will be charged applicable taxes. Offer not valid in Quebec. This offer is limited to one order per household. Not valid for current subscribers to Love Inspired Historical books. All orders subject to credit approval. Credit or debit balances in a customer's account(s) may be offset by any other outstanding balance owed by or to the customer. Please allow 4 to 6 weeks for delivery. Offer available while quantities last.

Your Privacy—The Harlequin® Reader Service is committed to protecting your privacy. Our Privacy Policy is available online at www.ReaderService.com or upon request from the Harlequin Reader Service.

We make a portion of our mailing list available to reputable third parties that offer products we believe may interest you. If you prefer that we not exchange your name with third parties, or if you wish to clarify or modify your communication preferences, please visit us at www.ReaderService.com/consumerschoice or write to us at Harlequin Reader Service Preference Service, P.O. Box 9062, Buffalo, NY 14269. Include your complete name and address.

Nurse Catherine Stanway is kidnapped by Drew Wallin's brother to help their ailing mother...but she soon realizes that she's also been chosen by Drew's family to be his bride!

Enjoy this sneak peek from
WOULD-BE WILDERNESS WIFE by Regina Scott!

How could his brother have been so boneheaded? Drew glanced over his shoulder at the youth. The boy had absolutely no remorse for what he'd done. Where had Drew gone wrong?

"I'm really very sorry," Drew apologized to Catherine. "I don't know what got into him. He was raised better."

"Out in the woods, you said," she replied.

"On the lake," he told her. "My father brought us to Seattle about fifteen years ago from Wisconsin and chose a spot far out. He said a man needed something to gaze out on in the morning besides his livestock or his neighbors."

She smiled as if the idea pleased her. "And your mother?" she asked, shifting on the wooden bench. "Is she truly ill?"

"She came down with a fever nearly a fortnight ago. I hope you'll be able to help her before we return you to Seattle tomorrow."

"You did not seem so sure of my skills earlier, sir."

With Levi right behind him, he wasn't about to admit that his fear had been for his future, not the lack of her skills. "We've known Doc for years," he hedged.

"My father's patients felt the same way. There is nothing like the trusted relationship of your family doctor. But I will do whatever I can to help your mother."

Levi's smug voice floated up from behind. "I knew she'd come around."

Drew was more relieved than he'd expected at the thought of Catherine's help. "As you can see," he said to her, "my brother has a bad habit of acting or talking without thinking."

"My brother was the same way," she assured him. "He borrowed my father's carriage more than once, drove it all over the county. He joined the Union Army on his eighteenth birthday before he'd even received a draft notice."

"Sounds like my kind of fellow," Levi said, kneeling so that his head came between them. "Did he journey West with you?"

Though her smile didn't waver, her voice came out flat. "No. He was killed at the Battle of Five Forks in Virginia."

Levi looked stricken as he glanced between her and Drew. "I'm sorry, ma'am. I didn't know."

"Of course you didn't," she replied, but Drew saw that her hands were clasped tightly in her lap as if she were fighting with herself not to say more.

"I'm sorry for your loss," Drew said. "That must have been hard on you and your parents."

"My mother died when I was nine," she said. "My father served as a doctor in the army. He died within days of Nathan."

Drew wanted to reach out, clasp her hand, promise her the future would be brighter. But he couldn't control the future, and she was his to protect only until he returned her to Seattle. He had enough on his hands without taking on a woman new to the frontier.

Don't miss WOULD-BE WILDERNESS WIFE
by Regina Scott,
available March 2015 wherever
Love Inspired® Historical books and ebooks are sold!

SPECIAL EXCERPT FROM

Love Inspired.

A young Amish woman yearns for true love.
Read on for a preview of A WIFE FOR JACOB
by Rebecca Kertz, the next book in her
***LANCASTER COUNTY WEDDINGS** series.*

Annie stood by the dessert table when she saw Jedidiah Lapp chatting with his wife, Sarah. She'd been heartbroken when Jed had broken up with her, and then married Sarah Mast.

Seeing the two of them together was a reminder of what she didn't have. Annie wanted a husband—and a family. But how could she marry when no one showed an interest in her? She blinked back tears. She'd work hard to be a wife a husband would appreciate. She wanted children, to hold a baby in her arms, a child to nurture and love.

She sniffled, looked down and straightened the dessert table. And the pitchers and jugs of iced tea and lemonade.

"May I have some lemonade?" a deep, familiar voice said.

Annie looked up. "Jacob." His expression was serious as he studied her. She glanced down and noticed the fine dusting of corn residue on his dark jacket. "Lemonade?" she echoed self-consciously.

"*Ja*. Lemonade," he said with amusement.

She quickly reached for the pitcher. She poured his lemonade into a plastic cup, only chancing a glance at him when she handed him his drink.

"How is the work going?" she asked conversationally.

"We are nearly finished with the corn. We'll be cutting hay next." He lifted the glass to his lips and took a swallow.

Warmth pooled in her stomach as she watched the movement of his throat. "How's *Dat?*" she asked. She had seen him chatting with her father earlier.

Jacob glanced toward her *dat* with a small smile. "He says he's not tired. He claims he's enjoying the view too much." His smile dissipated. "No doubt he'll be exhausted later."

Annie agreed. "I'll check on him in a while." She hesitated. "Are you hungry? I can fix you a plate—"

He gazed at her for several heartbeats with his striking golden eyes. "*Ne,* I'll fix one myself." He finished his drink and held out his glass to her. "May I?"

She hurried to refill his glass. With a crooked smile and a nod of thanks, Jacob accepted the refill and left. The warm flutter in her stomach grew stronger as she watched him walk away, stopping briefly to chat with Noah and Rachel, his brother and sister-in-law.

Annie glanced over where several men were being dished up plates of food. She then caught sight of Jacob walking along with his brother Eli. The contrast of Jacob's dark hair and Eli's light locks struck her as they disappeared into the barn. They came out a few minutes later, Eli carrying tools, Jacob leading one of her father's workhorses.

As if he sensed her regard, Jacob looked over and locked gazes with her.

Will Annie ever find the husband of her heart?
Pick up A WIFE FOR JACOB to find out.
Available March 2015,
wherever Love Inspired® books and ebooks are sold.